DEATH'S ASSASSIN

JANEAL FALOR

To Erik
I love you. Always.

CHAPTER 1

TATTERED.

Hopeless.

Broken.

That's my life now, ever since Daros poisoned me. It's hard to care about anything when I have no life left in me. "The crowd is going to hate me. I don't even look like a queen."

"It won't matter that you can't move well," Inkga says as she wraps my hair around a simple crown.

Perhaps, but it matters. I haven't been able to do much. I can still feel everything but lack the ability to move—except for lifting my finger and head a little—and this feeling of helplessness has been overwhelming. "I don't want to be carried to Wilric's funeral by servants." Saying his name chokes me up. Tightens my throat like a rope.

If only he'd stayed safe. If only Daros hadn't killed him. If only I'd been faster.

Too many *if only*s.

"I want to stand in front of the people on my own two feet and address them properly," I say.

"You'll command their respect whether or not you stand in

front of them. You always do." Inkga adjusts a few strands of hair and declares me finished.

I look so different than when I first became queen almost a year ago. My cheeks are rounder, fuller, and my eyes are more green than blue. My hair is longer and a lighter brown—almost a dirty blonde. I resemble the First Queen more and more. She's taking over me.

The First Queen. What am I to do about her?

After coming to my dreams for almost a year and offering to help me rule, the First Queen has shown her true colors. I need to eliminate her. We've spent too long under her oppression, with queens going bad after some time with her influence.

Her presence draws near. My lip pulls into a half-snarl without my permission.

"Don't you like it?" Inkga asks.

I force the First Queen's presence away and smile, though fear consumes me. Inkga deserves more gratitude than I can give her. Besides, she doesn't know about the First Queen and certainly doesn't know I'm being taken over. Being haunted. Only Jaku, Daros, Nash, and I know what's going on. I force my attention back to Inkga. "You've done a splendid job. Thank you for helping me."

She beams. "It's a pleasure."

When she turns around to make my bed, I let my expression fall. She's been nothing but kind, helping me with literally every-thing. I can't even eat or take care of the necessary myself. There are some things another person should never have to do for me, yet here I am, in a lounge chair a servant carried me to after several maids helped me change into a black mourning dress.

The sneer creeps back. This time, it's my own.

There's a knock at my sitting room door, and Inkga leaves the bedroom to get it. When she doesn't come back right away, I swear under my breath. She could be attacked, and I can do nothing about it. The image of her lying bruised and bloodied on the floor makes my heart pound. "Inkga? Are you all right?" I ask.

"Fine. Be there in a moment," she calls back.

I growl, but not so loud she can hear me. As I wait, I work on lifting the pointer finger of my right hand and lowering it again. It barely rises. There's no point to this. Daros knew what he was doing when he developed this poison and stabbed me with a dagger laced with it. I should be grateful I lived through it with the help of Venda from Faner and her magic. Thanks to her, I cheated death once again, only to be bound to this body, too weak to do anything.

The urge to throw a dagger is overwhelming. It's been too long since I practiced. Since I exercised.

And there's not a blasted thing I can do about it.

Not even magic can fix my circumstances. At least, not as far as we've been able to tell with Venda trying.

Inkga pops her head through the doorway, barely noticeable in the mirror. I wish I could turn around so my back wasn't to her. Not that I don't trust her—I got over that a while ago. It's the principle of the thing.

"Nash has a surprise you're going to love." She dances into the room and comes around to the front so I can face her. "He's putting the finishing touches on it right now while Puneah sniffs around. He'll be here in a moment, to take you to it."

I hadn't noticed Puneah leave my side. Despite my being uncertain about her when Venda first gifted her to me, she's become something of a comfort. I shouldn't have gotten so lost in my despair that I ignored the sleek, giant, cat-like creature.

But it's difficult not to.

"What did Nash do?" I try to put enthusiasm in my words, but they come out flat. Everything we've been through together—the hurts and comforts, the love we've shared. It is true that we could never be a couple, but now we can't even steal a secret touch.

"Nuh-uh. I'm not telling, or it wouldn't be a surprise." She grins and does a happy dance.

I want to growl at her ease of movement, but I refrain.

My mood doesn't dampen her spirits one bit. She does a little two-step and hurries back to the door. A moment later, Nash comes in with no surprise in sight. My heart gives an odd squeeze, like I'm not sure whether I want to run to him or run away. Either way, I'm stuck in this chair. No running happening.

His smile is shyer than I've seen on him before, a hint of mystery in his eyes. "Good morning, Ryn."

There's so much I want to say, but I settle on, "It's good to see you."

He walks around to my side and bends his knees until he's eye level with me. "May I have your permission to carry you into the other room, my queen?" The way he says the last two words is like a caress against my heart.

"You may," I reply.

We can make contact without getting into trouble. Of course, that's only because I can't get around without help, and it often becomes necessary for people to carry me. The council gave their permission for these circumstances. Some were reluctant to do so, but enough members were on my side, and between that and my inability to do anything, they didn't have much of a choice. They wanted to assign a single person to move me around, but it felt strange to have one servant waiting on me all the time. Not even Inkga does that, and she works harder than anyone else I know.

It's not ideal, but it's all I have.

"You may," I reply.

Nash swings me into his arms like I weigh no more than a bird, though I've put on some weight since becoming queen, and I'm no longer skin and bones. I'm nestled against his shoulder and chest, where I feel nothing except for the unforgiving metal of his steel vest. Despite that, tingles race across my skin at his nearness.

I take in the scent that's all Nash—metal and earth. I want to

4

get lost in it and pretend that nothing else exists. That I can stay here forever.

Only that's impossible.

Puneah comes to our side and follows along as Nash takes me to the other room, Inkga close behind. Nash has been so good to me, but I can't help wondering how he's doing deep inside. He won't talk about his problems and is just there for me. I wish there was more I could do for him. Perhaps if I get out of this melancholy that's overcome me, I'll be able to see his needs better.

He stops a few steps inside my sitting room, and Inkga skirts around him to the other side, bouncing on her toes. Nash swivels me around so I can see the room.

At first, I don't notice anything. All I want to do is hide back under my covers and sleep. Forget about a world where I can't move or love the man I chose. Where I'll soon be under the control of a mad woman. Of course, she's in my dreams too, although I haven't dreamt of her since I discovered her real intent.

Besides, I can't go to sleep because I can't get to my bed without help.

Nash tilts his head to the side. "Do you like it?"

It takes me a moment to figure out what he's talking about. There's a chair next to him I haven't seen before. It's polished elm, with a high back and sides. Thicker than most, it has four wooden wheels—two large ones in the back, and two smaller ones in the front. Wait. Wheels? On a chair?

"What is that?" I ask.

"I like to call it a wheelchair. Want to try it out?"

"It's mine?"

"Made it myself. Well, with some help."

"I…" Don't know what to say. He made this for me?

"It's fine if you don't want to use it, but I thought it might be better if there was a chair we could push you around in, so you didn't have to be carried around."

"Thank you."

"Don't thank me without trying it." But his smile has grown wider. "Here you go." He leans down and helps me settle into the chair, his nearness making my heart sing until he lets go. "I thought you might appreciate having it before Wilric's funeral."

I stare at the chair. I still won't be able to move myself, but it will give me less shame than having to be lugged around. "Thank you. Again."

"We'll have a servant push you. Inkga could even do it. It's not the same as walking, but it may give you some freedom."

Or the illusion of freedom.

It's more than being transported on a litter and not being able to get off it. This way, I'll be a little more respectable.

Still want to stab Daros for doing this to me, though.

I shove thoughts of him away. He can wait until we've mourned Wilric properly.

The guarded hope Nash and Inkga watch me with makes me want to hide. I can't be happy. Not now, anyway. But maybe I can fake it. "This will be wonderful. I'd much rather have a chair to sit in. Thank you."

"You're welcome." He leans in closer before pulling back. I have the feeling he would have kissed me if Inkga wasn't in the room.

I've missed our stolen kisses.

"If we're all ready, we should proceed so they don't wait for us," I say.

"I need to go on ahead of you, to take my place," Nash says. "I'll see you soon."

Not soon enough.

When he's out the door, Inkga asks if I'm ready, and I give her an affirmative reply. She pushes me out into the hall, where my guards are waiting, hands on their swords. Their black outfits and capes as well as the steel vests are a reminder of what Wilric always wore around me. That he gave up his life defending me.

The attacks probably haven't stopped. I don't know for

certain; I'm not told much anymore, and none have made it all the way. But I can't imagine that they've come to a halt.

I'll make certain Wilric's life wasn't given in vain. I'll get what I need out of Daros, get rid of the First Queen, and get this country back on track.

If I can live through it all.

* * *

A MOURNFUL KEEN vibrates through the air—the howl of pain over a loved one's death. Wilric's mother has the perfect voice for a funeral call, low but dynamic. When it's time to take up the mourning call with her, it feels natural, although I've never done so before.

The wordless music moves through me, pulling at my soul and calling to Wilric's. If only there was a way to speak with him after death, instead of having him hear our broken hearts. I would tell him how grateful I am for all he did for me. That he was more than a guard. Tears fill my eyes, and I blink them back, letting my voice ring louder.

The call goes on for some time, but not nearly as long as Wilric deserves. Voices drop off until his mother, his only remaining family member, is the last one holding the call. Her voice goes high, vibrating through the last notes until it ends as a low whimper.

The Neula comes forward—a woman painted black as death, darker than the darkest cave, wearing a black dress and veil that reaches down to her waist. She stands at the head of the crowd, close to me. I've met Neulas before but not at a funeral. No matter how many people I killed, I never attended anyone's death rites. I didn't understand until recently that it took several days to prepare the body for this final stage.

"Wilric Tulkon was a beloved son and friend. He will be

remembered dearly." She steps forward until she's leading Wilric's remains.

For the first time since I arrived, I bring myself to look at him. There's no sign of his injury, his torso hidden beneath his guard outfit. He lies on the wooden board that will be his final bed, looking the same as in life, though painted with death. The only things not black on him are his steel vest and ingoula; even his skin has been painted black, the same as the Neula's skin. The ingoula covers his face like a mask, the pieces coming together to form studded cheeks, with points on his forehead, chin, and nose. The metal gleams in the sunlight against the painted skin.

"Queen Ryn, please grace us." The Neula points to something behind me.

A servant comes forward, carrying a tray that holds my worst nightmare.

The Mortum Tura.

The blasted drink that got me into this mess in the first place. I start to say *no*, but before I can get the word out, the First Queen shouts through my mouth, "Give it to me."

The servant brings the cup to my lips, and I'm helpless as the First Queen swallows, the pounding of her victory dancing around my head.

Everyone stares at me. Now I'm not only an oddity in the chair; I'm glowing. I am thought to be a goddess, when I'm nothing but a weakling.

I turn my gaze to Wilric and focus on him and his sacrifice, while the others look on. The First Queen may have won this round, but I will not let her conquer my spirit.

If only the Mortum Tura made me stronger as it makes the First Queen... But it only feeds her, not me. I wish I knew more about how it worked and why Daros knows what it does.

The Neula turns around, and the men and women who've been given the honor of carrying Wilric to his last resting place surround his body. Nash is at Wilric's head, bending down to pick up the board Wilric was laid on.

Once those chosen have lifted Wilric's body, the Neula steps toward the Tomb of Zaco, the first known fallen royal guard. All other guards have been laid to rest in it since, their bones constantly being pushed back as new bodies come. Now it's Wilric's turn.

The people are still staring at my chair and my useless body. It would be nice if I could have brought Puneah with me. Her comfort is needed now, but I didn't want to scare anyone or take attention away from Wilric. She would have been something to ogle at besides me, though.

I shove thoughts of them away as I scan those who matter most this day. Wilric's mother follows after the Neula.

Inkga rolls my chair forward, but before we turn to trail after the procession, I spot Jem close by through a gap between my guards. Her expression is blank. Stoic. Unyielding to what's happening around her. Whatever was going on between her and Wilric, she's closed herself off.

It's the first I've seen of her since he was killed. It's terrible of me. I should have asked to see her sooner. I've been too wrapped up in myself to do anything of worth. Anything to help a friend. I want to catch her eye, to give her a look of understanding, but she doesn't glance my way before Inkga turns my wheelchair.

The walk—a bumpy ride for me—is long, befitting the journey Wilric's soul will take to reach its final destination. I believe and hope he's going to a good place, but there's no way to know for certain. Only the First Queen's soul didn't follow along with the rest, wherever souls end up, leaving me to deal with her.

We start in a park in the Medi part of town, near where his mother lived, and wind our way through the streets. The palace grows nearer, but we're heading to the left side of it, instead of entering its walls.

When we enter the tombs' row, there are structures almost as far as the eye can see. Even the Poruah have a place to be laid to rest here. Generations of people are buried within these buildings and catacombs. The greatest tomb of all lies before us. The Hall of Queens.

The building is expansive, resting among the tombs of the guards who served their rulers. Not only has it been added onto throughout the ages, but rumor has it that the building goes deep beneath the ground, to provide enough room to house all the queens.

I will end up there some day. Strange. I always thought I'd wind up in a pauper's tomb, shoved against hundreds of other people, with no paint or ingoula to send me on to the next life. But when my time comes, I'll be given a funeral fit for the queen that I am. I'd almost rather have a pauper's rites and save the people the expense.

We continue to the newest Tomb of Guards and enter, following those who carry Wilric's body. Nash's arms may be growing tired, but it's an honor worth every ache and pain.

The torches along the way are lit, shining bright against the white stone. The Neula takes up the keening wail, singing Wilric to his final resting place. The sound echoes around and through me, leaving behind the feeling of despair.

One less person I trust in Valcora. One less person I can count on. One less good man gracing our presence.

And I'm to blame for it.

Daros and I.

As the keen reaches a high pitch, I know what I have to do. As soon as the ceremony is finished, I will go to Daros and demand answers. I need to know what he knows about the First Queen. Every little detail. Wilric will not have died in vain. If Daros is to live, he will be put to good purpose, serving until his final breath.

CHAPTER 2

I SIT outside the room where Daros has been kept with numerous guards the last several days. I should have come sooner, but I let despair about my situation overcome me.

No more.

I won't allow Daros and the First Queen to win, not without a fight.

After steeling myself, I tell them to go in. Nash pushes my chair, and Jaku is by my side with his shoulder in a sling. With their help, I will do this. Daros doesn't stand a chance under our pressure. We will find out how to take down the First Queen and restore this country to the glory it deserves, instead of letting it be ruled by a tyrant who's taken over queens since the beginning of her reign.

That's what I tell myself.

In reality, I'm scared of him like never before, my insides quivering. What secrets does he hold? What does he know of the First Queen? How is he going to use it against me?

"Are you ready to do this?" Jaku asks before he opens the door.

Not sure. "Past ready. This needs to be taken care of." Though if I lose the connection to the First Queen, will I lose my access to a world where I can move? Will the nightmares return? So far, despite the First Queen no longer visiting my dreams, my sleep has been heavy and dreamless, but the worry is still there, hovering.

Doesn't matter. I will do what I'm called for on behalf of my people. Besides, I want to live my life, not be under the rule of someone inside my head.

Jaku opens the door and orders the guards out to wait in the hall with the rest of my escorts—Julina, Eldim, Afet, and several others. None of them have been told what's going on. Only Jaku, Nash, Daros, and I know about the First Queen and the full extent of her reign of terror.

Once the guards exit, Jaku enters, and Nash pushes my wheelchair inside. The room is dark, lit only by a couple of torches by the door. There's a bed on one side, a pot in the corner, a small table, and by the far wall is Daros, tied to the chair multiple times. At Jaku's orders, he's not to be around me unless he's incapacitated. Orders I agree with, not for my sake, but also for all those around me.

"Finally come to see me?" Daros's voice is hoarse, as if he's been talking or screaming for a long period of time.

He was not to be tortured, so he shouldn't have been screaming, and I can't imagine what he would be talking about. His dark eyes are sunken under his thick eyebrows, and his cheeks are leaner, as is the rest of him. The bulk of fat and muscle has been replaced with a thinner, weaker Daros. He'd lost weight before his captivity, but I'd never bothered to care why. Part of me wants to ask what happened to him, but I can't let his appearance distract me. Just because he looks weaker, it doesn't mean he is.

I wait until the door is closed behind us before saying, "It's time for you to give us some answers."

He looks me up and down, taking in my chair before he darts his gaze to Puneah and back. "Seems like you figured out a way to get around. Good for you. Too bad you'll never throw a dagger again."

I want to snarl. To poison him with my words, but it's what he wants—me to defy him and him to berate me, so we can go back to the way things used to be. I won't allow myself to give into it again.

It doesn't stop the fear from snaking along my spine or the spool of terror from wounding inside me at being so close to him, even when he's tied up. "The First Queen—what do you know about her?"

He stares at Puneah. "Is this a fila? I've heard they existed, but I was never lucky enough to get my hands on one. Seems as if someone is favoring you."

He wants to focus on the wrong thing? Fine. I'll play that game. "Puneah, search him."

She stalks forward, her sleek movements hard to follow in the low light. Daros has been searched, but I'm looking for something the guards may have missed.

Daros laughs as she moves closer. She growls, the sound reverberating through the air, making him shut up for once. It brings me deep pleasure, but I don't let it show.

Puneah sniffs him. To his credit, he doesn't flinch even when she nears his face. Her great fangs could do great damage, but I don't think she would attack without my word or being in danger. I think she wouldn't. It's hard to know for certain, when I'm still getting accustomed to the fact that she doesn't bite.

She sniffs his entire body before coming back to me. Never once did her tails twist into the sign that would tell me he's carrying magic on him. So far, it looks like nothing is here.

"Nash, help Puneah search the room. Leave nothing untouched."

I can't see them as they go behind me. There's no sound either, as both of them move silently.

A moment later, Nash says, "Found something."

He moves to my right and holds out a hand to show me a thick-chained gold necklace with a green gem set in it. Puneah puts her nose to the gem and twists her tails together. "Trying to sneak something past us, is he?"

Daros doesn't react, save for a slight tightening around his eyes—enough to let me know he's upset by what we found and that I'm taking it away. Good. Maybe he'll be more likely to tell me what I need to know now he understands I'm serious.

"What does the necklace do?" I ask.

"What makes you think it's anything more than simple jewelry?" His look is innocent, but I know better.

I'm not about to admit what Puneah can do, even if he's guessed it. The necklace will have to wait until more immediate things are dealt with.

"You don't wish to share? No matter. We'll put it somewhere for safe keeping." To Venda or the treasury, probably. Without knowing what it does, there's no saying that it would be safe to wear, and I don't trust Daros enough to keep it in his presence.

What am I thinking? I don't trust him at all.

"What do you know about the First Queen?" I wish I could stand. Get rid of this weak sensation. I'd feel much more imposing if I was taller than him. And if I need anything, it's the chance to gain the upper hand.

The corners of his lips twitch upward. "Androlla has been bothering you, has she?"

"Androlla?"

His grin widens. "I see she hasn't deigned to tell you her name."

There's a compression on my chest, like someone's taken a hammer to it. The First Queen's presence is near. A rightness hums about that name being hers. I glance at Jaku, and then Nash. "I believe he's telling the truth."

Nash hasn't taken his gaze off Daros since he returned to my side, and that doesn't change now. His hand is white on the hilt of his sword. What he's been through has affected him more deeply than I wanted to admit.

He's scared, like I am.

Scared of a frail man, tied to a chair.

"What else do you know about Androlla?" Nash asks.

"That's *Queen Androlla*." The retort rolls off my tongue before I know what's happening. A shiver of fear crawls over me.

Those were not my words.

Nash looks at me, but Jaku keeps an eye on Daros. I clench my jaw, wishing I could have kept the statement in. It's bad enough I have no control over my body. Now I can't even control what I say.

Where's a throwing dagger when I need one? Not that I could use it.

I shake my head and force my gaze back onto Daros. "What do you know about her?"

"I know she's taking you over already. Faster than usual, but then, you're probably the biggest threat she's faced."

"Why am I a threat? I can't move. All she has to do is wait for the next queen, and she'll control them."

"Ah, but you know about her. What's more, even before that, you were strong-willed. Always have been. I assume she's taking control because you aren't as easily swayed."

He swayed me to kill people more effortlessly than I'd like to think. "How do I get her out of my head?"

"You could always try to kill yourself again."

Nash jumps forward, swinging his arm. He just stops himself from punching Daros in the face. "You will not speak to Queen Ryn that way."

"Seeing how I'm the only one who knows what she needs to do, I'll speak to her any way I like." Daros's voice is gleeful.

I want to tell Nash it's all right, but I won't do so in front of Daros. I don't want him to know he's getting to me. That his stinging words met their mark. Before Nash can speak or hit

Daros, I say, "What can I do to get her out of my head without her killing me and without her doing any harm to the country?"

"That's the right question to ask."

When he says nothing further, Nash prompts, "Well? What can we do?"

"You believe I'm going to give the information to her? That I'll hand over every detail she needs to get rid of Androlla, without anything in return, so she's then free to have me executed? I think not."

Despite my promise not to kill again—one I've unfortunately broken but still strive toward—I wish to do him in right here, right now. Lucky for him, I don't have the physical ability to. "What do you want?" I ask.

He takes his time responding, letting his gaze bore into mine. "Why, my freedom, of course. For starters. You'll find my list of requests quite extensive."

"No." The single syllable is out quicker than a blink.

"Pity. I'll have to watch you lose yourself while the country turns back into what Androlla wants. I can do so from the comfort of my very own cell. And who knows? Maybe when she gets back into power, she'll have use for my particular skill set."

"You'll be lucky if she lets you live, if you know what you say you do." Jaku's words of reason are comforting after Daros's statement.

"He's right. The First Queen won't let you live if you know what you say you do. I can feel her hatred toward you while she plots against you."

He shrugs, or tries to. The way his skin whitens against the bindings as he tugs at them indicates he's having a difficult time doing much of anything, yet that smug smirk won't leave his face. "Doesn't matter to me. You kill me, she kills me—either way I'm dead. If you want help, on the other hand, I'd be willing to give it to you. For a price."

And that's what we come back to. I'm not inclined to let a

madman loose for the chance he knows something that might save me. Especially not one whose cruelty I know so well. "Not happening."

"Guess you're stuck with her in your head, then. That is, of course, until you are stuck in her head. I wonder if you'll still be there, watching all she does through you, or if you'll disappear completely."

My throat thickens, making it difficult to swallow. Neither option is acceptable, but I can't let Daros go free. There has to be a way to compromise. A way for us both to get what we want. Well... me more than him.

"Jaku, Nash, I'd like to speak with you outside," I say.

Without a word, Nash moves back behind me, and Jaku leads us out of the area, the guards replacing us. We go to another room several doors down. There are no windows or furniture, just the door and the stone floor. As soon as that door closes, I ask, "What do you think?"

"We can't let him go," Nash says.

"But we have to do something about Androlla." Jaku shoots a worried glance my way before covering his expression. "We can't let her take over Ryn or the country again."

"Agreed." Nash looks at me, his features hard to read. "It's your call."

I was afraid of that. Despite being the queen for a while now, I hate being in charge. I give myself a moment to think about it, trying to come up with something that will work, but I have nothing. "What if we find a middle ground that Daros is comfortable with, while still getting as much information from him as possible?"

"Can't you keep him locked up and force the knowledge from him?" Nash asks.

I give him a level stare.

"Right. This is the king of assassins we're talking about. That would never work."

The room is quiet as I mull over options. Will my idea work, or would torturing him be a better option? As much as I want to torture him, it wouldn't be right, nor would it give us what we need.

"We should go for an exchange, though I'm afraid we're going to give him more than we want and get little in return." Nash's thoughts mimic my own.

"Agreed." Jaku motions to the door, and Nash rolls me back to Daros's room, where we exchange places with the guards.

"Ready to give me my freedom?" Daros asks. "Make me your Head Advisor? Pardon me?"

All three options leave me feeling sick. "No."

"Then say goodbye to your freedom," he says.

What little I have, I'm not willing to give away. "I have a different proposition for you."

"Oh? What is it you want to offer me? I must tell you, I'm feeling rather picky, since I hold all the knowledge."

"I will pardon you if you give me the information I seek. Nothing more."

His expression remains neutral. "You will pardon me of all crimes, including any I may commit in the future, and I will give you *some* of the information you seek."

"No deal. I will pardon you of past crimes, plus I save your life by not having you executed, and you give me most of the information I seek."

"You will pardon me of all crimes in the past, save my life now and in the future, and I will give you some of the information you seek."

I don't want to give in, but what other choice do I have? If I don't go forward with this, I will be under the First Queen's control sooner, rather than later. "You'll have a deal, if you can keep Androlla from controlling me."

"I can't promise that, but I'll do my best."

Is his best good enough? It'll have to be. "I'll take it."

"Good. Now bring some papers for me to write up the pardon."

"You mean, for my Head of the Guard to write up."

"I meant what I said."

Though we're done with the main negotiation, I have a feeling I'll be here for a while yet. At least I have some hope of getting rid of the First Queen.

She simmers in the background, scheming. I wish I could read her mind. More than that, I wish I could ban her from me, but our connection is strong. This deal with Daros had better make a difference.

We procure parchment and a quill and agree on the terminology. Daros concedes to let Jaku pen it. Jaku writes it out in surprisingly beautiful penmanship with the hand that's not in a sling.

"Before this is signed," I say, "tell me what I need to know."

"I don't think so. There's no saying you won't go back on your word once I've told you what you need to know," Daros says.

"Out of the two of us, I'm the more trustworthy one."

"Might I remind you that you punched Fulla after declaring she wasn't in trouble?"

I hold back a growl. How does he even know about that? Probably servants gossiping. What doesn't he know about? "Fine. I'll sign this, and you will tell me."

"Some of what you need to know."

I roll my eyes. "Fine. Some of what I need to know."

He smirks. "We have a deal."

While Jaku keeps an eye on him, Nash brings me the pardon to sign. He places the parchment right up to my hand and puts the pen in it. I scratch my name down as best I can. It comes out scraggly and from moving my fingers the tiniest bit makes me tired, but it's signed. I'm grateful the name I choose is so short. It's not the first document I've had to sign since Daros poisoned me.

"There you have it." Nash shows him the document, as I say, "What do I need to know?"

He smirks. "Androlla is going to get more aggressive."

I want to growl but refrain. "There has to be more you can give me than that."

"That's the information you get for my pardon."

A scream tickles my throat. I was already figuring that out. Instead, I look at him calmly. "Then enjoy this nice room."

His smile falters. "But you pardoned me."

"I did, but I said nothing about your freedom. You will not be executed or held accountable for your actions. Despite that, you will remain in custody of the crown."

"You can't do this."

"Until you give me more information, I can." I glance at Nash and tilt my head toward the door.

He rolls me toward the exit.

"It's your loss," Daros says. "Androlla will command you before it's realized. You'll get no help from me."

His words sting, but I don't say anything. Nash takes me outside, and the guards reclaim their place.

I've lost this war before it even began.

CHAPTER 3

INKGA PULLS the blankets over me, and Puneah jumps up beside me and curls into a ball, except for her head, which she rests on my chest. Despite the weight, which is less than I expect, it's a comforting feeling.

Inkga shakes her head. "Never thought I'd see an animal so taken with someone. Let alone a fila."

I let a small smile slip out. "Neither did I. I'm not entirely sure about her, but she seems to be good with me. It's nice to have her company. Just not as nice as yours is. Thank you for staying with me and taking care of me."

She tucks a lose strand of hair behind her ear. "It's nothing."

"No. It's something. Nash told me you wouldn't accept a raise."

"Don't be silly. There's no reason for one."

"There are plenty of reasons, the biggest being that you do a lot more work now that I'm…"

She waves me off. "It's nothing I wouldn't do for any of my friends. Not everyone can claim friendship with the queen."

"Then you will accept the raise."

She chuckles. "That's not how friendship works."

I sigh. She has to make this hard. She's done literally everything for me. No one deserves earning more as much as she does. "I didn't want to go here, but you leave me no choice. As your queen, I order you to take the raise."

Her eyes widen. After a moment, she curtsies. "Yes, Your Majesty."

"None of that, now. We're still friends." I hope I haven't scared her away.

"You can't have it both ways, Ryn. Either you order me about, or we're friends."

"I can too have it both ways. It's how it's been almost since the beginning."

"But you've never ordered me to do something before. Not really."

She's right, and it feels rather odd. "Let me get away with it this one time."

She sits in a chair next to my bed and looks me straight in the eye. "I promise it's not a burden. I know you worry about that, but you needn't. I'm happy helping you."

I blink away the sudden stinging in my eyes. "I appreciate that more than words can express, but it doesn't change the fact you're getting a raise."

With a laugh, she sits back. "You are so stubborn."

I smirk. "You have no idea."

"Fine, then. I'll take it, but if I choose to use it to help others, there's nothing you can do about it."

I should have known. I yawn. "Fine. But make sure you're saving for the future, too. I won't always be around."

"Don't talk like that."

"But it's true." I want to tell her about the First Queen. To warn her away, for when Androlla takes over, but there will be time enough for that later. Now I want to be with my friend.

"I refuse to discuss it further," she says. "Would you like me to stay with you?"

"Yes, please."

She puts her elbow on the arm of the chair and props her head on her fist. "Then rest now. Just rest."

But I don't want to.

Despite my resistance, heavy eyelids limit my vision. I'm extra tired because a healer came in and worked each of my limbs before I settled in to bed. Besides, ever since Daros poisoned me, I have needed more sleep than I ever remember getting before.

Except I fear sleep.

No matter that the First Queen has left me alone since I discovered her true nature, I dread the moment I dream of her again. I have the uncanny feeling she's ready to spring on me tonight.

Puneah gives a rumbling purr, vibrating my chest. She seems content. Comfortable. Yet I know she's ready to pounce the moment someone tries to hurt me. If only she could protect me the same way in my dreams.

If only.

The night wears on as I fight sleep. My eyelids become heavier and heavier, yet I resist. Inkga begins a song, soft and low. It's one I've never heard before, about the stars and moons, and how they look down on us as we sleep.

Despite my fighting it, my eyelids close and don't open again.

"Took you long enough to fall asleep." The First Queen's words echo through the air.

I ignore her, in favor of marveling over my body. It's free of weakness. I give a little jump, pumping my fists into the air. The movements are quick and precise, like they used to be before I was poisoned.

I break into a run, going as fast and far from Androlla as I can. Ignoring that she's the reason I'm here, I run until I'm gasping for breath. If I didn't know any better, I'd say I have my old body back.

It's perfect.

Once I catch my breath, I break into a run again, adding spins, jumps, twirls, and flips as I go. Stretching my body is so natural. So right. I wish there were walls to bounce off. Then again, if I can make up a chair in this place, why not a wall?

I picture two walls framing me, far apart enough to give me running room. I get a running start before jumping onto the first wall, hurrying across the path, popping up onto the second wall, and doing a flip off it.

It worked. Blessed daggers, it worked. I continue my jagged path, only slowing down when my muscles burn and my lungs heave. Despite being just a dream, I'm feeling the strain. It must be a mental thing.

I slow to a stroll before I stop all together, bend at the waist with my hands on my sides, and take deep breaths.

"Are you quite finished?" The First Queen asks.

I don't reply. She's not worth it.

A tinkling laugh flows through the air. "We both know the only one here not worth anything is you. Why else would you be in this position? Had you behaved in a manner that said you cared about your life, you never would have crossed paths with me."

Something in me snaps. I glare. Although I understand she is trying to take away my free will, she doesn't look any different. Doesn't look as evil as her actions would suggest. "I'm worth a hundred times what you are, you lying, despicable scumbag." Not that I haven't had doubts, but I have learned better now.

"Pretty words from one whose own parents didn't want her. Who tried to kill her."

The reference to my parents makes me cringe on the inside. I don't want to go there. My father's latest betrayal is still too raw. I decided I was worth something previously. I won't let a few harsh words make me forget that.

"So you think. We'll see how long your confidence lasts as I take over your body. Then again, you're of little use to me, now that you're broken."

I clench my teeth. "There's nothing you can say that will hurt me."

Androlla glides to me. Instinct says to flinch away, but I've dealt with much worse taunting from Daros. This is nothing.

"Ah, right," she says. "Daros. Claims he knows how to defeat me,

24

when all he knows is that I exist. Seems to me he's getting the better end of the deal."

There's that niggling doubt inside me, which she's tugging on. I shut off my thoughts. I can't deal with her reading them.

She gives a low, throaty laugh. "That's right. I'm in your mind. You can't get rid of me or your thoughts. Then again, which thoughts are yours and which are mine?"

Through gritted teeth, I say, "You are not allowed here."

She turns her back to me, like she hasn't a care in the world. "I can go wherever I want in your mind. It might as well be mine."

"It will never be yours." I let venom ooze through my words.

She laughs again. "If you weren't so annoying, I'd think you were cute. What you don't understand is that I'm already a part of you. There's nothing you can do about it."

There has to be something.

She sits on air, crossing her ankles. "Not one thing. You're slowly going to lose yourself to me. And since you now have friends, I'll enjoy getting rid of them."

"Don't talk about my friends. You have no right."

Her pearly white teeth shine as she speaks. "I have every right. They are but a nuisance. You've changed more laws than I hoped you would, but it'll get right with time. I'll pick out my next victim to become the queen before having you killed off. Pity you didn't work out. With your skills, we could have lived a long time."

There's a knot in my stomach that keeps getting bigger. I don't know what to do with it. I want it gone. I want out of here. And yet, I don't. This is the first time I've been able to move in around a week. Really move. I don't want to give that away.

"I suppose there's a chance you'll heal, but it's so small, it's not worth considering." She looks at her nails.

I should kill her here and now. I can move fast, so she won't have time to counter. I grab a dagger from my belt and slash it at her. She casually raises an arm to block me, and a thin red line appears where the metal hits. She smiles.

Pain screams through my arm.

I wake up groaning in pain. My left arm is dripping blood on the bed and some on Puneah. My hurting Androlla in my dream injured me. But did it hurt her?

Her presence becomes known in a strong, hard laugh.

Apparently, the only one hurt is me.

CHAPTER 4

"Let me in." Nash's voice comes from outside my bed chamber. I know a guard is stationed there with Jaku and Inkga in here while the healer wraps my arm. It's tricky business, since I can't help her lift it, but she manages fairly well.

I nod to Jaku, trying to ignore the lightheadedness plaguing me since I woke. He opens the door, letting Nash inside.

The man I love has pale, dark circles under his eyes. Has he had a hard time sleeping again? "I heard they sent for a healer. What happened?" His voice is frantic as he inspects the healer's work.

"She woke up with the wound," Inkga says. "I swear no one came in the room to hurt her. Do you think it could be related to the poisoning?"

"It's not." I speak for the first time since I got Inkga's attention to grab a healer.

"Then how did you get this wound?" the healer asks. "It's a clean cut, like it's from a sharp blade."

I do like to keep my blades in prime condition, and that goes over into my dreams. I keep my lips firmly pressed together and glance at Jaku, not daring to look at Nash. This isn't the time to discuss it. Can't have rumors going around that the queen has gone crazy. I'm not sure many people would believe me, except Nash and Jaku. Inkga, maybe. The council would probably see it as an excuse to have me executed, so they could pick a sane queen. It's a stringent rule that must have the entire council's approval to be enforced. It's cruel to those who grow old and senile, but no queen has had a problem with the law that I'm aware of —until me.

Yes. Definitely time to keep quiet.

The healer *hmpf*s. "Fine. Don't tell me. But you'd better tell your Head of Guard. He needs to know how to keep you safe, as I'm sure this was knife work."

"I swear I didn't let anyone in," Inkga says again.

"I know," I tell her.

She wrings her hands as the healer packs up her equipment, leaves a few instructions about how to care for my wound, and is out the door, claiming she'll be back later to check on me.

Inkga says, "Is there anything I can do for you? Anything I can get you? Say it, and I'll make it happen."

My old body back. Saying that would be unfair. "Would you check on Puneah? I want to make sure she gets washed all right, without biting anyone."

"Of course." She stops moving her hand. "I'll get right on it, and I'll bring some breakfast up with me on my return."

"Thank you."

She hurries to go before turning back to me. "I'm glad you're all right. I don't know what I would have done if you were hurt seriously."

I nod, words eluding me.

She leaves, and we're alone with a single guard outside my room. Jaku and Nash each approach a side of my bed, coming close, probably so we won't be overheard.

"What happened?" Jaku asks. "How did you get sliced on the

arm when no one was in the room but Inkga? Are you sure it wasn't her?"

"Of course it wasn't." I'm getting tired of telling him that. It's all he's been asking since he arrived. "The cut came from me," I say.

Nash's face scrunches up. "Ryn, I thought you were over hurting yourself. And how did you move enough to make that happen?" His face lightens. "Are you getting your strength back?"

"No." The word comes out of me more harshly than I mean it too, but the pain in my chest is so great, it's difficult to be anything but harsh. More calmly, I say, "Sorry. No. Let me explain. I was dreaming of Androlla and had full use of my body. We were talking, when I got the idea that I could kill her and be done with everything. Except, when I cut her arm, I woke to pain and my arm bleeding."

Both men are silent, as they exchange a glance. Jaku says, "I think it's safe to say you can't harm Androlla in your dreams without hurting yourself."

Nash curses. "Sorry. This whole thing has me frustrated. I can't believe it hurt you. Do you believe she was injured as well?"

I think back to the moment I cut her. How she lifted her arm. Her smile. The pain. "I don't know. I think so; her arm was red. But she didn't mind. She grinned at me like she hadn't a care in the world. However she's defeated, I don't think it's from something happening in a dream."

Nash looks down at my bandaged arm. "What do we do now?"

"I'm afraid I know the answer, but no one is going to like it." When I have their full attention, I say, "I need to speak with Daros again." I could have him tortured, but would that give the First Queen more of an upper hand? More of a footing to overtake me?

"Are you having a joke?" Jaku asks. "He played you last time. What's to keep him from doing it again?"

"I'll make him give us the information first this time. But he's the only one who knows what to do. I have to work with him if there's any chance of getting rid of her. I could tell him lies, but I wonder if that's giving the First Queen more power." The First Queen's presence draws near, dark and heavy. "She doesn't relish the idea of me meeting him again either, which makes me think it's a good one," I say.

"I don't like it," Nash says.

"I think you've lost this one, Ryn," Jaku says.

"Except you're both forgetting one thing."

"Which is?" Jaku runs his free hand over his stubble. Probably didn't get a chance to shave this morning.

"I'm the queen. I get to do what I want."

Nash huffs.

"As one of your council members, I would advise against it," Jaku says.

"As your Head Advisor, I also advise against it." Nash's tone is firm.

"Then what should I do?" Out of habit, I try to point to my head, but my hand only twitches. "There's nothing stopping her from taking over. It's a matter of time. I don't like having to deal with Daros, but for once, he's the lesser of two evils."

Which is rather disgusting.

"When do you want it arranged for?" Jaku says, sounding resigned

"You mean you're agreeing with this?" Nash yells.

"I have to do as the queen desires," Jaku responds.

Nash lowers his voice, but it still holds a hint of tension. "And I have to do what's best for my queen."

"Which is talking to Daros," I say. "I know you don't like it. I don't, either, but we have to get some answers."

He shakes his head. "Fine."

"Now that we're all agreed, I'd like to go see him."

"Let's wait for Inkga to come back with Puneah and food," Jaku says. "You need something in your system, and I'll feel better if Puneah is with us when we go talk to Daros."

"The creature doesn't unnerve you?" I ask.

"Oh, she does. That's why I want her around. Besides, she seems attached to you, and I want you to be surrounded by those that care as much as possible."

Sounds like a good reason. The truth is I'd be more comfortable with Puneah around as well.

"I'm going to make arrangements." Jaku looks at Nash. "You've got her?"

"Nothing will harm her while you're gone. I promise you that."

"And I'll hold you to that promise," Jaku says.

"I'm right here." Because they're talking around me, like I'm not or can't hear.

"Sorry," Jaku says. "I want to make certain you're taken care of."

"You're forgiven." He does have the right thought, but I wish to be included in plans about my own safety. Though it's something I'll probably never be able to do again. I clench my jaw, to keep from spouting off how I feel about it.

Jaku leaves, and Nash stands and presses a kiss to my forehead —a faint, feather-light kiss, but there, nevertheless. I close my eyes reveling in the safe, secure feeling—the love that I feel for him and he shares with me, even if we can never be together. I need that. I need to feel his love for me. His strength.

There's a soft touch on my hand, and then the pressure increases slightly as he squeezes it. I open my eyes to find him looking right at me. "What?"

"Wishing I could take this away."

I sigh. "You and me both. I don't know what I would do if I didn't have you."

He wraps both his hands around mine. "You'd have Jaku, Inkga, and Jem."

The thought of them being here to help me threatens to close my throat, so I quickly switch topics. "How is Jem?"

He squeezes my hand more. "She's managing. She thinks she's

hiding her feelings from everyone, diving into work with the other ladies-in-waiting and training them to fight as well as practicing, but it's obvious there's something missing from her life."

I wish it didn't have to be like that. That Wilric was still here for her to flirt with. To learn from. And if my suspicions are correct, to love.

"Can I tell you something?" I ask.

"Anything."

I bite my lower lip, unsure I can tell him. But if I let it fester inside, where only the First Queen knows of it, she'll use it against me. "I feel like it's my fault Wilric died."

"What? No. Why would you say that?"

"Because he died saving my life. He died protecting me. If I had never come here, he wouldn't have been in that position."

"I understand, but think about it. It was his job to protect you. More than that, if you hadn't come along, it's unlikely that he would have met Jem. That they would have formed a relationship. That he would have found such joy in serving and loving. Or that he would have died in such an honorable way, saving you, which I know he wouldn't want any other way." His eyes are wet, but the tears don't fall.

Part of me feels at peace from his words, but I'm still conflicted. "You don't know that. There's no possible way you could."

"That's where you're wrong, my queen. He may have died suddenly, but we spent long hours talking whenever we got the chance. One of the things we talked about was death, and he mentioned how he would rather die in the service of the crown, especially for such a worthy queen, than any other way. He was pleased he could be of such use."

I think the words over. Can it be true? I know he can't have wanted to die—not like I did when I first came to the palace, but in another way? A way that left him honored?

"What's more," Nash continues, "I know he was happy. He

had an excellent life, a good family that he got to see sometimes, and he was falling deeply for Jem. Even if they could never marry, they could touch, which is more than what we could have in public. There was peace in his life and service. He was happy. What better time to go than when everything is as you want it?"

"But he could have had more. A wife and children. A long life."

"Yes, but in the guard you know your time isn't long. Protecting the queen is dangerous when things are so unstable, and your life is constantly in danger. I'm just sad to see a good man—a friend—go." This time a couple of tears do drop down his cheeks.

I wish I could wipe them away with my kisses. That I could take away the pain of losing a friend. Instead, I cry with him, mourning the loss of one so brave and true. One who should have had a long life, full of the people he loved and the things he enjoyed doing.

But Nash is right. It's not my fault.

It's Daros's.

And there's nothing I can do about it.

I pardoned him for all crimes. There's no way to punish him without breaking my resolution. Despite that, I'm probably about to give him even more, since I need his help so desperately. Perhaps I should give into torturing him. But no. I won't go there.

Nash runs a thumb across my face, drying my tears before his own. Once that's done, he leans down, his mouth right next to mine and his breath warm against my lips. "I promise to take care of you. We'll find a way through this."

"And if we don't?" I whisper.

"Then I'll still be at your side the entire way."

He brushes his lips against mine, soft at first, but firmer as the moments tick away. I press back, grateful I can do so, but wishing I could run my hands up his back and neck. That I could pull him closer to me.

As if reading my thoughts, he does move closer, puts a hand on my cheek, and deepens the kiss.

Everything going through me—every thought, feeling, touch—is like a bolt of energy rushing through me. Making me feel alive in a way I haven't since long before I was poisoned. I'm full of so much feeling, I don't know what to do with it.

I let myself get lost in the kiss. Lost in the feel of him. In the touch of his skin against my face. The way his fingers move toward my hair, then through it. I've never been so grateful I have control over my lips as I am in this moment. Talking is nice. Kissing is better.

He pulls away from my lips, and I'm about to protest, when his kisses trail along my jaw, up into my hair, and back down again.

I ache for him. To be with him. To love him. To marry him.

But those things can never be.

He breaks off, but only by a few inches. "What's wrong? Why are you crying?"

"Because my heart is torn to shreds over the fact that we can never be together."

He squeezes his eyes closed, as if in pain. "I know." He kisses the wetness from my skin. "I know."

To my sadness, he stands, brushes the remaining tears from my face, and grabs my hand once more. When he sits next to me, I have the most insane urge to jump on his lap and kiss him until I can't remember a thing.

But I can't lift my own hand.

There's a knock at the door. Nash has barely enough time to pull his hand from mine when it opens. Guess it's a good thing I couldn't climb on his lap after all. It's Inkga, which explains why she didn't wait for me to ask her to enter, since I've given her permission to come in at all times. Though we haven't told her about our relationship, I'd like to think she'd be happy for me and Nash and keep our secret. It's not something I'm willing to test, though. Although I think of her as my friend, it's still difficult to trust anyone with that secret.

Puneah noses her way between Nash and me, sits on the ground next to my bed, and lays her head on my bed, next to my hand. My fingers twitch but can't reach her.

Inkga sets a tray on the nearby table. "What would you like to start with, for breakfast?"

Anything that will get rid of the heartache blossoming inside me.

CHAPTER 5

DAROS SITS BEFORE ME, bound like before, eyeing the bandage on my arm. "Had a little run-in, did we?"

I ignore him. I won't give him the satisfaction of letting him know I hurt myself trying to kill the First Queen. "I need more information."

"She did that to you, then. I knew you'd need more."

Next to Daros, Nash balls his hands into fists.

On his other side, Jaku remains calmer, but the lines in his neck are tense. He says, "You will respect Her Majesty."

Daros shrugs—or tries to. "She hasn't earned my respect."

Nash's fist goes flying.

Before it can land, I say, "Not yet, Nash."

He pulls back, shoulders heaving. It can't be easy, putting up with Daros attacking me. If our positions were reversed, I would have let that punch land, instead of pulling back.

"That's right," Daros says. "Listen to the girl. That's all she can do anymore is talk. Might as well make her think it means something."

This time, Nash doesn't hesitate. He punches Daros full on the mouth. Daros reels back fast and hard, the front two legs of the chair lifting off the ground.

I don't bother saying something to Nash. I wanted to do the same thing.

Daros turns his head to the side and spits. "Not a good way to get information out of me."

I say, "I need you to tell me how to defeat the First Queen. None of this nonsense I already know. You *will* give me the information I need."

"Fine."

"Fine?" He's going to give it to me without a fight?

"On the condition that you give me my freedom and my house back."

Of course there's a catch. There's always a catch. He wants a bargain. "You know I can't do that."

"Why not? You pardoned me. Might as well set me free, like you should have done."

"Why do you even want to stay in the city?" Everyone knows him here and now they realize what his job is, if they didn't already.

"My reasons are my own."

I hold in a huff. "We both know you're going to wreak havoc in this country if I set you free. I can't have that happening."

"It's your death."

I clench my jaw. He's right. I glance at Nash and Jaku. Neither is looking at me, both staring daggers at Daros. Too bad it doesn't intimidate him in the least. I could take them out of the room and discuss it with them again, but I don't want to. It's clear it's up to me and they'll support me with what I decide, even if they don't like it.

"Fine. You want your freedom and your house back?" Not that his house was left in very good condition. Another reason not to care if I give it to him. "You can have them, if you take a dozen guards with you wherever you go."

"Not much freedom then, is it? Besides, you could have your Head Guard here stab me in the back as soon as we part ways."

I try to act nonchalant, but if he doesn't take it, I don't know what I'll do. "You'll have to trust that we aren't like you. Besides, it'll mean more freedom than you have now."

He purses his lips as the room turns silent. It's so quiet. I can hear my own breathing, my stress, dripping from me. It's not what I want, but then, none of this is. He says, "Three guards, in exchange for another piece of information."

I don't let my relief show on my face. Besides, he's only offering a piece. I need the whole, but I have a feeling it's going to take a lot of time and persistence to get it out of him, and more giving in to his demands. "Six. And when I summon you, there's no delay in your coming," I say.

"Done."

That was too easy. What has he planned? I don't trust him at all. At least with the guards, I can hope everything will go as I want. "Tell me what I need to know."

"Not until I have what I want."

"That may have worked last time, but it's not going to work now. Tell me."

"Let me out of the bands first."

I clench my jaw. He's right, I have to let him go, but I don't wish to. I want to keep him locked up forever. We're far past that alternative if we're going to continue getting information out of him. I give Jaku the *go ahead*. He leans down next to Daros's ear and whispers something I can't hear before sawing through the ropes.

Once he's free, Daros shakes out his arms and rubs them down, before standing and stretching. "You don't know how good that feels."

"Answers, Daros." My words are crisp. "Now."

It's strange, looking at him when he's so much thinner. Though we've been feeding him, it hasn't been enough time for him to put the weight or the muscle back on. He saunters forward, but Nash darts out a hand and shoves him back by the shoulder.

Daros doesn't glance his way. "You'll need magic to defeat Androlla."

I should have known, but it's a shock. "Where do I get it?"

"I'm not sure it's worth telling you without more of what I want."

I glare him down. "And I don't have to give you what you want, without something more to go on. How do I get magic?"

He taps his lip with one finger as he looks at me. Nash and Jaku are tense, their muscles bunched, poised to grab him the moment he missteps. Daros may be weakened, but so is Jaku from his shoulder wound. I'm not sure who'd have the upper hand if it came to a fight. Though Daros wouldn't get far, with all the guards outside the room, and no other way of escaping.

When Daros speaks, his voice is deceivingly calm. "Practice simple spells to start with. A charm for good luck. A charm of protection."

Both spells sound useful, but not like something I can use to defeat the First Queen. On the other hand, if it's going to take magic to defeat her, I have a lot I need to learn. "How do I do that?"

"You are a simpleton."

Puneah growls. Can she understand what we're saying? Either way, I'm happy she's on my side. "Tell me what I need to know."

He rubs his nails against his shirt, as if he hasn't a care in the world. "You'll need an object to focus the magic on. A rock. A piece of jewelry. Clothing. Anything that doesn't have life to it."

"So no plants?"

"No plants or animals."

"Fine, then what?"

"Let's start with a spell for luck. Besides the object, you'll need something green, rosemary, and a mirror. Grind up the first two ingredients on the mirror. While doing so chant *ohma lo*, then place the object you're going to use on the mirror and rub the grindings into that object while saying the same phrase. When you get it right, the object will glow for a brief moment, and then it will be enchanted with luck."

"That's all I need to do?" It sounds simple enough.

"No. You need to believe it. Not a little, but truly think it's going to work. The object will not take to the spell unless you do so."

"You're not instructing me to build a curse, are you?" Because I wouldn't put it past him.

"Would I do such a thing?"

That doesn't make me feel better. Perhaps there's another way I can get the information I want. "What does *ohma lo* mean? Why do I need to chant that?"

"You ask too many questions," he snaps. "It needs to be done if you want Queen Androlla gone."

His rebuke stings, but I don't let it show. I have to focus on the task, and not on his trying to make me feel inferior. "I can do that."

"Right." The word comes out like he doesn't believe me. "In the meantime, if you'll excuse me, I have a house to set up."

I want to ask if he'll come back when called, but I can't bring myself to seem that weak. Besides, he'll have guards to make him. I hope they can. With his skills, including magic, there's little I can do about forcing him to return. I have to believe I have things he wants, which is why he's staying in town. There has to be a reason why he's so insistent on having his house back.

Jaku and Nash on the other hand have no problem stopping him, both getting in his way to the door.

"You'll have to wait until we can arrange for the guards to be with you," Jaku says.

"Very well," Daros replies. "But you won't tie me up. I refuse to be bound again."

Jaku looks at me. I give my consent. We leave and shut the door on Daros after the guards join him.

As I'm being wheeled away, I ask Jaku, "Who will you put on him?"

"I'd like the best, but they need to stay with you. I'll try to split it in a way that you're still protected, but Daros won't sneeze without a blade making it to his throat."

"Perfect."

While we journey back, I think about magic. Is it true there's a healing spell? One that can undo the damage Daros did to me? If there is one, I doubt he'd give it to me, since he was the one to put me in this predicament in the first place.

Back in my rooms, Jaku excuses himself, and I request that Nash roll me by the sitting room window. When I'm settled, he asks, "Would you like me to get everything together for the spell?"

"The sooner, the better. Also, I would like to speak to the Head Librarian."

"Consider it done." He draws nearer long enough to give my hand a squeeze and is out the door.

I want to ask him how he's doing, if he's handling things better, but I don't think I'll like the answer when there's even less I can do about it now that I'm confined.

Moments later, Inkga enters. She is kind enough to chat with me a while, but it's hard to focus on what she says. My mind is busy trying to figure out how making a protection charm or luck charm will help me defeat the First Queen. Why type of protection will it offer? And how will a luck charm help me if I can hardly move? I'll have to concentrate on this as the first step and believe it will assist me better when we get to the harder spells.

Her presence is near, leading me to believe I won't be able to keep this from her. What will she say about it when I go to sleep next? Will she even care?

No matter what she says or does, I should ignore her and enjoy the little time I have my free will.

I force myself into conversation with Inkga, getting away from thoughts of Androlla. There's more there that I want to think about anyway.

Nash joins us after a while, laden with a bag and joined by a tall woman with big eyes that take everything in.

"This is Wula Hendri, the Head Librarian," Nash says.

She gives a pretty curtsy. "How may I help you, Your Majesty?"

I glance at Inkga and make a quick decision. I'm not ready to tell her about the First Queen, but letting her know I'm interested in magic will be a good first step to see how she reacts. "I would like all the books you have on magic."

"Magic? But that's unheard of." Wula puts a hand on her hip.

"Mostly unheard of," I say. "It's not all gone as evidenced by Venda from Faner." I should consider enlisting her help as well, if she's willing.

The librarian lifts her eyebrows. "I heard rumors, but I didn't know they were true."

"Very. What I need from you is any and all books you can find on the subject."

"I will do what I can."

"As quickly as you can, please."

"Yes, Your Highness. Will there be anything else?"

"That should do it. Please keep quiet about it."

"Very well. I will personally deliver you what I can and will report back when I can't find anymore."

"Thank you."

As she exits, I glance at Inkga. Her eyes are wide, but the rest of her seems calm. When she notices I'm looking at her, she says, "I didn't know magic still existed."

"It does, though there's not much of it in Valcora at the current time." It's almost as if someone has tried to snuff it out. The First Queen, perhaps? If it's the key to defeating her, I can understand why she would be reluctant to let it continue.

"That's amazing," Inkga says. "Can I learn with you?"

I can't help but laugh at the eagerness in her voice. Maybe she'd change her mind if she knew it was to defeat an evil queen who's been ruling for a thousand years. Or maybe she'd think I am crazy. "If you like. I'm trying to make a luck charm today."

I explain to her what Daros told me about simple spells without divulging my source, without telling her it was Daros that did the telling, as Nash pulls items out of his bag and sets them on a nearby table. Once he's finished, he rolls me closer.

"How are we going to grind the items down without breaking the mirror?" Inkga asks.

I'm more worried about having enough strength to grind them in the first place. "That is a concern. We'll have to be careful."

"Who wants to try first?" Nash asks.

"We should let Ryn try," Inkga says.

Something in me doesn't want to touch the stuff. Instead of giving into that feeling, I try to push myself forward and fail. "I'll need some help."

Nash nods. He grabs a sprig of rosemary and another plant I can't place.

"What's the other green plant?" I ask.

"Dried hathwa." He sets them both on a mirror and pulls a pestle out of his bag along with a rock that he sets on the mirror besides the other two ingredients. "Here, Ryn."

I love the sound of my name coming from his lips. There's little time to ponder it, though, as he sets the mirror on my lap and helps me grab hold of the pestle. I flicker my gaze to Inkga, who's watching intently.

Nash says, "Go ahead."

I attempt my best to grip onto the pestle and move it toward the mirror. The jerky movement causes the pestle to go flying out of my hand to the floor. "This is going to take a lot of practice."

Inkga grabs the pestle and places it back in my hands. "That's all right. We have time."

Nash winces. Time is one thing I don't have.

I try several more times with the same results, and my hand feels weaker than ever. "Why don't you give it a try, Nash? Or Inkga?"

He looks to her. "Why don't you try it first?"

"All right." There's a hesitation in her voice, but she takes the mirror and pestle and begins to grind the plants up while chanting *ohma lo*. After a moment, she stops. "I feel a little silly, doing this."

"You have to believe in it for it to happen," Nash says.

"All right." She resumes until the mixture is a fine powder, and then proceeds to rub the material into the stone while continuing chanting. A minute passes. Then another.

She shrugs. "Maybe I don't have an affinity for magic."

"Do you need it?" I ask.

"You just need to believe, I think," Nash says. "It will work. It has to."

His voice is so intense, I expect Inkga to question why it matters so much, but she remains silent. Nash goes through the process, starting with a new batch of hathwa, rosemary, and a rock. When he starts rubbing the mixture into the rock, I watch on with eager eyes.

Nothing happens.

After several minutes, he leans back. "I don't know what I'm doing wrong."

"Maybe we should request Venda's help," I say.

"Do you think she'd be able to guide us?" Inkga asks.

"She prevented me from dying with magic. I don't see why she couldn't help us along."

Inkga hurries to the door. "I'll go get her." She doesn't wait for me to respond; she leaves the door at an almost run.

Nash glances at me. "You think Daros kept something from us?"

"I don't know."

"I'll whip him if he did." The venom in his words matches the poison in my heart toward Daros.

"I wish I could help."

His expression softens. "How are you feeling?"

"Truth be told, tired. It's been a long day, though it's still early afternoon. I'm afraid it's taken a lot out of me."

"Why don't you close your eyes and rest for a while? Do you want me to take you to your bed?"

"I'd rather sit here with you, but maybe I will take you up on your offer." I watch his soft smile, until my eyes close. The next thing I know, I'm waking to the door opening. A quick glance at the clock shows it's been over an hour. I yawn as Inkga and Venda enter.

This is ridiculous. I've never been so tired in my life. I don't think I was even this sleepy as a baby. I'd ask Shillian about that, except I'm not talking to her since Carver's betrayal. Trying to kill me for Daros. I want nothing to do with either of them.

"I found Venda," Inkga says. "She's willing to help us."

"I hear you are trying to make a luck charm." Venda's voice is melodic as ever, but there's an undercurrent to it that I don't understand. A tightening that's not usually there.

"We are trying to learn magic in general. A luck charm sounds easy enough." If it's too difficult to learn, I can't imagine I'll get what I need in time to stop the First Queen.

"It is simple, once you understand magic." She glances around the room. "Where is Puneah?"

"Probably sleeping in my room, on my bed or under it. That's her favorite place." She's usually on it when I'm there, but it's not a given.

"She must be comfortable with you, to have made your bed her nest."

Charming. "Do you know what we need to do for the luck spell?"

"I do." She glances down at our ingredients. "Hathwa?"

"We were told to use something green," Nash says.

"From whom?"

We remain silent as she and Inkga look from me to Nash.

Nash finally says, "Our source that's helping us with magic."

She sniffs, lifting her chin. "If you need advice, you should come to me. No one in your country knows enough. Something green will work, but bark of an urta tree would work better."

"An urta for luck?" Inkga asks. "Like the superstitions say?"

"Just like that," she replies. "Superstitions exist for a reason."

"I'll fetch one, if I manage to find some," Nash says.

"They are rare, but check with the cook's assistant. I've been able to acquire several rare ingredients from her," Venda says.

While he's gone, Venda questions me about what I know of the spell, and I tell her all Daros explained to me. I'm getting good at it, now that I've heard it once and retold it twice.

"Very well," she says.

"So this spell will really work?" I ask.

"With a few adjustments, yes."

That's a relief. If Daros is mostly telling the truth, perhaps we'll be able to get to the bottom of this with Venda's help.

Nash comes through the door. "The cook's assistant didn't have any but knew of a gardener that might have some, and he did." He pulls a piece of dark bark from a pouch.

Nash pulls a piece of dark bark from out of a pouch.

"Very good. It is true that believing in it is an important part of magic, but you must also find a part of yourself to give to the spell. A part deep inside here." Venda pumps a fist on her chest.

"What about *ohma lo*?" I ask. "What does it mean, and why must we say it?'

"In the ancient tongue, it means *luck be given*. You could say just that, but I and other enchanters feel the magic is stronger when using the ancient language. It helps you to concentrate. To focus on something specific."

She gathers the ingredients on the mirror, forming a pile of each. "The pestle will help break down the rosemary but isn't strictly necessary. It just takes combining them. Their oils, you might say. They should mix as you chant, and you have to feed them your belief and the part of you." She smushes them together with her fingers, chanting *ohma lo*. After a minute or so, she takes the mixture and transfers it onto the rock, while she continues to chant. It takes a moment, but then the stone glows, and she stops, wipes the mixture off the newly made luck charm, and holds it up for us to see.

"I can't believe it worked," Inkga says.

"And that is why you fail." Venda hands her the rock. "That is yours to gift to whomever you choose. You may not keep it for yourself or give it to Ryn until you make one on your own. It will mean more if you make it. It will still be lucky, just not as strongly. Since we are in Valcora, I would decorate the charm and tell the person you are gifting it to that it is something special you made them, and not that it is magic. People here do not like magic."

Inkga takes it reverently. "It's hard to believe they don't like magic, when it can create good things."

"It can also cause harm"—Venda looks straight at me—"but it seems your leader would like to bring it back to this country, which I commend."

It is for the best purpose—to get Valcora out of the hands of a mad woman.

CHAPTER 6

A KNOCK on the door makes me jump, and I'm surprised by the movement. How did that happen? Deep inside, I must have the energy to move my body. I hope. A servant enters, and Venda, Inkga, Nash, and I stare him down.

He bows. "Your Majesty, forgive me, but an emergency council meeting has been called. They are requesting your presence and that of your Head Advisor, Nash Zorris."

I glance at the clock. It's almost dinner time, the part of the day the council loves to eat. It must be an emergency indeed if they called a meeting now. Have they heard about Daros's pardon and release and are angry at me over it? I try not to worry about it. "Thank you. We will be there shortly."

Once he leaves the room, I tell Venda, "Thank you for your assistance. It is invaluable. Would you come again, to teach us more?"

She lowers her bald head. "It would be an honor."

"I assure you, the honor is ours," I say.

Nash takes her hand and bows over it. "We owe you more than words can say."

Venda flicks her gaze to me, before turning it back to him. "I will delay my return home to help you in this matter."

"Thank you," the three of us say as one.

I glance at Inkga, and we both giggle, though it doesn't feel like the best of times to laugh.

We give our *goodbyes*, Inkga says she'll be ready with my dinner when I return, and Nash takes me out. With my guards surrounding me, I'm wheeled through the halls until we reach the far-off council room.

When we enter, all faces turn to us as the council members stand around the table. Their expressions are a mix of solemn and worry.

I swallow my fears as I'm rolled into place at the head of the table and Nash takes his place at my side. "Please, be seated," I say. Once they're settled, I ask, "What was this meeting called for?"

"A problem has been brought to our attention," Timit, my Head of Treasury, says. "The Kurah are refusing to sell their goods until taxes have been lowered."

I don't know whether to be relieved it's not about Daros or furious that the Kurah have gone this far. "They can't do that."

"They can, and they have," Timit replies.

"I'm afraid it's true," Mina, Head of Foreign Relations says. "They're quite insistent. We must give in, or all will suffer."

There has to be a way around this. "How will anyone get what they need if they are refusing to sell? Won't they be affected just as much if they don't sell their goods?"

"It's not that simple," Timit says. "They are trading with each other for the supplies they need."

"So the Medi and Poruah will be the ones to pay." How can anyone do such a thing to another person?

"We need to act fast, whatever we decide," Nash says.

"Agreed," Jaku says. "We can't let the majority of people suffer because a small group is hoarding their resources."

What do we do? I don't have the answers. There has to be something. If I don't act on this, I'll have the Medi and Poruah fighting against me as much as—if not more than—the Kurah. The country will be thrown into even greater chaos, and the threats on my life will increase, as will the assassins coming for me. I won't have someone else die in my stead, and I refuse to go, so I have to figure this out.

"Any suggestions?" I ask.

The room is silent. No shuffling papers by the advisors. No one taking notes. Just the sound of my own breathing. *Gah.* This is as useless as I am.

I can only think of one thing. "Bring all the Kurah you can to the throne room tomorrow afternoon. I will speak to them. If they have a spokesperson, they may bring them."

"Forgive me, Your Majesty," Timit says, "but what is speaking to them going to do?"

"We'll find out tomorrow."

* * *

I'M EXHAUSTED. I spent all night running in my First Queen dream —running because I could and because *she* was there. No matter how far I went, though, Androlla was always there, hovering.

Inkga helps me get ready through my sleepiness. A healer comes in to help move my limbs, to keep my muscles active. Then a servant picks me up and puts me in my chair. Inkga wheels me into the sitting room, where Nash and Venda are sitting with a big pile of books. Nash is holding one open partway through.

"What have you there?" I ask.

"Wula brought them in while you were getting ready," he says.

It's so good to see him up and about, without having to request his presence. I hate that it's because I was poisoned, but some good seems to have come of it. "Wonderful. I want to try the luck charm again, but afterward, I'd like to read through some of those books and see what we can find before I have to go to my meeting this afternoon."

"Sounds like a good plan." Nash puts his book down and gets out the supplies.

Inkga places me by the table and then takes a seat next to Venda, eagerly watching Nash's movements. Would other people be this excited for magic, or would they really cower in fear of what it could do?

I'm not sure I'm brave enough to find out.

It doesn't matter, anyway. I need the magic. The country needs it, to get out from under Androlla's control. I don't have to force it on anyone, but it still has to come about. The fingers of my left hand twitch, and I realize I'm trying to twist the wooden ring I found in the treasury on my right ring finger. At some point it became a habit to twist it, and I didn't know it.

Nash brings the urta bark, rosemary, and mirror to me. While he holds the mirror with one hand, he uses the other to help me grasp the ingredients. I crunch it, working to squeeze my hand together over and over again, chanting like Venda did last time. It doesn't take long before my muscles grow sore and my fingers tremble under the strain, but I am moving them, which is more than I did yesterday.

"Is that enough?" I ask Venda.

"If you have placed some of yourself in it, then yes. Otherwise, you need to keep going."

Everything else was so hard, I forgot to put some of me in it. I concentrate on the words on making them feel as if part of me is coming out on my breath and onto the plants while I speak. I don't know if it works or not, but it feels good enough and my fingers are giving out, so I stop crunching but continue chanting.

Nash assists me, moving my hand to a pebble. I press the mixture into the rock, imagining the little part of me I put into my words going into it. I press as hard as I can, my arm shaking, even with his support.

Nothing happens.

Androlla is laughing at my efforts.

"This is pointless."

Nash puts everything down and cleans my hand with a damp cloth. "The Ryn I know is a fighter, not a whiner."

I clench my teeth. He's right. I have to work harder.

"It will not come without practice," Venda says.

My exhale is louder than I mean it to be.

"Do you want to try again?" Nash asks.

If I must. "Yes."

We attempt it three more times. By the end, I can barely move my hand, and there's still no glow on the rock. "I think I'm ready to do some reading."

Nash nods his approval. "I made something for you. One of us might still have to turn the pages for you, but it should allow you to read for yourself."

Which will not only be quicker but nice to not have to rely on others as much. I'll have to work on turning pages myself, though there's no telling if I'll ever be able to do it.

He goes out of the room and comes back carrying an odd contraption. It's a stand, but it has a length of wood sticking out at a ninety-degree angle that stretches across, parallel to the floor. He sets it next to me and swings a part of it like a stand over my lap. Inkga hands him a book, which he opens and places on the stand.

"Do you like it?" There's a note of hope in his voice.

"Like it? I love it. Where did you get the idea for such a contraption?"

"They have something similar in some libraries, but without the bend for sitting. I got a hold of one and adjusted it for you."

"You're more accomplished than I could hope for." I long to give him a hug and kiss, to let him know how much this means to me. Both it and the chair with wheels have far exceeded my expectations.

Inkga clears her throat, and I realize I've been staring at Nash a little too longingly. She says, "I'll try with the magic while you read. If you don't mind my chanting while you do so, that is."

"I don't mind at all." I focus my attention on the book in front of me even if the words are blurry for the moment. Anything to get my attention off Nash.

Venda helps guide us as we try magic or find something in a magic book, and Nash and Inkga flip pages for me.

After three hours, it's almost time to meet. "What have you found?" I ask after a particularly trying round of attempting to enchant the pebble.

"I found a spell for giving someone warts." Nash sounds frustrated, but I can't help but laugh, along with Inkga and Venda.

"It's funny," I say. "I came across everything from destroying an object to beautifying." Both seemed surprisingly easy. Destroying an object only required the object and beautifying only required the petal of a daisy over what you wanted to enchant.

"I found one that helps you amplify your cleaning tools, such as a broom," Inkga says. "That'd be useful."

"All those spells are simple enough, if you believe," Venda says.

Is that really all it takes? Believing in the magic? There are spells with ingredients difficult to find or chants that look hard to pronounce, like *uni'plifnuo*, but otherwise they seem straight forward.

I look over more books while the others eat lunch. My excitement has overshadowed my hunger.

When Inkga goes to tell a servant we're finished with lunch, I say to Venda, "We have a necklace we know is magic. Could you tell us what it does?"

Nash stands, pulls out the necklace we confiscated from Daros, and hands it to Venda.

"I can try." She threads the necklace through her fingers, closing her eyes.

Several moments pass in silence. Is she going to find something, or will Daros's magic stay hidden? It would be nice to know he can enchant items for his own use. It would confirm he knows what he's speaking of.

"Indeed, it has magic. It is a charm of stealth." She hands the necklace back to Nash. "Quite a strong one. You may wish to use it, Nash."

That makes perfect sense. I should have guessed something along those lines. It's a wonder we were able to catch Daros. "Thank you," I say.

"I must go. I will be back to teach you more later," Venda says.

"I look forward to it." And to her company.

After she leaves, it's time to meet with the Kurah. I hope I can express what I need to.

CHAPTER 7

THE THRONE ROOM is full as Inkga wheels in my chair. The people are restless—noisy and writhing. There are three unbreakable lines of guards, and more surround me, including Jaku. They must be almost all the guards we have for the palace.

I wanted to bring Puneah but didn't dare expose her to such a large, and probably hostile, crowd.

The room isn't as full as I expected. There are lots of people, but about half as many as at the last meeting I had in here. Not all the Kurah are here, but I'm glad those who came did, even if they're loud.

I'm rolled into place where the thrown used to sit. Someone smart must have removed it—probably one of my ladies-in-waiting. I wait for the people to settle, but the noise continues building. It would be good if there was a way to amplify my voice.

Yelling as loud as I can, I say, "My people, I brought you here today to discuss your needs."

No one pays me any attention. A guard I don't recognize says, "Maybe we should have you drink the Mortum Tura. That way, they can see you are meant to be the queen. That might quiet them."

"No," Jaku and I say at the same time.

The guard raises his eyebrows but doesn't press the issue.

What can I do to get their attention? If I had my full capabilities, I would throw my dagger over their heads.

"Silence," Nash calls out from somewhere behind me. The crowd simmers, though there's still some noise. "The queen wishes to speak with you."

The crowd simmers, though there's still some noise.

I have the urge to run away. Good thing I'm stuck in this chair, or I might do it. I don't know how I'll convince them to release their goods to the Medi and Poruah. Because this is something that has to happen. "I know you have issues with your taxes being higher, and that is what we're here to talk about."

I take a deep breath. "I know your grievances, and I understand that taxes are a burden you haven't had to shoulder until I came to be queen."

"That's right," yells a man in the front row. "What are you going to do to fix this?"

"We are working on plans to ease your tax burdens." I put as much sternness into my words as I can. "But we will not—I repeat, *not*—give in to threats. If you want your taxes eased, you must return to selling your wares and helping those who aren't as fortunate as you."

"Why should we?" a woman several rows back yells.

"Because it's the right thing to do."

"Right for who?" Another woman from the crowd calls out. "You? The Medi and Poruah? Not for us. We demand you lower our taxes, and lower them now."

How do I handle this? How do I help them see? Or is harshness the only thing they'd understand?

If Daros was the ruler, he'd beat them or kill them into submission. I don't want to go that route, but I do want them to grasp how serious I am. "I promise you again that we are working hard on making sure your taxes are lowered. There will be arduous times ahead, but if we work together, we can make the best of a tough situation. If you continue to threaten and demand, I will no longer fight for you."

"Why should we listen to you?" a male calls out.

"Because I am your queen."

Silence rains down for the first time since I arrived. The Mortum Tura might have worked better and faster, but they are calming down. "You will open trade, or you will face the consequences," I say.

I'm about to tell Jaku I'm ready to go, when I feel a little funny. It's always hard to move, but this is almost like I can't move at all. Like I have no control.

Like the First Queen has taken over.

No.

I fight against her, to prevent my lips from opening, but they do so anyway. "One more thing. I declare that my Head Advisor, Nash Zorris, and my Head of Guard, Jaku Hanka, are both to be stripped of their jobs and imprisoned. Nurf Pluno will be my new Head Advisor."

I strain against her control. I can't let her do this.

"Furthermore, I order the death of Daros Durkin."

I'm finally able to clamp my lips shut. I try to open them again, to take back what she said, but they won't budge.

Guards head for Jaku and Nash. I look on, agonizing over their imminent capture, as they both stare at me with shocked expressions.

CHAPTER 8

DAROS MAY AS WELL HAVE POISONED my heart. For all the good I try to do, it never works. Stupid Androlla and her control over me. She gloated to me all night long while I slept, even as I ran from her. Now as I wake, I want nothing more than to stab her in the throat.

"Inkga?" My voice is harsher than I meant, but I can't help it.

She stirs. "Sorry. I fell asleep." She won't look at me. "How can I help you?"

"Please see to it that Nash and Jaku are let out of prison, and the bounty on Daros's head is taken off. Write the order, and I'll sign it."

She looks at me, her eyebrows crinkling together. "Yes, Your Highness."

"*Ryn*. It's *Ryn*." Tears come to my eyes, and I blink them away for a brief moment before they return full force. Inkga looks at me as if I'm a barbarian from another country. I can't help the words pouring from me. "I'm just Ryn."

"It's all right," she says, her voice soothing. "I don't know what's going on, but I understand things must be stressful for you. I'll get everyone you need. Be back in a moment." She exits.

Crying was a dumb thing to do. Now I can't wipe the tears off my cheeks. Everyone who comes to visit will know I lost it. As if I ever had it to begin with.

I sniff and try to gain control of my feelings. Puneah comes out from under the bed and jumps up next to me, then bumps my hand until it rests on her head. I flex my fingers, letting the soft feel of her fur soothe me.

When Inkga returns, I'm in control again, if not completely calm.

"I have Afet coming. He should be able to take care of both requests. He's acting Head of the Guard, with Jaku in jail." She looks at me. "Would you like me to dry your cheeks?"

If only she didn't have to. "Please."

She grabs a handkerchief and dabs at my face. I focus on the silky feel of Puneah's fur. It makes me want to close my eyes and go back to sleep, only *she* will be there to haunt my dreams. Then again, I'll be able to move.

Doesn't matter. I've got things I need to take care of.

"There," Inkga says. "That's better."

"Thank you."

"Mmhmm." She twists the handkerchief through her fingers.

"What is it?" I ask.

She looks at the floor. "I'm sorry I grew cold with you this morning."

"I don't blame you. Not after the way I acted last night."

"If you forgive me for saying so, it didn't seem like you. It was almost like you were channeling Queen Deedra."

Should I tell her? Does she have a right to know? Do the people have a right to know? I know she won't reject the thought of magic, but Androlla. She's a threat to anyone who knows. And the people... They'd reject me. I don't know what they could do about it, without sending the country into natural-disaster chaos, but they already push me away enough without thinking I'm crazy.

Actually, I do know what they would do. They would have me killed, for such crazy talk. A new queen would be elected, and things would go back to the way they were. Better than being ruled by a crazy person, if a bit more unstable.

I probably shouldn't put that pressure on Inkga, though the thought is tempting. She's looking at me with an expression like she's trying to figure me out.

There's a knock, and Afet enters. "You wished to see me?"

"Yes, I would like Jaku and Nash released, and the death sentence on Daros lifted." I try to say I want Nash reinstated as Head Advisor, but it won't come out. The First Queen has my lips locked down tight.

"Of course, Your Majesty." He bows and leaves the room.

The honorific makes me pause. Did he add it because he's nervous around me, like Inkga? Are they afraid I'm going to turn into a tyrant, like their last queen? I can't blame them, since that's what Androlla is trying to turn me into.

Inkga helps me change into a dress, which is always an ordeal, but I'm glad to be out of my night gown once it's over.

"Should I get your breakfast?" Inkga asks.

"I'm not hungry." Farthest thing from it.

"You need to keep up your strength."

I hold back a growl. She's right, but that doesn't mean I like it. "I'll be back soon."

She leaves the room, and in her place comes Julina. To guard me or keep me company, I'm not sure. Either way, she's not looking at me.

"It's a fine morning," I say, trying to start a conversation.

"Not for Jaku and Nash." She's upset.

"I know. I'm sorry. I've got Afet on it, trying to correct the situation."

"Why did you do it in the first place? That's all I want to know."

My chest tightens. What do I tell her?

"Why don't you have a response?" she asks.

Still at a loss for words, I stare at her like I'm stupid. Maybe I am, to have gotten in this situation without a way to correct it. Maybe *stupid* is the wrong word for it. *Foolish*, perhaps? Or too depressed to think straight.

My mind goes back to the portraits of all those queens who came before me. How did they explain the fact they were changing to others? Or didn't they notice it? Perhaps it came on too slowly for any of them to realize what was happening.

"It's difficult to explain," I say. "I wish I had an answer for you, but the most I can say is that I didn't mean it and I'm sorry."

"At least you got one thing right—ordering Daros's execution. I don't know why you didn't do that sooner."

I wince. "Actually, I'm taking that back as well."

She tosses her hands up in the air. "Don't expect me to like it."

"I don't." My voice is small. I make it bigger. "Things are tough. We have to deal with them as they are."

She cocks her head to the side. "Forgive me for speaking out of place, Ryn. We're all frazzled this morning, wondering who's next."

"If I had it my way, no one would be next."

She furrows her eyebrow.

"I promise you I'm trying my best. You have been an excellent guard and a good friend. I don't want you going anywhere."

"Thank you." She gives a shy smile. "You've been a good friend too, even when I sneeze at the wrong time."

I chuckle. It'd be nice if we could have more of those moments.

Inkga returns with breakfast and helps me eat. To my surprise, Julina doesn't leave the room. She stays while I eat, which is a little embarrassing, since Inkga is feeding me. The feeling soon passes. I can't do anything about it anyway.

By the time Afet returns, I've finished eating. Nash and Jaku enter the room after him, looking worried.

"Thank you, Afet. That will be all for now," I say.

He bows and leaves the room, Julina after him. I glance at Inkga, who says, "I'd better put this tray away. I'll see you soon, Ryn."

"Thank you, Inkga."

Once she's gone, Nash and Jaku start talking at once, both questioning in their own way what's going on. I go to raise my hand, to stop them, but it only moves a bit before falling back to the bed. Thankfully, they stop anyway.

"It was Androlla," I say. "And I'm sorry, Nash. I tried to—" My mouth clamps down, not letting me finish. Stupid First Queen. When my jaw relaxes, I say, "As you can see, I'm having some difficulty."

"Ryn." Nash's face crumples in pain.

Jaku does a better job of staying together, but there are still stress lines on his forehead. "We'll fix this. I promise we'll find a way, for both your good and the country's."

"Thank you. And I'm sorry. I hope your night in the dungeons wasn't too bad."

They exchange a smile. Nash says, "We were there, but we weren't locked up. No one could bring themselves to do it."

I laugh. "Good." I grow more serious. As much as I don't want to, some things need to be done. "Get Daros and his guards in here. Or my sitting room, rather, as soon as you can."

"I'm on it," Nash says.

As he leaves, Jaku asks, "Would you like me to help you into your chair and wheel you to the sitting room?"

"Please. I'd rather not meet Daros in here again."

He scoops me into his arms and sets me down in my chair. I expect Puneah to follow, but she stays hidden under the bed. Once I'm settled in the sitting room, he stands in the corner, where he can watch both the doors and the window. I knew I liked this man.

"Tell me a little about yourself, Jaku. I don't know much," I say.

"There isn't much to tell."

"There has to be something."

He shrugs.

"What about your family? Do you have anyone?"

His lips twitch upward. "I have a wife and three sons."

"Do you live with them?"

"I visit often enough."

I frown. That doesn't seem fair. "What are they like?"

This time the twitch turns into an actual grin. "My wife is the sweetest thing in the world. She's lovely and a wonderful mother. Our boys are grown now, with homes and jobs of their own, though none took a chance to be in the guard with me. They were rambunctious little things when they were younger, but they've grown into fine men."

"They sound nice. Though I think you should have your wife come here, to live with you."

His gaze darts to the window. "Thank you for the offer, but we're happy. Two of my sons live close to her and take good care of her. She knew what type of life she was getting into when we married."

Still, I can't imagine being far from your loved ones, only to visit when you have a day off. Now I have people I care about, I want to see them every day. Except Shillian. I'm not sure what to do with her. They haven't found any evidence she was helping Carver or knew his plan to attack me, but I don't know how to trust her despite that.

She is my mother, though, and now I know where she is, I should do something with her. Carver, on the other hand, I couldn't care less about. The council hasn't decided on his punishment, for attempting to off me and working with Daros. If he's not imprisoned for the rest of his life, it will likely be a death sentence. I don't wish that on anyone, but he did try to kill me, even if he did a bad job.

The dungeons are full of people who've tried to kill me. Far too many.

"Forgive me for getting lost in my thoughts," I say. "How long have you been married?"

"Long enough to know my wife is always right."

I laugh.

Nash enters the room. "Daros and his guards are here. Are you ready to see them?"

I'd much rather keep talking to Jaku. "Send them in."

And hope he's not so angry at me that he'll stop helping me out.

CHAPTER 9

DAROS GLOWERS AT ME. "We had a deal."

"We'll discuss that in a moment," I say. "For now, I want all of you to know that, no matter who says what, Daros is not to be killed. Do you understand?" I look at each of the guards in the eye as they give an affirmative.

"Good. Even if the order comes from me, you are not to kill him. Now I need a moment alone with Daros, Jaku, and Nash."

The guards file out. As soon as they're gone, Daros rips into me. "Girl, you'd better not think I'm going to tell you anything else if you're going to play games like this. I won't have my life in your hands. Your life is in my hands, do you understand?"

He takes a step toward me, hand raised. Past memories make me want to cower, but I give him a defiant glare. Before I can lash him with my words, Nash slams a hand down on his chest. "You will not speak to Her Majesty that way."

Daros looks down at Nash's hand on his chest, the one missing half a pinky. "I can take you down as easily as I can take her down."

"But you won't, or I'll kill you." Jaku's voice is quiet but piercing.

I've never been as glad he's my Head of Guard as I am now. "And I will order him to, and Jaku will listen to me, no matter what I said previously." Not entirely true, but Daros doesn't need to know that. "You may know what I need, but I would rather rot in my own mind than let you harm the people I care about again."

Daros steps back, and Nash's hand falls to the side. Daros says, "So be it, but don't expect help from me."

"Then don't expect your house or other nice things," I say.

His nose flares, but he doesn't continue to argue.

"Now that's settled, I want you to know it wasn't me who ordered your execution; it was Androlla."

"Figured, since these two went to prison." Daros motions to the other men. "She wants me dead because I know how to defeat her."

"Tell me, so I can get rid of her before anything else happens." I'm getting desperate. I need to know the people I care about, and my country, are safe.

"Have you been practicing the luck spell?" he asks.

"I have."

"Have you accomplished it yet?"

If only. "Not yet, but I'm getting close."

"Until you do, there's nothing else I can help you with. You need more than basic magic to defeat her."

The First Queen moves close, listening in on every word Daros says.

He goes on. "You need to master this before we can move on. Send for me when you do so."

He heads to the door, and no one stops him as he leaves to join his guards and do only daggers know what. Probably something sinister I don't want to know about. Letting him go is such a bad idea.

But what other choice do I have?

"I need to speak with Nurf." The words pop out of my mouth, surprising me, but it's true; I should speak with the man who is now my Head Advisor, since I can't force the words past the First Queen to reinstate Nash.

Nash's expression is oddly blank, like he's trying to hold back a greater emotion. "I'll get him for you."

"And if you don't need anything else from me," Jaku says, "I have a few things I need to attend to."

"By all means," I say.

The men leave me alone, but with the door ajar, so I can see my guards and they can see me, though none of them look my way. I'm sure one of them, if not more, is paying attention to my room.

A while later, Nash returns with an unfamiliar man I assume is Nurf. The man has beady eyes that take in the room but mostly focus on me, long legs under a wide belly, and short, wavy hair.

Nash opens his mouth, but before he can say anything, my lips move. "Leave us alone. I want to talk to Nurf by myself."

Oh no. The First Queen is taking over again. I knew there was something wrong when he was put in place, but I planned on remedying that this morning, not dealing with Androlla.

"Are you sure?" Nash focuses on me.

"Of course, I'm sure. Leave us," Androlla says through me. "And make certain you shut the door on your way out."

Can he hear the difference in my voice? The regal edge to her words? Though subtle, it's there. *Please let him hear it.*

"Well, then, I'll leave you to speak with your new Head Advisor." He bows—much too formal for him—and leaves.

Did he suspect something, or was he putting on a show for Nurf? Either way, he's gone, and there's nothing I can do to get him to come back. It's hard enough, being unable to move my body. Being unable to speak for myself makes me rage inside. Scream and fight. But it does no good. Androlla ignores me, like I'm nothing but an ornery sheep, way off in the distance.

"Thank you for coming, Nurf."

"Of course, Queen Ryn. How can I assist you?"

"I know you were loyal to Queen Deedra."

His eyebrows twitch.

What is she getting at? What does Deedra have to do with anything?

He says, "Until her death, Your Majesty."

"I know you think I killed her, but it doesn't matter. You need to trust me like you trusted her. As if I am her."

"A—alright."

"Can you do that, or must I remind you what the punishment is?"

He straightens. "Whatever your command is, I shall follow."

"Good. Kill me."

His jaw drops. Mine would too, if I wasn't busy trying to mentally punch her. Why wouldn't she try to kill me in my sleep, other than the fact that my skills are better than hers? Either way, if I'm dead, Daros will secretly put someone he wants on the throne, and then he'll oust her.

I feel her pause. Using the opportunity, I try to speak, but it comes out as a mumble.

"What was that?" Nurf asks.

"You heard me. You will kill me, and you will do it now." Androlla has gained control again. I fight against her, but it's hard when I'm half focused on Nurf and whether he's going to heed her instructions. "There are daggers in my top drawer, under all the clothes."

He slips out of the room and is back a minute later. He pulls out one of my daggers. The blade is shiny, but he holds it in a way that makes me think he's used it before. Many times. No, no, no. He can't be doing this. I can't die by my own blade.

He hesitates. "Why do you want me to kill you?"

"Just do it."

He stalks forward. Inside, I scream at him to stop.

Outside, my body doesn't twitch.

He scowls, as his pace increases. He reaches me, pulls back his arm, and jams it forward. Inwardly I flinch, waiting for the pain. But Puneah jumps out of my room and locks onto Nurf's forearm with her sharp teeth.

Nurf cries out, and the door bursts open. Nash and Julina rush into the room, one after the other. With movements quicker than I've seen him use before, Nash is on my attacker, pulling him back with a sword to his throat. Julina adds a second while Puneah clings to his arm, dragging it to her level so he's hunched over.

"Are you all right, Ryn?" Julina pulls the dagger out of the man's grip. She searches him for more weapons and comes up with half a dozen—all mine that he must have stolen from my drawer.

Who is he?

The First Queen won't let go of my jaw. There's no way for me to respond, and she doesn't either, just glares them down.

More guards pour in the room, and Eldim checks me for injuries. "Did he hurt you?"

Still, she won't give me control. Instead, she sneers at him. He backs away, as his eyebrows crease together.

The guards surround Nurf and drag him toward the hallway. Puneah refuses to let go until they reach the doorway. Once they're out of sight, she comes to me and nudges my hand with her head.

"What happened?" Julina asks.

I try to move my lips, try to give some type of response, but Androlla doesn't release me. She attempts to say who knows what, but I clamp my teeth together, so she can't speak.

Nash takes one look at me and says, "Everyone out."

"But the queen was just attacked," Eldim says. "We need to protect her. Neutralize any other threats."

Nash flexes his jaw. "Julina, check her bedroom. Eldim, make sure the window is secure, in case he let more people in her rooms."

They hurry to do as requested of them, while the rest of the guards stand around with their swords out. Nash strides over to me and stops before his legs would brush against mine.

Once Julina returns and both she and Eldim give the *all clear*, Nash says, "Out."

Julina's lips thin. Everyone moves out of the room, albeit rather slowly.

As soon as the door shuts, Nash leans in closer. "Ryn?" he asks.

"Ryn?" he asks.

"You have no idea who you're dealing with," Androlla snarls from my mouth.

A crease appears between his eyebrows. "Ryn, you have to fight her. Come back to me. You can do it. I know you can."

I struggle harder, trying to gain control of myself. It's not fair that she can do this to me. That she can leave me a prisoner in my mind. She should have been wiped out ages ago. Inside my head, she laughs before letting go of her control over me.

"Nash?" The word is shakier than I meant it to be.

"Is that you, Ryn?"

Emotions sit heavy in my chest, trying to eek their way out. "It's me."

I'm back, thanks to Nash. Is this why the First Queen doesn't wish queens to have lovers? So we don't have help fighting her off? Whatever the case may be, I'm extraordinarily grateful he's here.

"Thank all of Valcora. I thought I'd lost you for good." He bends down and presses a hard, quick kiss to my lips. "What happened?"

I struggle against the tremble trying to take over my voice, and make it come out strong instead. "She took over and asked Nurf to kill me."

Nash whips away from me, to pace the length of the room. "I should have never left you alone."

"It's not your fault."

"In any case, I'll make sure someone we trust is with you at all times. Jaku is going to be furious we left you."

"I think Nurf may be an assassin."

Nash swears.

"I say that as a warning, not to upset you. We need to keep a close watch on him, even if he's in the dungeons," I say.

"I understand." His voice is tight.

If only there was something I could do to protect myself from *her*, then he wouldn't have to worry so much. I wouldn't worry so much. This is ridiculous.

Shoving the thoughts aside, I flex out my hand next to Puneah and rub her nose. The movement is difficult but comforting. "Thank you for saving me. You're more amazing than I could have ever hoped for."

Nash stops pacing. "I'll see to it that she gets some big, fresh fish for lunch."

"Thank you. And we need to call a council meeting, so I can re —" Return him as my Head Advisor. The First Queen struggles against me, keeping me from talking until I change the direction of my thoughts.

His face tenses up, as if in pain. "It's her again, isn't it?"

"She won't let you be who you should be at my side. I'll have to make someone else my Head Advisor."

"I understand."

I search his expression, but it's impossible to read. "I'm sorry."

He moves closer, and my heart beats faster. "Don't be. None of this is your fault. We'll figure out how to win this together. All right?"

I blink several times, to keep from crying. Dagger it all, I'm stronger than this. "All right."

"Good. Now let's get the council together, so we can get this straightened out." He moves to the hallway. His voice rumbles, but I can't make out the words. He returns and gets behind my chair.

Puneah struts by my side as we move. I say, "Did you tell them how dangerous Nurf is? That he's an assassin?"

"I did. How did you know that, by the way?" Nash asks.

Guards encircle me, as we continue through the hall toward the council room. "It was a guess, really. The way he held himself —his dagger—gave it away." Plus, the way he knew Queen Deedra, probably while under the control of Androlla, seemed like they had a sort of working relationship. Just a guess, though.

Nash is quiet. The slap of feet, including Puneah's claws, is the only sound echoing off the walls.

The council room is a busy hive of activity. The council members are on their feet when I enter, giving bows or curtsies.

I wait until Nash rolls me into place before saying, "Please be seated."

There's a collective shuffle as they get back to their chairs.

"I would like to call"—I try to say Nash's name, but the First Queen won't let me—"Jem Surah as my new Head Advisor."

"Very well," Timit says. "But how many times are you going to change Head Advisors? It's an important position that needs stability."

I wish I could give it that. "As many as I need."

Now to find out Jem's response.

CHAPTER 10

JEM STANDS STRAIGHT AND TALL, like a board. Her expression is neutral. I can read people, but I can't get a feel for her other than a slight tightening around her eyes that belies a calm emotion.

Nash and Julina are here in my sitting room, and Puneah is at my side. She hasn't left it since Nurf attacked me several hours ago, though Nash did bring her a plate of fish.

"Have you heard?" I ask Jem.

"That I'm to be your new Head Advisor? Yes." Her tone is sharp. "What about Nash?"

I need to have him do something that will keep him close. Both him and Jaku are vital. They're the only two I can fully trust to help me with the First Queen. And Inkga, but she doesn't know anything about the First Queen. "Nash will return to being my guard. He's well-suited for the job."

She opens her mouth, and I expect a litany of complaints. Instead, she snaps it shut again.

"What is it?" If she's to be at my side more often, I have to know what she's thinking. My last Head Advisor before Nash tried to kill me, after all. Not that I expect that from her, but the more I know, the safer I'll feel.

"I'm certain Your Majesty doesn't wish to hear it," Jem says.

Ouch. "Tell me anyway."

Her gaze drifts first to Nash and then to Julina. "It's not my place."

"I'm making it your place. Now, what is it?"

Still, she hesitates.

This isn't like her at all. "I would excuse Nash and Julina, but you'll have to forgive me if I don't. Due to recent developments, it's prudent to have a couple guards around me at all times."

"I understand about the circumstances."

"They will keep your confidence. I can promise you."

"It's not that." Her stoic expression breaks into a rage of hurt and anger. "Why didn't you have Daros executed? Why did you let him go free, back to his life? He tried to kill you, he outed you as the Shadow Wraith, and he's killed countless people, including Wilric." Her voice breaks on his name.

I soften my voice as much as I can, like Inkga taught me. "I'm sorry, Jem. I promise you I would like nothing more than his execution, but there are reasons I can't disclose as to why this can't be."

"I don't understand."

"There's nothing I can say that will help make sense of it. I'm sorry."

She purses her lips, looking much more like the Jem I knew when I first arrived at the palace. "Does he get to know?" She motions to Nash.

Not the question I expected. I thought she would fight more. "It doesn't matter."

"Yes, then. Why can't you tell me?"

Because you'll think I'm insane, for having another person in my head. "It's a secret. I'm sorry."

"Stop saying that. If you were really sorry, you'd tell me. I'd convince you otherwise, and we would execute the evildoer."

"I wish it was that simple." More than words can ever express.

The man has a black heart with a need for power that can never be cured.

"Fine."

"Fine, what?" I ask.

"If you won't tell me, that's your prerogative, but don't expect me to go along with it."

Chills wash through me. "You can't hurt him."

"There's more than one way to deal with him." She plays with her dress, where I know she hides a dagger.

"You can't use your dagger on him."

"Never said I would." Her eyes are dark.

This isn't a battle I can win, mostly because I want to join her side. I can tell her this, though— "His time will come, but for now, we need something only he can give us."

Her lips thin, but she doesn't argue further.

"Let's talk about some situations that need dealing with."

"Excuse me, Ryn," Nash says.

"Yes?"

"If you don't need me, I'd like permission to interview your attacker."

"Certainly." I may join him after I'm done with Jem. I want to know more about Nurf.

"I'll send Eldim in," he says.

"Thank you."

I pretend not to pay attention to him as he leaves. It's hard, when all my thoughts are attuned to him. As Eldim switches with Nash, I tell Jem, "Please have a seat."

She sits nearby and faces me. "What would you like to discuss?"

"The Kurah have me worried. Do you know all that's happened with them?"

"I'm caught up to speed. Were they the ones behind Nurf attacking you?"

That'd be easier to deal with. "Not this time, but they've tried on several other occasions, and the last word I have is that a few released their goods to be sold, but some are still hoarding them."

"It's a conundrum."

"Indeed. I need to know who their leader is."

"A Kurah in a cloak, right?"

"Yes, and by all accounts, a man. I need to find out who it is and get this country back on track." And hope I can get the First Queen out of my head, so it makes a difference.

"What do you suggest?"

"I want you to know so we can be on the lookout for things." If I had full control of my body, I would be out searching for the problem. With a limited body, there are limited things I'm able accomplish.

"I'll see what I can do about getting people on finding more information."

"That'd be good. Someone out there knows who it is. We need to find them." Puneah bumps against my hand, making me give her some attention. Can't believe I was ever scared of her. "The other thing we're dealing with is the purchase of the mine. We have the couple who owns it coming in sometime in the next couple of weeks to finalize the details." I'm looking forward to seeing the woman who taught me to read.

"I heard you found a mine to purchase. I admit I wasn't expecting that."

"Why not?"

She glances down. "The Kurah are so angry I didn't think any of them would relent to sell to you. Do you know why they're angry?"

"Over taxes." I changed the taxes almost as much as I changed my Head Advisors.

"I believe you'll be able to fix it better than you think. Your heart is in the right place. It's time to let the people know."

Her words give me a spark of hope. "Any idea how to do that?"

Her fingers tap on her leg. "Let me think about it."

"Very well." I'll be thinking about it too—when I can, with everything else going on. There's so much, it's hard to keep track of it all. No wonder I have an entire council to help. "How is your training going? I know I haven't been much help since…" I'm too weak to move.

She ignores my breaking off. "I'm still training, but it's hard without Wilric." Her voice cracks.

"I miss him too."

She dabs at the corner of her eyes.

"Were you—" I almost ask her about her relationship with him. If she cared for him as more than a friend. But I hold myself back. Though I trust Julina and think Eldim is pretty trustworthy as well, it's not my place to out Jem's feelings.

"Was I what?" Her mask is back on, clouding her feelings.

"Are you ready to be finished with our meeting for today?" It's the best cover I can come up with.

Her eyebrows twitch. "Certainly." She stands.

"Jem, if you ever want to talk… about anything, you can come to me. I'd be happy to—you know—speak with someone about… well, anything." That was awkward.

"Thank for the offer, Ryn." She gives an almost smile.

As she leaves, Inkga enters the room. "Would you like some lunch?"

"No, thank you. Would you please wheel me down to the room Nash is interrogating Nurf in?"

"Of course."

When we arrive at the room with my entourage, I hear a muffled noise, almost like a grunt. It sends a chill through me. Eldim opens the door, and Inkga rolls me in after him. He stops, and Inkga rolls me past him but halts as well.

Nurf, my attacker, is dangling by his arms in Nash's grip, bruises already forming and blood dripping from his lip and nose. His breathing comes in gasps.

What has Nash done?

CHAPTER 11

"Nash?" The word comes out more uncertain than I mean it to.

He meets my gaze before he quickly drops his—and Nurf, who falls to the floor with an *oompf*.

"Eldim, see to it that Nurf is returned to the dungeon and taken to a healer. Everyone else, leave us." I don't know how I'm going to deal with this, but I have to. Somehow.

If Nash did what I think, if he really beat this man, I have to make sure it won't happen again. If I do have feelings for Nash. I can't let my love for Nash get in the way of doing what's right.

No one moves.

"Get to it now." My voice is stern.

"Your Majesty, we can't leave you when…" Eldim doesn't continue, but I know he means when Nash has just beaten a man. He should know Nash would never hurt me, though.

"I'll be fine. Leave," I say.

Slowly, everyone moves out. I keep an eye on Nash the entire time, though he won't look at me. I give it a minute once the door is closed, and then I use my softest voice. "Nash, what happened?"

He looks at his fist. "I—I didn't mean to. It just happened."

"You can't hurt people like that, even if they are bad."

His response is so low, I almost miss it. "I know."

"Is this because of your torture?" I don't want to ask, but I have to.

His shoulders crumple in on themselves as he makes a sound so anguished I want to rush to him. To comfort him. To tell him we all make mistakes.

But I can't.

I'll have him do the next best thing. "Come here."

He closes his eyes, the muscles in his jaw working.

"Nash? Would you come here, please?"

"Leave me alone." He rushes from the room, shoving the door open and sending it slam against the wall with a *bang*, and then there's nothing I can do to help.

I'm left in silence, trying to decide what to do. The weight on me is so heavy; my shoulders want to slouch. Maybe that's why I can't move—not Daros's poison, but having so much going on.

As much as I want to go after Nash—as much as I love him—I have to do what's best for my country. I can love him, but it will have to be from far away. That was a hard lesson learned. It also means I can't have him running loose around the palace; I need him to heal. To come to terms with what he went through. He'll never be the same again, but dealing with his anger this way only makes things worse.

"Ryn?" Inkga's voice is small, coming from behind me.

"Sorry. Please take me back to my sitting room and send someone for Jaku. I need to speak with him."

"Of course." She sounds a little more certain, as if direction is all she needed.

I wish someone would give that to me. I don't know what to do or how to fix this. I want to call everyone in and tell them not to speak of what happened, but it's futile. At least Nash was only my guard and not my Head Advisor when this happened.

As Inkga pushes my chair down the hall, with my guards sticking close, I wish there was something all these people could do to heal me inside. To heal Nash. My heart hurts, but there's no time to dwell on it. I have to fix the situation with Nash, the Kurah, and the First Queen, and decide what would be best for my country.

Once we're in my sitting room, and it's me, Julina, Eldim, and Inkga, I let myself sigh, releasing some of my pent-up emotions. It would be easier to let the First Queen take over. Easier, but not right.

Jaku storms in without his sling on. "I heard what happened. Are you all right?"

"I'm fine. Nash didn't hurt me. He would never." I force my words to be confident, even if I'm broken, emotionally.

"Before, he would never have hurt a man without it being in defense."

True, but— "He was doing it because the man tried to kill me. I don't think we need to worry about what's going to happen to me when Nash is around. But that's something I'd like to speak to you about." I take a deep, grounding breath. "I want Nash relieved from the guard and sent home. I'd also like it if you would find someone who can talk to him about what he's been through. Someone who can help him."

My eyes burn, and my throat is tight. I love this man so much. I can't imagine what he must be feeling—the shame and embarrassment and anger. He must feel so alone, which I can relate to, but clearly he doesn't want to talk to me.

"I know who," Jaku says. "I'll get to it as soon as I leave here."

"Thank you. It means more than words can say."

He glances at my escorts and presses his lips together. I won't push him on it, but there is one thing I want to know. "Who do you have in mind?"

"Me."

Him? I didn't expect that.

"Don't look so surprised. I'm the Head of the Guard. Lots of guards see things that are tough. I've been through hardship myself. I've helped good men and women heal from this sort of thing before. I've tried a little with Nash already, but he wouldn't let me. Now I can tell him it's at the mandate of the queen if he doesn't listen, but I have a feeling that, after today's episode, he'll be more willing to talk."

"You think so?"

"I believe so. Yes. From what I heard, he had quite a shock."

That I can agree with.

"Is there anything else you need of me?" he asks.

"That will be all."

"Then I will go see Nash personally and get things moving."

"Thank you, Jaku."

He nods before leaving the room.

I'm grateful to have him on my side, helping with what he can. He's more useful than I would think a Head of Guard would be. I should find some sort of way to reward him for a job well done. The only thing I can think of is money, but I'm not sure that's what he wants or needs. His loyalty seems to run deeper than what I can pay him. I wish there was something I could do that would have a deeper meaning.

But for now, I need to focus on getting my country back under my control. To do that, I'll need some help. Now that Nash is no longer under my service and Jaku is busy, can I convince the others to leave me alone so I can practice magic? I'll have to try because the alternative is telling them.

While I don't know Eldim that well, other than he's helped save my life, I know Julina. Part of me still worries what she'll think of me and what she'll do if she finds out I'm hearing a voice in my head that sometimes takes me over. No, I'll have to convince them to let me do this without them.

"Inkga, would you please get Venda?" I ask.

"Of course."

While she's gone, my mind is busy worrying about everything

I need to do and take care of. As soon as Inkga and Venda return, I ask Eldim and Julina to leave.

"No." Julina's voice is firm.

"I agree," Eldim says. "It's not safe. There could be a secret tunnel we don't know about."

I want to roll my eyes, except I've been attacked in this very room. "I know things seem dangerous, but there are some confidential matters I need to discuss with Inkga and Venda. Puneah will protect me, though I hardly think it'll be necessary."

"We can keep confidences," Julina says. "It's part of our job."

"That may be"—and I do really want to tell her, but I can't have her thinking I'm crazy, practicing magic—"but this really needs keeping under wraps for now. If it works out, you will learn about it in time."

"And who will protect you while we're not here?" Eldim asks.

"Like I said, Puneah will. She's proven her worth, and you'll be right outside."

Julina shakes her head. "Unless this is a ploy by Faner to get you comfortable before they murder you."

"Glad you put that so bluntly."

She has the grace to look down, cheeks reddening.

I continue. "Faner has no reason to attack me."

"That we know of," Julina mutters.

"I promise I'll be safe." I put as much emphasis as I can on the last word.

Julina looks at the ceiling, like it holds all the answers. "Fine. But we'll be right by the door. Call out if you need assistance."

"I will, and thank you."

They huff as they leave the room.

Once they're gone, Venda says, "You needn't defend me."

"I had to get them out. Besides, I'd like to think it's true that your people don't wish me harm."

She simply looks at me, making me wonder if I'm mistaken.

"We should get started," Inkga says.

Venda speaks as if Inkga said nothing. "Why do you not wish it to be known that you are doing magic?"

"My reasons are my own."

"They will be more accepting than you think, once they get over their initial shock. Look at Inkga. She's done well."

How can a woman so entirely different from me read my fears when I keep them closed up? Either I don't keep them locked up as tight as I think, or we aren't so different after all. "May I ask you a question?"

"You may ask." The implied, *but I might not answer* stands out.

I'm not sure it's something I should say. My ladies in waiting would be shocked if they heard me ask such a thing, but I'm so curious. "Why does your skin almost shimmer? Are all the people in Faner like that?"

"That is two questions." She goes so quiet I don't think she's going to say anything further, but before I can nudge her to continue, she says, "Most people in Faner have skin that almost shimmers, as you say, unless they are from another country or have bred with those of another country too much. We retain our essence. That is all I can say."

Their essence, huh? Interesting. I wish she could say more, but we all have our secrets. "Very well. What spells are we learning today?"

We work through several spells together, practicing enchanting objects. My movements are stronger than before, inching closer to what I thought I'd never be again, but still oh-so-far away from it. I force the issue to the back of my mind and work on feeling the magic. Inkga holds the mirror and my wrist while I work my fingers to smash the ingredients together.

I chant, focusing on that feeling inside me that hums with life. I need to use it. Believe it can do the job.

It moves through me, and I want to pull back in shock, but I force myself to continue. To know this will work.

The thing moving through me grows stronger, heading toward

the ring I'm trying to enchant. I push it forward, believing it can work. Believing the information Venda has given us will do the job. I've seen it work, after all. It has to work this time.

With one final push, the ring glows.

"I did it." My hand falls to my lap and the glow fades, but there was no mistaking it. "I finally did it."

"You have succeeded." Venda picks up the ring. "This shall be your good-luck charm. We will put it on a necklace for you so you can always have it on."

Good luck is something I desperately need.

While Venda pulls a chain from a bag at her waist, Inkga draws my attention. "You did it. I knew you could; it was a matter of time."

"And with the help of you both," I reply. "I couldn't have done it without you. Now we need to get you a luck charm of your own."

She grins. "I can't wait until it works for me as well."

We continue using magic, though Inkga isn't successful. The work is soothing, after the day I've had, and though it's not easy, it feels like there's a purpose behind it. A way to defeat the First Queen. I just need Daros to tell me how.

CHAPTER 12

WHILE JEM GOES over the things I'll have to deal with for tomorrow, I try to press back a headache that worsened as the day passed. I can't decide if it's stress or something else.

"Are you listening?" Jem asks.

"No. Sorry. I wasn't. Tell me again, and this time I'll pay attention."

"I said that Kada has arranged for a meeting with the couple selling the mine to the government."

I perk up. I'm looking forward to seeing Kapeni again. "When do they arrive?"

"A couple of weeks."

I try not to look devastated. I was hoping they'd be here before I completely lose myself to Androlla. Her presence is near, mocking me. "Very well," I say.

She clasps her hands before her. "That is all. Would you like me to call for Inkga?"

No—that means going to bed. And yes, it means going to bed. Freedom in my body, but trapped by an evil queen. I both fear that and love it. "That would be good. Thank you."

Jem takes a step toward the door but stops. "I want to say

you've come a long way since you first started ruling. You're becoming a great leader, and it's obvious you care for the people more than you care about yourself. But don't get so lost in taking care of them that you forget to take care of yourself."

She doesn't give me a chance to respond before leaving the room. I glance at Julina, but she's studiously ignoring me. Ever since I kicked her and Eldim out, she's been cold. Another guard is with her now—a woman I don't recognize, lithe and muscled. She looks as if she'll be able to take good care of guarding me, but looks can be deceiving.

I wish there was a way to take care of myself in this body. I hate leaving everyone else to defend me, when there's nothing I can do. Though they've done a fine job so far, it's not the same as doing it on my own.

A woman enters the room and helps me move my body like she's been doing three times a day since I was poisoned, keeping my muscles strong. I don't talk to her. Don't say a word. I appreciate what she's doing, but I'm just so exhausted.

Once she's finished, Inkga comes in to get me ready for bed. It's such a process now. I can't believe I ever took throwing on a nightgown for granted. Once I'm finished, Julina and the unfamiliar guard put me into bed.

"Can I get you anything else?" Inkga asks once I'm settled.

"Thank you, no. I'm fine." Ready to run and jump in my dreams.

"All right, then. Let me know if that changes." She heads out, leaving me with the guards watching over me.

It's almost like when I was attacked before, and they worried so much they kept a constant guard on me, only this time I can't move, and I really do need them. Is it such a bad thing, to need other people?

It's hard to let other people take care of me when I was forced to take care of myself my whole life. If only there was a way to find a happy medium… a way to be all right with their helping, but still able to do things on my own… I doubt it will ever happen.

I squeeze my eyes shut tight, wishing I could roll over. So much for being exhausted. I lie there quietly for some time, trying not to think of all the things I need to do. Letting my mind clear itself.

As soon as the sunset colors come into focus, I hit the ground running. My body, my freedom—it's all here, where I'm trapped in a colorful prison. I stretch my legs out reminding me how good it feels to move.

I take out my daggers and practice moves as I go. Thrust my dagger into space while I run. My muscles sing at the chance to be used. They've been denied the chance to go like this. I swing back my arm and punch it forward, only to jerk myself back as the First Queen pops into view in front of me.

That was close.

If I didn't stop myself, I could be seriously injured or dead. Would it kill her?

"What does it matter?" she asks. "You can't move, anyway. You live a useless life, making those around you work harder to pick up the slack you leave behind."

I press my lips together and hold back from punching her in the face.

"You don't have to hold back. There's no point. Use me as your dummy. It's better than fighting air."

"Nice try."

She smirks.

I stash my daggers, turn around, and jog away from her.

"There is no away from me," she says, her voice sounding as if it's next to me, though she's not.

I grind my teeth, trying to ignore the pain of how right she is—and failing.

"That's correct. You are stuck with me. Soon, the only time you're able to do anything will be when you're sleeping. Then you'll be here

with me. The rest of the time, you'll have to watch from the corner of my mind, while I get rid of everyone you care about and take back my rule."

She's done a bad job of it this far. Besides, everything is so volatile; my body will be killed soon by an assassin, only to be replaced by another she doesn't yet have control over. By the time she gains control over that body, that person will probably be assassinated. It's an endless cycle that will prevent her complete destruction of my country until she gets things back under control, though I'm not certain how she'll accomplish that.

She laughs—a tinkling sound that has me wincing. "It wasn't always like this, you know. The people have grown restless. It will pass, and then I will have one long rule after another again."

I stop running and do a sort of dance while I punch at the air, careful not to go so hard that I'd hurt myself if she popped in front of me.

She appears on my right side as I pass, and then my left. I ignore her. It's getting harder and harder not to pay attention to her, though.

"That's right. I'm getting in your way, aren't I?"

I stop, drop my hands to my sides, bend over, and gasp for air, out of habit. "Why did you enact a law that senile queens be executed? Doesn't it go against what you want?"

She pouts. "That was the council, not me. Long ago, they were figuring things out, and that was their way of dealing with it. Of course, those years are long gone and forgotten, even if I wasn't able to get that law overturned."

That explains a lot. It would seem at one point, others tried to get rid of her.

"Yes, and they didn't get very far. Just like you won't."

It doesn't matter. I will defeat her.

"Oh, yes. Those little parlor tricks you've been doing... You will fail."

I stand upright. "Maybe, but you can't rule forever."

"Yes, I can. I practically already have."

"You've never dealt with me before."

Her tinkling laugh fills the air. "Tell yourself whatever you want. You will soon be fully mine."

I wake to the sound of her laugh in my ears then the tink of another sound.

It's dark. Why am I awake? I can't see my clock to know for sure, but it feels very early morning. "Julina, are you awake?" I ask.

"I am." Her voice comes from somewhere in the corner.

"Could you light a candle?"

She doesn't respond, but there's a shuffle of movement. A moment later, there's a faint light. The glow flickers over her eerily.

"Thank you. Would you see what time it is?"

Before she can move, the sound I think woke me comes again. A light ping, like something tapping on glass. A pebble hitting my window?

"What was that?" I ask.

There's a flash of movement by my window, and then it slides open.

"What do you think you're doing, Milni?" Julina asks, her voice stern.

The other guard doesn't reply.

"Close the window," Julina says.

Although there's a nice breeze coming in with it being open, something in my gut agrees with her. This is bad. Especially when instead of replying or closing the window, Milni draws her sword.

Julina strides forward as she draws her sword as well, swifter than the other guard. Before Julina can reach the window, a shadow appears in the opening and hauls itself into the room.

Julina curses and runs to me. Puneah is out from under my bed, growling at Milni and the stranger. A second shadow appears at the window. How many are there?

"What do you want?" I try not to show my fear despite being incapable of protecting myself.

None of the three answer as a fourth person climbs in. Julina shouts for help.

Milni laughs. "I blocked the door earlier, when I took a bathroom break. No one is coming."

Julina pulls out a dagger with her free hand. "You're not going to hurt the queen."

"Oh, I think we will." Milni steps closer, brandishing her weapon.

Puneah's on her in an instant, clamping down on her sword arm.

She screeches, "Get off me, you stupid animal."

Julina calls for help again, and all chaos breaks loose. Julina moves her sword faster than I can keep track of, my body begging to help her but my muscles refusing. Attackers burst forward, two males and a female. A second attacker comes at Julina, and the other two approach the free side of my bed.

Julina throws her dagger at her attacker. It pierces in the man's shoulder, and she jumps on the bed, a foot on each side of my waist.

Puneah clings to Milni. Milni reaches down, to get her sword off the ground, and Puneah finally lets go, aiming for her other arm. Now free, Milni pulls a dagger out of her belt.

"Puneah, to me," I call out.

Like a streak of lightning, she's on my bed by my head, blocking my view of that half of the room. Julina's fighting off an attacker on that left, while at the same time, staving off attacks from the right.

Milni jumps on the foot of the bed. Not knowing what else to do, I scream as loud and long as I can. Not out of fear, but in the hope someone will realize how urgent this is and work harder to get to us.

"Shut up," Milni yells.

I take a deep breath and scream again while the fighting continues. Julina's got more skill than I've given her credit for in the past. That, or she's been training harder than ever when she's not with me. She moves like a dancer. A lethal dancer. A body crumples to the floor, but a sword is coming at her thigh.

It slices through. Julina grunts and stabs at the attacker. Her blood drips on my hand. As much as I worry for her, I say nothing. Whatever words I have would only distract her. Besides, I'm busy screaming for help.

The banging on the doors is heard above my yelling, but I don't know if they'll get through before Julina and I are dead. Milni dives forward, driving her blade toward me under Julina's legs while the others keep Julina busy. The candle flame flickers over Milni's face for a brief moment before Puneah attacks, snarling.

The door bursts open. Finally. I shout, "Attack."

Whether I mean I'm under attack or that they need to attack, I'm not sure, but the guards rush in, full tilt. The sound of metal pounding against metal fills the room, along with voices calling out in pain. Milni's sword goes into Puneah's shoulder.

The animal makes a pitiful howling noise. Milni withdraws the sword, and the moment she does, Puneah jumps at her and bites her hand.

Within moments that feel like forever, it's over. Julina's still above me, dripping blood. Puneah won't let go of Milni's hand, even as a guard takes the traitor by the arm. The other attackers are dead or hurt so bad they're incapacitated on the floor.

And I... I'm in the middle of it all, doing nothing.

Julina just saved my life.

CHAPTER 13

"How did this happen?" I demand of my guards the next morning in a secure room. It's bland—nothing but white walls, wooden floor, and my chair. "How did a traitor get in your midst?"

There may be more. It's difficult to tell, though none would be among the group who saved me last night. That, or they're biding their time.

A headache is forming.

"I spoke to all the guards early this morning," Jaku says. "We had no idea Milni was a traitor. She showed no indication of it at any point, to anyone."

"Not that they're saying." I tap my fingers, grateful I can do so but wishing I could do much more. "How did the attackers get on palace grounds?"

A muscle twitches in Jaku's jaw, but he looks at me steadily. "We don't know, which is why I'm suggesting that we move your rooms. Away from stairs, for your convenience, but still on the second floor and on the inside, with no windows, for mine. We'll do our best to make certain there are no secret tunnels."

I go outside so little as it is. Partly my own fault, but still, I don't want to lose that one connection I have to it. If it means

Puneah and Julina are safer, though, I'm for it. "Please, go ahead and have it set up. But how did they get in my room without anyone outside noticing?"

Jaku's fist tightens. "The guards who noticed were either killed or incapacitated, and then a ladder was used to climb to the second story."

I grit my teeth. The damage done was far too great. "Send my condolences to the families of those lost, and send one of my ladies-in-waiting to see those injured."

He nods. "I'll see to it personally."

He probably knew the men who died. Is he hurting? Now isn't the time to ask, and I doubt he'd answer, anyway, but it does make me wonder what he's going through.

"How did they get a ladder?" I ask.

"I'm looking into it, but it appears one was hidden nearby in the bushes for them."

"And the prisoners? Are they saying anything?" Only Milni and another male attacker made it out of the fray alive. None of my people were lost, but Julina has been with a healer all morning, and Inkga informed me that Venda was taking care of Puneah. I hope Venda isn't furious with me for letting Puneah get hurt.

"Not yet," Jaku responds. "I'm going to interview them personally when we're finished here."

"I would like to go with you."

I expect him to fight me on it, but he nods his approval.

"As for the rest of you… Thank you for helping save my life. I'm sure Jaku already spoke with you, so I won't belabor the point. I appreciate all you've done to protect me."

We wrap up the meeting, and I make sure to give thanks to each guard personally as they leave. They take it silently for the most part. Eldim is the last and says, "It is an honor to serve a queen who cares about her people. We would all give our lives for you."

He's gone before I can respond. I glance at my lap. What would I say anyway?

Once I'm alone with Jaku, I ask, "How's Julina?"

"She needs some time to heal, but she'll be fine."

"Not too deep of a cut, then?"

"No."

Sing praises. I don't know what I'd do without her. Not just because there are so few people I can trust but because I like her. She's kind and loyal. She saved my life. "There should be a reward for her."

"She won't want it, like I didn't want the raise you gave me."

I smile. "You earned it, though, so you get it whether you want it or not."

He shakes his head, but a faint grin hides in the movement. "Shall we go interview the prisoners?"

"Yes. Let's. Can you call one of my servants to wheel me there, please?"

"I'll do better. I'll take you there myself."

"You don't have to do that."

"You're right; I don't. But I want to." He gets behind me, where I can't see him. "Besides, you're quickly becoming the daughter I never had."

I don't know how to deal with the sudden onslaught of emotion. His statement was so unexpected but welcome. How would I handle life without him? Before he can open the door so we can wheel our way out, I say, "And you're like the father I always wanted."

He pauses before opening the door and wheeling me down the hall. Eldim and Afet escort us.

"Where are the rest of the guards?" I ask.

"I no longer trust any of them with your safety. We'll find a way to make this work."

"When are you all going to get some sleep?" Because they can't guard me night and day, as much as Jaku probably wants them to.

"You let us worry about that. You've got more important things to take care of."

While I want to argue, he's right. There's so much on my plate right now, I can't add another thing to it. First I need to find out who was behind the attack and have them taken care of. Then I'll deal with Androlla.

Currently, she's laughing at me. Mocking my almost death.

I do my best to shut her down. When that doesn't work, I switch to ignoring her.

The halls are empty as we trail through them. When we get to the stairs, Eldim picks me up, and Afet carries my chair down. Eldim is strong, the metal breastplate hard against my side, but he's nothing like Nash.

I wish he was still here. Wish I knew he was getting the help he needed. With Jaku spread so thin, is he going to have time to speak with him? I hope the time away from me does Nash some good, because I ache for him.

Eldim sets me down in my chair, and we're off, twisting through halls until we reach the area by the dungeons. We don't go down the stairs, but instead, Jaku wheels me into an interrogation room.

I don't want to be here, remembering Nash beating up my would-be murderer. The thing that broke us apart. Not that we could ever be together.

I force myself to think of something else. "Which prisoner will we be interviewing first?"

"The man. We don't know his name," Jaku says.

"Good choice." This way we can gain as much knowledge from him as possible and use it against Milni.

Afet goes to tell someone we want the prisoner, and we wait in silence. When he finally comes in, heavily guarded, my personal guards stick close by my side, Jaku between us and the attacker. The man is set on the only chair in the room and bound, and his guards leave to wait outside.

"Who sent you?" I ask.

The man glares at me but doesn't respond.

Jaku stalks forward. "You will answer Her Majesty."

"I refuse to speak to that garbage, who treats my Kurah employer like they have no importance in the community."

Whether he knows it or not, he gave us two vital pieces of information—it was another Kurah attack, and he has an employer.

I keep my expression neutral. "I'm trying to help all the people, not only Kurahs, though I do value what you can bring to this country. I don't know what we'd do without you."

He spits at me, but it falls short of hitting me.

"Who sent you?" Jaku demands. "Who is your leader?"

The man presses his lips closed.

Jaku lowers his voice. "Did you hear about the last person who tried to kill the queen?"

The man goes very, very still.

"I guess you have, then. Would you like to become him, beaten until you give us the answers we want?"

The reminder of what Nash did makes me a little ill, but it if that's what it takes to get answers out of this scum bag, I'll handle it.

But he doesn't open his mouth.

Jaku continues to question him, trying different angles— threatening at one point and offering the man a lesser sentence if he speaks. But the man doesn't say a word.

After what feels like a very long time, Jaku says, "Fine, then. We'll see what fate awaits the man who tried to kill the queen and won't give us any information."

The man has the decency to look scared as Jaku gets the guards, and they take him back. Once he's gone, Jaku asks, "What do you think?"

"He's in league with the Kurah," Eldim says. "Their attacks are getting more dangerous, if they reached Her Majesty's room."

"We'll make sure that doesn't happen again, but I concur."

"How will we convince Milni to give up the leader? If she knows who that is." I'm worried that she doesn't. That we'll be led back to the same man in the cloak. He could be almost anyone.

"We'll do our best to suss it out. There's something else to consider," Jaku says.

"What's that?" I ask.

"There were no attacks while Daros was in prison."

"Not even ones that didn't make it to me?"

"Not a one." Jaku studies me hard, searching my expression.

If something's going on with Daros, I'll have Nash kill him. I wish I could do it myself. "There's one problem—Daros is capable of orchestrating an assassination attempt while in prison. Even if it's him in the cloak, he would have found someone else to do the job while I was weakened."

"True. So if it is him, is he trying to kill you?"

"After last night?" Eldim asks. "I'd think so. That was a fierce attack. If we hadn't gotten through the furniture Milni stacked in front of the sitting room door, Julina and Her Majesty would both be gone."

I clench my teeth. Never did I think I'd be almost taken out by four people. Before, I could handle them, especially with Julina and Puneah at my side. But now... It doesn't matter. They saved me, and I'm grateful for that.

Jaku tells Eldim to get Milni. When she arrives with her guards, she's scowling, hands and feet manacled. They were not playing around when they brought her to the dungeons. They place her on the chair across from me, with my men in the same positions as before. Once her guards leave, I ask, "You need to tell us everything you know, and you need to do so now."

She purses her lips and shakes her head. "Not going to happen."

"We know a lot from what your man told us. Might as well make it easier on yourself," Jaku says.

She pales. "He told you nothing."

"You'd wish," I say. "Tell us what you know."

"And if I refuse? You'll what? Threaten me? That's all you ever do. I doubt you were ever an assassin; you don't have the guts to do anything."

I have the strongest urge to smack her across the face. It's a good thing I'm stuck in this chair because I'm trying to be better, something she wouldn't know a thing about. "Your fate will be left in the hands of the council. I'm sure execution is on their list of appropriate punishments."

She smirks. Not the reaction I expected.

"If that's how you want it to be, we'll make sure they know you didn't cooperate." Jaku clasps his hands behind his back.

"If it makes you feel better, go right ahead." Her tone is so snide, I'm not sure what to do.

"I never took you for someone who'd betray the crown," Jaku says.

"You're blind. I didn't betray the crown. I'm trying to fix it."

"What do you mean?" We're getting close to discovering something. The question is, will she let us?

She snorts. "I'm through talking to you. I've said more than enough. Do whatever you want to me."

"Then you wouldn't want to tell us anything about the Kurah?" I say.

She flinches. It's small, but it's there if you're looking for it.

"Hit a pressure point, did we?" Jaku asks. "Might as well tell us the rest."

"You're guessing." But there's fear in her gaze that wasn't there before.

Jaku moves closer and leans over her. "You'd like to think that, but you know it's wrong."

He says something else I can't hear and places his hand on her shoulder.

She shrinks away from him. "I'll tell you nothing." She winces, but otherwise keeps a straight face.

Jaku lets her go and gets her guards. After they take her away, he says, "What do you think?"

"We should let her escape, and then follow her," Eldim says.

"You think she's going to try to escape?" I ask.

"Just a hunch, but she might. She knows this palace really well and has lots of connections, which I know you have plans to interview, but they might not know anything. If anyone can escape, she can."

"All right," Jaku says. "Set it up, but make sure you have someone you trust on her. I don't want to lose her if she gets out."

"I will keep Ilko on her."

"Perfect. He's almost as much of a shadow as Ryn."

As I was, he means, but that's good to know. If he trusts this Ilko to stick to Milni, I'll have to trust him to do so as well. I wish I could send one of my more trusted men, but they'll never go for it. I can only send good wishes that they find the leader.

CHAPTER 14

"Shillian Nilmac here, requesting an audience, Your Majesty," Kada says.

She doesn't often come personally to tell me these things, but she must think my mother's ask for an audience is worth attending to in person.

When was the last time I saw my mother? It's been a long time. I don't want to see her again, but part of me is curious. What is it she wants?

Most of all, do I want to reconcile with her?

By all accounts, she hasn't been doing anything suspicious, but it's hard to trust her. Hard to believe she wants what's best for me. "Did she say what she wanted?"

Kada shakes her head. "There was no word, other than that she wished to visit with you."

I glance at Eldim in the corner. If I agreed to see her, at least I wouldn't be alone. I have others here, and it's unlikely that she'd try to hurt me.

Kada says. "She's been quite insistent on seeing you."

"But you can't get out of her why she wants to see me?"

"I'm afraid not."

"Send her in." Where did those words come from? I'm not certain they were mine. Does the First Queen want Shillian in because she's a danger to me? Or am I the one who wants to see her?

"Very well." Kada bows and is out of the room.

If I could walk, I'd pace now. It would do some good to stretch out my legs and get my worries worked out. I don't know how to deal with her coming. Instead, I drum my fingers, trying to think of what Shillian could want.

There's a knock. I'm about to find out. I stop drumming my fingers as Kada peeks her head in.

"Shillian Nilmac, Your Highness," she says.

My mother enters the room, her gaze not leaving me even as she curtsies. "It's so good to see you well, Ryn."

I almost snap at her not to call me Ryn, but I was the one who told her to call me that in the first place. Better than the birth name she gave me, Keera. I'm mostly angry she thinks I look well when I'm stuck in this chair. "What is it you want?" I ask.

She flinches.

My tone was a bit harsh, but I have a hard time caring.

"I wanted to make certain you were well," she says. "I heard about the attack and was worried for your safety."

Is that all, or does she have some hidden agenda? "Or you were hoping I was about to die."

She flinches. "I deserve that. I know it's hard for you to understand, after everything you've been through, but I want what's best for you. I want to know you're safe and taken care of, even if I can't be the one to do it."

"You proved that by giving me to Daros."

She hangs her head. "I can never tell you how sorry I am, but it's true that I am. I wish so much that things could be different."

Why do I feel like I kicked a puppy? I soften my voice. "I wish things could be different too."

She looks up, eyes wet with unshed tears. "Do you think you

can ever forgive me? I promise I knew nothing about Carver's plan to betray you. If I did, I would have done everything in my power to stop him. You're my daughter, and I haven't protected you like I should."

No, she hasn't.

It's such a confusing array of emotions. I don't know whether I want to welcome her back into my life or throw her in the same prison cell as Carver. I stare at her, trying to decide her fate in a way that's fair to us both. I don't know what the answer would be.

The First Queen is here, hovering close. I have the over-whelming urge to put her in jail. Because of the combination of the two, I find myself saying, "You are forgiven." Can't have Androlla ruling my life more than she already does. I add, "But I'm not sure if I can be around you yet."

"I understand. And thank you so much. It's difficult to express my gratitude for your words."

For the first time since she came in, I study her. Not just her expressions. It's difficult not to be shocked by what I see. She's thinner, her clothing frayed. She reminds me of the way Daros has been falling apart, and the comparison bothers me. I don't want the two of them to be in the same category, so I find myself asking, "What has happened to you?"

Her cheeks are stained red. "I—I didn't want to tell you, but I've been living on the streets since I was turned away from the palace."

Guilt stabs at me, and I brush it aside, though it's hard. It's my fault she was on the street. No house. No food. "We should change that."

Her eyes widen, and her eyebrows jump higher.

"I mean it," I say. "I want you to come back and live at the palace." Perhaps not near me, but there's plenty of room. She should be able to live here without me seeing her at all.

And if I did see her, would it be so bad?

"You don't have to do that," she says.

"I want to."

This time, her tears let loose. "Thank you. So much. Thank you. It will only be until I can find work and have an income."

I hesitate but wave away her concern. "It's not a problem to have you here. I'll make arrangements, and you can stay for as long as you need."

"Thank you. I'm truly indebted to you."

"Nonsense. You housed me for a couple years. It's only fair I do the same." Though I don't plan on giving her away to an assassin master when I'm done having her around.

"Nevertheless, I owe you all my gratitude. I'm afraid I haven't earned your trust as a mother, but I will do everything in my power to do so." She stands and gives another curtsy. "Thank you for seeing me. I appreciate all you're doing for me."

I nod. My throat closes, so I can't make a real response. She exits the room, and even as I make mental plans to have a servant take care of her, I wonder if I'm doing the right thing.

CHAPTER 15

INKGA and I are getting ready to practice enchanting objects when a servant announces Venda.

"Good timing," I say. "We were about to try more magic." Since Jaku is the only one guarding me at the moment, I feel safe in saying so.

"I will be happy to help, but that is not why I came," Venda says. "I would like to join your personal guard."

"You want to what?" Surprise drips from my words.

"I want to join your guard. I know it is unorthodox, since I am not of your country, but I assure you I have your best interest at heart. Until you can again protect yourself, I would like to assist in keeping you safe."

What do I say to that? Inkga, with her wide eyes, looks as surprised as I feel. I say, "That's very generous of you. Please forgive me, but I don't want you to think you have to help. I know you were only here to teach my people about Puneah."

"If I may be honest—I believe you trust these people and gather that they will not break my confidence."

"You'd have to ask them."

She looks at Inkga, who says, "I'm apt at keeping secrets. I can keep yours as well as Ryn's."

Then Jaku. "I, as well, will keep your secret, as long as it will not harm Ryn or Valcora."

Venda turns her unnerving gaze back on me. "Very well. Much like you, I am an assassin."

Inkga gasps. Jaku has had enough training to not look stunned —or maybe he already knew. I think about her grace and ease. Her use of magic would be a great tool, and a fila would also be a good tool to work with. The more I think about it, the less it surprises me.

"I have the skills to help," she continues.

"We can test those," Jaku says. "But why would you and your country want to save our queen? Why did they send you and place you close to the queen, where we're supposed to trust you?"

"My ruler does not know about this yet; it is my choice. I was sent here to deliver Puneah, yes, but also to discover what type of queen was on the throne. One we could work with, to widen the passage between our countries and open trade, or one for whom we should block the passage. Valcora has been bouncing between an unknown and a perceived danger for a long time, and Queen Swaja, my current leader, would like that to change, as would I. The last queen was seen as a threat, making our country nervous.

"I have discovered you are a queen with a lot of heart, despite what some may say. In contrast to your predecessors, you are endeavoring to do what's right for your countrymen, even if you don't always succeed. I see you opening trade among your people, and I think it would work well to do the same between our countries. That may not happen if another queen takes the throne. I'm determined to see you live until either you can take care of yourself or I die."

I was mostly following along with her words until the last line. Sure, I don't think I'm the best queen, but I do work to do what's best for the country. I also want to open trade between countries. But is that enough for her to be willing to die for me?

It's a bigger statement than her being an assassin.

Giving your life for another is the highest honor of love and respect.

That's what Wilric did for me.

I don't want to lose another person like I lost him, but my guards could use the help. If I'm honest, I could use the help. "I want to see what you can do, and then we will decide if you can join the guard."

One moment she's standing in front of me, the next she's at Jaku's side with his own dagger to his throat. "My skills are sufficient."

"Clearly." I'm surprised Jaku is taking it so well, not moving an inch, even to glare at her. "Please let my Head of Guard go."

She releases him, flips the dagger around, grabs the blade, and hands him the hilt.

Jaku takes it. "Thank you. But it begs the question—how do we know we can trust you? We can't even trust our people. What makes you different?"

Venda finally looks at him. "I have had opportunities to kill Her Majesty and I did not. I could have had Puneah harm Ryn early on, yet I did not—the fila would be the last creature to harm her now, though."

"Fair enough."

I lift my eyebrows at Jaku, but say nothing. He says, "We would like you to join us."

"I would like it to be a secret," she says.

"It would give us an edge if she was with you, and no one knew of her skills," Jaku says to me.

She nods. "I will continue to act in a similar manner, saying I need to be near the fila, now that she is injured."

"Speaking of Puneah—is she going to be all right?" Concern laces my words, though I try to hide it.

"She heals fast and will be fine in a day or two. It's doubtful you will notice a difference when you see her next."

"Where is she now?"

"Resting under the bed in your old room."

"I'd hate to be a would-be assassin that stumbled in that room right now," Inkga says.

Everyone looks at her.

"Well, it's true. She may be a sweet thing when she wants to, but she's also ruthless. I don't think her injury changed that."

"Indeed, it has not," Venda says. "Shall we get on with your magic work for the day?"

"We should." It's urgent that I learn more than I have. I'm barely passable at making the luck charm that I've given to Inkga to be passed on to others. Once I get a little better at it, I'll be able to send for Daros and hopefully learn the real spell I need to defeat the First Queen.

Asking Venda about Daros's plan might be a good idea. I don't want to give her more information than she already has, but there has to be a way to gain knowledge from her. "Is it true you need to learn easier spells before bigger ones?"

Her keen gaze locks onto me. "You are planning a bigger spell?"

"Perhaps."

She continues to look me over, before saying, "It is much more realistic to learn easier spells first."

Makes perfect sense. Maybe I should tell her all about Androlla and ask for help. The question dances around my tongue, but I can't get it to come out. Can't risk her knowing.

I wish Nash was here. I could use his strength and knowledge. I sent him home, but I wonder when he'll come visit. Is he too angry at me to do so? My heart aches, but I do my best to ignore it. I have work that needs doing without my losing focus.

CHAPTER 16

Jᴀᴋᴜ sᴛᴀɴᴅs in my sitting room, ready to give his report. Eldim is the only other person here.

Jaku says, "So far, the prisoner has not attempted escape."

Drat. "Very well. Keep the guard on it."

I clench and unclench my fist as we talk. "Send Inkga and Venda in. Eldim, you're excused for the day. Go get some rest."

"Thank you, Ryn. Stay safe while I'm gone."

"Always do."

He snorts, but leaves the room without another word.

Venda and Inkga enter, and soon we're practicing enchanting different objects. We've been working about an hour when we decide to take a break.

Inkga goes to get lunch and returns with a lot of food. "All this has been through two tasters so we should be good."

Guilt that someone else is putting their life on the line for me punches me, like it does every time I'm reminded that I have tasters. I push it aside. It's their job. They accepted the risks that came with it. I can't do anything about it and should stop worrying.

Usually I eat alone or with Inkga, but Venda's here and I offer her food. Despite that, I'm about to protest, saying I'll eat later while they enjoy lunch, when she says, "Feel free to eat in front of me, Ryn. I know you don't like doing so, but it doesn't bother me."

"Oh. All right." I glance at Inkga, who gives me an encouraging smile.

"Sounds good to me." Inkga gets herself a plate and makes me one while Venda gets a plate of her own. I want to feed Jaku too, but know that he never eats on duty.

While we eat, I practice moving my hands as much as possible. It's a difficult task, but if I ever want to have full control of my body again, I have to do something. I flex my hand and let it rest on my lap as there's a knock on the door.

A servant enters with my mail. Inkga takes it and opens each letter for me to read one at a time while she discreetly looks away. She's the best. What would I ever do without her?

"This one's interesting," I say.

"What's it about?" Inkga asks, keeping her gaze averted from the note.

"You can put it down. I'm done. Thank you. It's from Inyi. She'll be arriving at Indell soon." I left my lady-in-waiting in a city after the old ruler there proved treasonous and took advantage of the people for personal gain. "It says that the people of Trentin have elected a new leader. She sounds like someone I'll be able to work with, and the people love her."

"That's good news." Inkga gathers my documents into a pile, to be taken care of later. "Dessert?"

Without exercise and with all this food, I may end up a fashionable size, though I'd rather be able to wield my daggers. "Not right now. You go ahead, though."

I don't have to tell her twice before she's digging into a puffy treat. Venda refrains and instead guides me through more magic.

"You must feel it," she says. "The more you believe, the easier it will be."

It's hard to believe something when I've spent my life thinking it didn't exist. I continue to try, though. Venda's words are soft as she takes me through the process. I strain to make the mixture, my hand cramping after several attempts. I do my best to shake it out and struggle through again until I feel something inside me move as I chant the words.

Venda places a little rock where I can reach. The words move through me, helping me focus on the part deep within. It flows out, and the rock glows. "I did it."

Faster than ever. I'm finally ready for something more advanced. Something that can take down the First Queen.

CHAPTER 17

A GLANCE in the mirror tells me my hair is lighter than it's ever been. I dart my gaze away. I don't want to see me become her. I want to be me.

The paintings of other queens never looked completely like the First Queen. They must have been made right after each woman claimed the throne, or there would be a hall of portraits that looked the same.

Mine hangs among them, and I look so different. Why hasn't anyone commented on this? Maybe they think I want to change my appearance. I wish Androlla wasn't overcoming me so fast, but I suppose I've given her no choice.

Inkga wheels me out to the sitting room, where Jem is waiting, Afet and Eldim trailing after us.

"What is the plan today?" Jem asks.

"I'd like you to send someone for Daros. I need to meet with him first and foremost."

Jem's eyes tighten. "Why do you need to meet with that scumbag?"

I wish I could tell her. "It's not something I'm free to disclose."

She stands, crossing her arms. "I don't know if I can be a party to this."

Inkga excuses herself from the room, and my guards look like they wish they could do the same.

What can I give Jem to make her understand without disclosing everything? "I know this is hard. Trust me, if I had any other choice, I would have him executed instead of working with him. But this is something I have to do, and I need your support if you are to remain my Head Advisor."

She paces. Though the walls have landscape paintings on them, it's not the same as having a window to the outside. The room is stuffy, almost closing in on me despite its large size.

Jem stops in front of me. "Why can't you tell me what's going on? I fear he's using you."

"He probably thinks he is," I admit, "but he has information vital to this country's security."

She shakes her head. "Are you certain he's not? He wouldn't help anyone unless it furthered his cause."

"Agreed. He definitely thinks it's furthering his cause, but that doesn't change the fact that I need him alive for the information only he has."

She rubs her temples. "I don't have a good feeling about this."

"Truthfully, I don't either, but there's no way around it."

She sits back down and gives me a wry grin. "You probably hate him worse than I do."

"Hate is a funny thing. It can morph out of control or ebb away. I think I've come to grips with what he did to me, but that doesn't mean I like him or trust him. Or even understand him, for that matter. What he did to me was evil, but it made me who I am today."

She nods. "I understand that, even if I don't want him living in Valcora anymore."

Maybe that's what I'll do. I'll get Venda to take him to Faner after all this is over, if I can convince her to. Then again, I don't know if I can bring myself to loft him off onto someone else. It doesn't seem fair. Why would another country want such a foul being?

"I'll have Kada set up a meeting with him." Jem makes a note.

"I'd prefer if you sent a message to him yourself."

"You don't trust Kada."

"It's not that." I don't know much about my Head of Relations with the Queen, other than that her position is a mouthful, and she seems to be warming up to me lately. "It's that I trust you."

She gives a little head-bob. "I'm honored, Ryn. I'll take care of it, even if I don't like it."

We discuss the rest of what we need to do today. When we're finished, I expect her to leave. Instead, she stays, playing with the fabric of her skirt.

"What is it?" I ask. When she says nothing, I persist. "You can tell me."

"I don't want to upset you."

Did something happen to Nash? "Just tell me."

She sits up straighter. "You haven't met with the people much since Daros poisoned you. You used to meet with them more often, to hear their concerns. I think they miss that."

She's right; I haven't. Due to my fears, more than anything else. "Do you think they want to see me... like this?"

"I think they want to see their queen leading them, no matter the circumstances."

I nod. "I'll take that under advisement."

"When you're ready to set up a meeting with the people, let me know."

When, she says, not *if*. Guess she has more confidence in me than I do. "All right."

* * *

I'm with Daros, Jaku, Nash, and Puneah. It's been several hours

113

since I spoke with Jem, and I'm feeling the weight of the country on me.

Jaku insisted on being in a different room, far from my own newly acquired chambers. He also wanted more guards here, and while I wanted to agree, this subject is too sensitive to have a bigger audience.

All I want to do is stare at Nash. It's the first time I've seen him since he was sent home. I want to tell him how sorry I am, but also how disappointed. That I hope he can do better. Become better. But he came in with Daros, so there wasn't a chance to speak with him. The only reason Nash is here is that I'm meeting with Daros.

Though I try to keep my gaze off Nash, the dark circles under his eyes are noticeable. Otherwise, he looks like my Nash. My chest gives a squeeze, and I force myself to focus on Daros.

"You've made a luck charm, then?" he asks.

"Several," I say. "I need to know how to defeat the First Queen."

He steps closer, and Jaku and Nash raise their swords in his way.

"I wasn't going to hurt her," Daros says. There's no telling if it's the truth. "I was getting a better look. Androlla is definitely taking over. Your hair and eyes show that clearly enough. She's assuming control fast. You haven't drunk any more of the Mortum Tura, have you?"

"Not since last we spoke."

"She must be pressing hard on you to make the change come about so quickly. Though, from what I heard, you have drunk a lot of the Mortum Tura, so she would have the strength to do so."

I clench my jaw. If only I'd known sooner the power the death drink held, I would have only drunk it once, and then demanded answers from Daros. Not that he would have given them at that point. And it doesn't matter; thinking of *what ifs* won't help me. "I need answers, Daros."

"And I have them. I'll even give you this one for free, since I'm feeling generous."

I narrow my eyes at him. "You never give anything for free."

"You make it sound like I'm not a nice guy. Didn't I take care of you when you were growing up, girl? Teach you what I know?"

Nash's sword is up in a flash. "You will address the queen respectfully."

Daros takes a step back with a hand up in the air, like he's innocent. We all know otherwise. "Sorry. Habits, you see." He looks right at me. "Habits are hard to break, unless you're like Her Majesty here and can't walk anymore. At least she won't be killing anyone else."

I work to keep my breathing steady and even. He's purposely pushing buttons, and I fear it's working.

Jaku puts a free hand on Nash's shoulder. That seems to calm him down just enough to withdraw his sword.

"Get to the point, Daros." My words are crisp.

"I wanted some conversation, but fine. We'll move onto business." He weaves his fingers together and rests them on his stomach, which is much tinier than when I lived with him. Is he eating? "Small charms aren't always effective, though depending on who makes them, they might be more or less worthwhile. You need to deal in bigger magic. Need to find a way to open your horizons to something big enough to defeat Androlla."

"Like what?"

"I'm getting there. Patience, little queen. Patience."

I have no patience for his lies.

Neither does Nash. He takes another step forward, but doesn't unsheathe his sword again. "Tell us what we need to know before I knock you unconscious."

"Do that, and you'll never get the information you want." Daros gives him a smug smile, before turning his attention back to me.

How unfair is it that Daros was the one to find out about the

First Queen and how to defeat her? The man is clearly getting what he wants. Though it's strange—the cuffs of his sleeves are fraying, his clothing worn. There has to be something to it I'm not seeing.

It doesn't matter what state he's in. He needs to give us answers, but I don't ask again. Speaking of how he needs to tell us just makes him happier.

He stays silent. It reminds me of when he would silently dangle torturing me as a consequence. The quiet doesn't get to me like it used to, but Nash's fist keeps flexing over the hilt of his sword.

When none of us speak, Daros's smile dims. He's a pathetic little excuse for a person. His joy in bothering other people is sickening, but somehow pitiful at the same time.

Finally, he says, "You need to practice bigger magic."

"What type, and how do I do it?" Not that I'll take him at his word. Comparing what he tells me with Venda's teachings will help.

"A healing spell, I would think," he says. "And don't go thinking it can heal you. It's very intricate and only does the most basic of healing. It will take a lot from you and give little in return."

I press my lips together. I *was* thinking of how a spell like that could heal me. Maybe it still can. Maybe I need to talk to Venda again, and she'll have ideas to make it better. Probably not, though. I'd like to think that, if she knew how to heal me, she'd have already done it. "Very well. How do I accomplish this spell?"

"You will need the pollen of a kew tree, fresh honey, basil, and a dollop of cream from a yak. Mix these together over bandages, chanting *plo fir muw*. That should do it."

At least I don't have to gather the ingredients. "Anything else I should know?"

"Next time I won't be so generous with my knowledge."

Well, that is a given.

I can't believe he knows so much about magic. "Why didn't you teach me magic when you were training me?"

"I have my reasons."

Reasons like not caring if I died. How much of his criminal talents are magic related? Will I ever know? Does it matter?

"Now, if you'll excuse me," Daros says, "I will be returning to my life." He practically pushes Nash and Jaku out of his way, though they let him.

As he goes out the door and joins his guards, I wonder what he's plotting.

CHAPTER 18

WHILE I WANTED to get started on the spell right away, there's no time. I meet with my council, see my ladies-in-waiting, have a late dinner, and it's time for bed. My eyelids are heavy, and my desire to run and be free is strong.

Inkga helps me get ready, as usual. I ask her, "Do you ever get tired of assisting me with this?"

She freezes, holding the blankets in midair, then slowly sets them over me up to my chest, and looks me square in the eye. "I will never tire of helping someone with such a good heart."

"Do you really think I have a good heart?" I try, but sometimes it feels like I fail.

"You're not perfect—none of us is—but the core of your desire is for the right."

"Thank you."

"You're welcome. Do you want me to stay with you while you try to sleep?"

"I've got Eldim and Afet to keep me company." The two are in a corner each, though it feels a little like overkill when there are no windows in my room and the only entrance is the door that others are guarding.

"All right, then. I'll see you in the morning, unless you need something sooner."

"Thank you, Inkga."

"Any time." She grabs a dirty linen set and is out the door.

It seems like she's the only maid who takes care of me. I've never thought about it before, but it makes me pause. Is it because of safety reasons or because others don't want to help me?

I suppose it doesn't matter either way, but it is odd. Whatever the case may be, Inkga is a loyal friend more than anything else. I need more people like her in my life.

I let my eyes close, trying to ignore the guards. Puneah makes a purring sound from under my bed that makes me relax more. I let my mind drift, and it goes to Nash. Seeing him today was hard. I wanted to reach for him so bad, to talk to him and see how things are going, but I don't want to push him if he's not ready.

I push the feelings aside and all goes dark.

"You won't conquer me," the First Queen says. "You should give up now. Surrender to me."

"Do I seem like the type of person to surrender?" I don't know why I'm bothering to talk to her. I stretch out my body, loosening my muscles.

"It was worth a try. It will be so much easier for you if you let me in. Allow me take care of all your worries."

"I can handle my own worries—thank you very much."

She laughs her tinkling laugh. It grates on me, so I break into a run. She pops in and out of my line of sight and then sits down on the side, watching me.

Everything blurs out as I feel each muscle in my body tense and move. I'm strong, as I should be, but realizing it won't last past the dream drains me. I try not to think about it, but the thought keeps coming to me.

"I can offer you escape from a body that no longer works."

It's tempting, but no.

Besides, I get a little better every day.

I keep going, moving on and on.

"You think your magic will work against me? You know nothing."

Is she right? Are we going in the wrong direction? "You are the one who knows nothing," I say. "You've been stuck in other people's bodies for a thousand years. You've forgotten what it's like to live."

She appears, standing before me. I can't stop myself; I knock into her and tumble to the ground, while she manages to stay upright.

She towers over me, seeming infinitely bigger than she is. "I know more about what it's like to live than you ever will." She reaches down to help me up, but I ignore it. "You'll find I can make even your dreams miserable if you don't cooperate with me."

I haul myself off the ground, keeping my mind blank.

"I know you're angry. I feel it rolling off you." She comes closer, until her mouth is next to my ear, and whispers, "I've won. Just give into me. I'll make your life easier. More pleasant. Together, we can do so much."

I whip around, getting some space in the process. "You mean like you killing me, since my body is no longer useful to you? No, thanks."

"Perhaps I was hasty to want you killed. We can still accomplish a lot from your position."

"We both know you're lying. You want a healthy body, so you have as much freedom as possible."

She shrugs. "Think what you like, but you'll find it much less painful to cooperate with me than work against me. I can make your waking hours a living nightmare if you're not careful."

They already are. My body's been taken from me. Nash has been taken from me. My country is fighting me.

I clamp down on those thoughts, but it's too late.

"That's right. You do have things rough. Let me ease your burden."

"By taking over my life? Not happening."

"You'll wish you'd taken me up on my offer."

I refuse to give into her. Ever.

CHAPTER 19

"THAT IS one way to enchant an object to heal someone—yes," Venda says. We're in my sitting room, with Jaku and Inkga. "But you must have lots of energy to cast it, and it's not the most efficient charm."

Great. Lied to again. Or maybe Daros doesn't know better. Either way, I'm grateful Venda's here to help. "What would you have me do?"

She looks down at the pile of ingredients Inkga collected at my request. I don't know how she managed to get them all on such short notice. Just one of the advantages of having her on my side.

"To these we need to add red weed and take away the cream." Venda leans back as she finishes looking over the pile.

"I'll fetch it right away," Inkga says. "I know where the red weed is, but it may take some time to collect."

Red weed is difficult to find, but if she knows where to find it, it would speed things up. "Thank you, Inkga," I say. "Be sure to take a guard with you."

"Ryn, I travel the grounds by myself all the time."

"Be cautious, then." Though I wish she would take a guard.

"I will." She gives a little wave and is out the door.

I focus on Venda. I know little about her, other than that she's from Faner and an assassin. "Did you leave any family behind in Faner?"

She searches my eyes, as if looking for something. Whatever it is, she must find it because she says, "Assassins are discouraged from having a family."

"Even parents?"

"We have them, but we are turned over to the assassins' guild when we are twelve, after showing some of the skills it takes to be in the profession." Her voice is matter of fact, but it reminds me too much of my being sent to Daros and growing up without parents.

"I can tell what you're thinking," she says. "It is different than what you went through with Daros. Yes, we are pushed, but not to the point of breaking. Our leaders can be harsh at times, but we have others in our lives, like the healers, who are kind and attentive."

What would that have been like? "Forgive me if this is too personal, but do you have friends?"

"Others in the guild, yes, but we are encouraged not to let those ties grow too close. If we get too close to someone, it's dangerous for both them and us."

So her life is not unlike my own, though I've found a way to cheat past some of the cards life dealt me. "How did you get assigned to bring me Puneah?"

The animal in question must hear her name because she comes padding out of my bedroom to rest her head on my lap and look up at me with those cat-like eyes.

"You have created a true bond with your fila," Venda says.

"What does that mean?"

"No one knows exactly. I do know she will give her life for you, as you've seen. She considers you an ally. Perhaps a friend."

I stroke her fur, not minding the concentration it takes to move my hand that much. She purrs—a deep, rumbling sound.

"Definitely a bond." Venda sits back and watches us. "As to your question, I am highly skilled at what I do. My queen sent me because I'd be able to handle myself if I got myself in a tricky situation."

"And yet, here you are, putting yourself in dangerous situations to save my life."

"There's no point in having skills if I don't use them."

That gives me something to ponder while we wait for Inkga's return.

Once she comes back with the two other ingredients, we get to work.

Venda pulls out a mortar and pestle.

"Where did you get that?" Inkga asks.

"From my country."

"No. I mean you don't have a bag with you, and I didn't see it earlier. How did you carry it here?"

"In the folds of my dress."

"Isn't it heavy?"

She shrugs. "I've brought it several times with me in case we needed it."

"And what do we need it for?"

"Instead of grinding things on the bandages, we will use this. It works well to mix what we need for the healing spell."

As she sets it down and arranges items on the table, I ask, "Will this spell heal anything?"

She lifts her gaze to me, eyes sad. "No. Only minor things. There are few who can enchant objects to heal major wounds."

"Why?" Inkga asks. "Why only a few? Why can't I do it?"

"Because it takes rare ingredients, but that can be overcome. More than that, it takes so much of yourself that few are willing to give, even when they think they are. Also, it leaves you weakened for months, unable to cast other spells or do much for yourself."

I know what that's like.

Inkga scowls.

Venda pulls together a small amount of the red weed, basil, pollen from a kew tree, and wheat into the mortar. "The honey is for the end. Also, this spell will make an enchanted item that will only work at casting spells for the caster."

"Why?" I ask.

"Because it is attuned with your soul."

She stands and brings the mortar and pestle to me.

"Is that how you stopped the poison from killing me?"

"It is."

"Then why couldn't it save Wilric?"

Her expression is down turned as she stops in front of me. "He was too far gone."

I nod, though I want to argue. What use would it do? It can't bring him back any more than she could save him before.

She places the mortar in one of my hands and the pestle in the other and helps me use them. "I don't know if you'll be able to press as hard as is needed for this enchantment to work, but we'll try. As you work the mixture, say *lew fa tee ro.*"

"Right." That doesn't sound ridiculous.

"If you're not going to take it seriously, it won't work." Her voice is stern.

"I'm sorry."

She studies me before continuing. "It means *to heal the wound.* It is an old spell, used by many generations to heal those who are unhealthy."

Being able to do such a thing would be a vast improvement. I do need to believe more.

I say the ancient words as I push my hand, moving it around a little. It takes some time to get the mixture as good as Venda wants it. By the time we are finished, my hands and arms are exhausted. I let them rest in my lap, where Puneah nuzzles them.

"Good," Venda says. "Now you must rub it into the object you want to use, chanting the same words. It will take more of a pull than your other enchantments so far. Your instinct is going to be to yank it back, to stop it from happening, but you must let it."

"I have a question," Inkga says. "Why do you have to chant while you do these things?"

"The chant isn't as important as it is to concentrate. You will find different people use different chants for the same spell. It's a process to help you focus on the magic." Venda puts a slim bracelet in my hand. "This is what you will enchant. Then you will be able to wear it and use it whenever you need."

I look more closely at the item. It's beautiful. An open circle of silver metal that fits around my wrist. In the center, a flower is carved. It matches my ring. "Where did you get this?"

"After seeing how you wear the ring all the time, I decided you should have something to go with it. I commissioned it, and it was finished yesterday. This should be the perfect spell for it."

"Thank you." She didn't have to do that. It's a kindness I've been shown so little of in my life. I'm not sure what to do with it.

Shillian pops into my head. Would she like it? Think it's befitting a royal to wear? I shake away my thoughts. My mother betrayed me almost as much as my father did. She may not have literally stabbed me in the back, like he did, to erase his debts, but she supported his being here.

Still, I did allow her to live in the palace. How much is she responsible for something she didn't know was going on?

Venda slides the mixture out of the mortar and onto the bracelet, and adds the honey when she's finished. "Rub that in and chant. Let the magic guide you to give part of yourself to it. It will not hurt, but it will be uncomfortable."

"Won't this ruin the bracelet?" I ask.

"It washes off fine after the spell has been cast."

All right. No more delaying. I think of everything she's said and begin my chant while using my aching fingers to rub the mixture onto the bracelet. Nothing happens, but I expected that from the previous enchantments we've done. I continue rubbing, focusing, and chanting until there's a tug inside me. Unlike before, it's rough, almost brutal in its hurry to get at me.

I stop. "What was that?"

"That was the pull on your magic. You think about what that felt like, and I'll help Inkga give it a try."

The magic was bigger than I expected. More insistent. How do I give control over to that? This is going to take longer than the time I have.

CHAPTER 20

TIME PASSES TOO slow and too fast all at once. There are so many expectations of me. I can't keep up with them all. I have council meetings, meetings with my ladies-in-waiting, reading, and filling out papers, all while I continue to do what I can to gain physical and magical strength.

None of it is going well.

And the whole time, not a word from Nash. Yesterday, I sent a note to his mother, hoping she wouldn't mind the intrusion.

Lunch just finished up, and I'm waiting for my council meeting. We'll probably go over more things the councilors are bickering over—things that don't matter. Maybe they'd matter more if I didn't have the weight of the First Queen on me.

"You look like there is a heavy burden on you," Venda says as she enters my sitting room.

I give her a smile, but it feels tight. "I didn't expect to see you today."

"I thought I would spend some time with you." Her gaze flits to Afet and Eldim.

The two need a break. They've been alternating standing

guard over me with Jaku, and I'm afraid it's too much. No matter what I say, though, they tell me they're fine.

Is there more than what she's saying? "That's kind of you." It gets frustrating, these little in-between moments I have that I usually spend by myself, unable to do anything except exercise my hands.

She sits on a chair across from me. "How are you?"

Is she serious? "I'm fine."

"You can be honest with me."

Frustrated that I can't defeat the First Queen. "I wish I could do that thing we were practicing earlier." I don't dare say *magic* in front of Eldim and Afet. Though I can probably trust them, I don't want to chance scaring them off.

"I know. It will come with time. Your strength will increase, and you will benefit from that."

Androlla will take over before then. Though she has left me alone the past several days, even in my dreams, it makes me more nervous than if she was bothering me. It's like she's gathering her power for something big.

I hold my head high. No matter what it is, I won't let her.

"I have a gift for you," Venda says, snagging my attention back to her.

"You didn't have to get me anything."

"But I wanted to. It seems well suited to you. I should have given it to you a while ago." She pulls a small object out of her pocket. It's a rectangular box, made of dark wood.

"What is it?"

"Something that will give you a little independence." She places it in my hand and shows me two small protrusions sticking out of the sides. "If you hold both of these down at the same time, it will shoot a dart laced with a quick-acting poison."

I look at the device with new appreciation. "It can do that?"

"Of course. And it has five darts loaded in it, so after you shoot one, another will take its place. You'll have to count to three for the mechanism to have time to move."

"I don't know what to say."

"*Thank you* will suffice." She stands and moves out of the way. "Go ahead and aim it at the chair, to make sure you can use it, then press those two buttons at the same time."

I hold the box between my thumb and middle finger, my pointer finger on top. A week ago, I wouldn't have been able to do that. Once I feel both parts that stick out, I press them down, aiming for the chair. A thrill goes through me as a dart goes flying out of the box and lands dead-center in the chair. "Thank you. More than words can express, thank you. This will help so much. The darts are so little, though."

"They'll feel like a prick. It's made to be light and easy, but that little prick will put the poison in your opponent's blood stream."

"What will the poison do?" I don't want to accidentally kill someone.

"One dart will knock them out. Two to three darts will do so more quickly, and they'll be quite sick when they come around. Four will put them in a coma for days, and five will kill them."

"Five is death. Got it." And will be very careful with that box. "This is a gift like I never expected."

"I hope it gives you some peace of mind. Just make certain you're willing to knock out and possibly kill whoever you're aiming at when you use it."

Daros flashes into my mind, but I don't want to kill him. Not only does he have the information I need, but I am over that need. His death isn't worth sullying my life. He's a pathetic excuse for a man who can find no joy except to play with others' lives. After all this is over, I hope to have him executed, not out of vengeance, but for the safety of others. I don't know if that'll be possible, though, given the pardon he had me sign.

"I will be careful to only aim it at enemies."

"Good. Now we eat."

"I had lunch," I say confused at her words.

"Yes, but you have not had lychee."

"What is that?"

She pulls a little red sphere full of tiny bumps out of her pocket. "It is a fruit from my country, which is where your gift came from. I had a package arrive today. You will find this fruit better fresh in Faner, but it is still good enough that I wish to share with you and your guards." She peels the red skin off to reveal an almost translucent whitish fruit beneath it. She cuts it in half with her fingers and pulls out a tiny pit. "It is ready now. If you will permit me?"

She wants to feed me since I can't bring my hand to my mouth. I'm more curious than embarrassed. "Of course."

She places the fruit between my open lips. It's delicious. A light, almost floral flavor. "I like it."

"I thought you would." She throws one each to Afet and Eldim and shows them how to open them before feeding me another.

"They are delightful," I say. "Thank you for sharing with us."

"Yes. Thank you," Eldim says.

"That's some good fruit," Afet adds. "Though we probably shouldn't be eating on duty."

She waves a hand. "Ryn is safe now. She has her dart shooter. Everything will be fine."

If only my dart shooter really could make everything fine.

Inkga enters the room. "I have your mail for the day."

"If you will excuse me, I shall be going," Venda says.

"You don't have to leave on my account," Inkga replies.

"I need to take care of a few things, but thank you for saying so." Venda gives me a faint smile before going out the door.

Inkga grins as she comes over to me. "Are you having a good day so far?"

"The best." Given the circumstances. "Venda gave me a new toy." I hold up the dart flinger and explain what it is.

"I'll be sure to stay clear of its path," she says. "I'm happy you have a way to protect yourself. I know that's been bothering you."

"Is it that obvious?"

She winks. "Let's take a look here. I thought you might like to read this one first." She opens the letter.

"Who's it from?"

"Slipa."

My interest is immediately piqued. Nash's mother wrote me back.

Kind enough to look away, Inkga places it before me. I eagerly take it in.

QUEEN RYN,

I was happy to receive your letter. Thank you for your interest in our family. We are all doing well. The girls are more settled now that their brother is home, though I have a feeling he won't be here for much longer.

Nash is doing well—better than he has been since he first returned—though I know he's still haunted by what happened to him. I appreciate your concern and have let everyone I know how kind you are. You are always welcome in our home, whenever you should desire to visit.

Thank you again, for taking such good care of Nash and of our family,

Slipa

HE WON'T BE home for much longer? What does that mean? I'm grateful to hear he's coming around, if it's true. It's hard to know for certain when it comes from his mother. Despite not trusting my own, I know they can be biased toward their children.

Maybe she doesn't know how bad he got, and he's worse than ever.

The thought makes my stomach churn. I don't want him

worse; I want him better. I need to see him myself, to know how things are actually going, but I don't dare call for him. Sending a letter to his mother would be showing him preferential treatment.

"Thank you, Inkga, I'm finished with that one," I say. Probably had her hold it way too long, considering how short it was.

"I thought—" She stops herself.

"Thought what?"

"Forgive me. It's not my place."

"We're friends, aren't we?"

She nods.

"Then you can tell me or ask me whatever you want." And I'll do my best to answer.

She bites her lower lip. "I thought that you would be happier about that letter—unless it was bad news?"

I'm very aware of Afet and Eldim in the room, though I trust them both. "It wasn't bad. I am happy, but I'm also still worried. There's a lot that could go wrong, and that seems to be all I can think about."

"I understand."

"Do you?"

She nods. "It's hard having people you lo—care about going through hard times."

Too true. It hurts to think about.

"Are you ready to read the next letter?" she asks.

I give her an affirmative. No matter how many letters from Shillian or ladies-in-waiting I read, they don't take my mind off the first one. Off Nash and how he may be doing.

CHAPTER 21

It's almost time for dinner as I'm wheeled into my sitting room. My mind has been on the letter regarding Nash for the past two days. I wonder how he's doing as I practice strengthening myself, my magic, and my country. It's a lot to take in.

I haven't been worrying enough about the First Queen because she's been leaving me alone. But what is she planning?

Inkga lights a candle and gives a squeal.

"What is it?" I demand, readying my dart flinger.

Her squeal of fear turns to delight. "A great surprise. I'm going to get out of your hair."

And he steps into my line of sight. Nash. My heart flutters wildly. I want to press myself against him. To give him my lips and remind him he has my heart. Instead, I point my dart flinger away from him and keep my voice formal. "Inkga, please go get Jaku. Nash Zorris, it's good to see you."

He winces. Whether it's because of how I look, my formal tone, or something else, I can't tell. My fingers twitch. Eldim and Afet each take a corner while Inkga sets me in place on the side of the room by some chairs and leaves the room.

"What is it you wish to discuss?" I ask.

"Mother got your note."

"And I received hers." This is so formal. I hate it. Why do I feel a need to set this tone? I wish we didn't have an audience, but I'm not sure it would be any better. There's so much standing between us right now.

He glances around the room, stopping on the unlit candelabra. "May I light this for you?"

It is rather dark with only one candle. Inkga usually lights more, but she must have forgotten since she left in a hurry for Jaku. "If you'd like."

Nash takes the lit candle and goes around the room, lighting more. As the room brightens, my heart grows heavier. He's silent. I'm silent. It's like there's a chasm between us that can't be crossed.

Nash nods at Afet and Eldim. They nod back, but otherwise, the room is still. Quiet.

Jaku enters the room. He takes one look at the situation and says to Afet and Eldim, "Why don't you take a break? Come back in two hours to relieve me."

"Yes, sir," they both say.

They exit the room, and Jaku says, "It's good to see you, Nash."

"It's good to see you too." He hesitates a moment. "Don't suppose it's possible that you give me and Ryn a moment alone."

"Afraid I can't do that."

"I didn't think so, but I had to ask."

Jaku gets in a corner. "Ignore me the best you can."

Like we'll start kissing in front of him. Not that it would happen anyway. He takes one look at me, and resolve hardens his face. He strides closer and kneels in front of me. "Ryn, I know I can't ever earn your full forgiveness for what I've done and how I've behaved, but I want you to know I'm trying hard. The time away and talking to Jaku were what I needed. I'm not perfect, but I'm doing better. You made the right decision."

The urge to throw myself at him is stronger than ever. "Why didn't you visit, then? Or write?"

He glances down. "I was ashamed of my behavior. Truth be told, I still am, but I'm hoping you can find it in your heart to forgive me."

"Of course I can, Nash. I forgave you the moment it happened. I just wanted you to get the help you needed, to get better."

His head jerks up. "You mean that?"

"I do."

"Thank you, Ryn. That means more to me than I can say."

And the fact that he's here, asking for forgiveness, means more than I can say. "You don't have to talk about what happened if you don't want to, but I need to know you'll never beat a defenseless man again."

"Never. I've gotten a hold of myself. What's more, after speaking with Jaku, I know the best option is to not put myself in that situation."

"Good. I'm glad that's settled." Now would be the perfect time to hug him, but I can barely move my hands. Besides, I'm not sure how keen Jaku would be on our touching. He might have told us to act like he wasn't here, but he wouldn't be all right with seeing us hug and kiss. Or fight. Oh, how I miss our sparring.

"I have to ask. How are things going with Androlla? I've been worried about it the whole time I've been gone, and wondered if..."

"If she's taken me over yet? No, she's left me alone for the past while. It makes me more nervous than if she tried to gain control all the time. I worry she's planning something."

Nash stands and paces. "I don't like the sound of that."

"Neither do I," Jaku says. "You didn't tell me that."

"Because I have it under control." And I'm scared to talk about it, but it has to happen sooner or later. Better it come from me, than they see it happen with their own eyes.

"Don't keep things like that from us," Jaku says. "We're trying to help you, but we can't do it if we don't have all the information."

"Sorry." I glance at Nash, to see how he reacts—and if I'm honest, just to look at him. It's so good to be able study him.

He shakes his head. "We need to get this figured out before she gains control permanently over you. How's the magic coming?"

"Inkga and Venda are doing a good job helping me, but it's been a struggle. Daros said I needed to learn a healing enchantment next, but despite practice, it hasn't come to me."

"A healing enchantment. Is that to help you?"

I hold back a grimace. "It' not strong enough."

"What could that be for, then?" Nash stops his pacing across from me, facing my direction.

"I don't know. I'm wondering if I'll need a huge spell that will help me heal myself. Heal her out of me? That, or it's practice for another big spell."

"Perhaps he's leading us on," Nash says.

"That's always a possibility," Jaku replies.

I hate to think like that, but it's been a wiggling worry in the back of my mind ever since Daros started taking me on this path. "We need a plan in case he's not being honest with us. I've been researching more magic with the help of the books you found me, Nash, and with Venda's assistance. The problem is I haven't found anything that would help us defeat the First Queen."

Maybe there's nothing. Maybe she made herself indestructible and that's why she's always mocking me.

"There's got to be something," Nash says.

"She's close now." I try to ignore her pressure in my head. "And mocking us."

He strides over and gets so close to my face that we're almost touching. My breath gets knocked away by his sudden proximity. "You tell her that we'll find a way, no matter what," he says.

My fingers twitch and flex before aiming the dart flinger straight for Nash and pushing the buttons on both sides.

CHAPTER 22

Nash cries out and scurries away. Jaku is asking what happened. I'm screaming on the inside because I can't control myself. I can't do anything but feel my hand aim for Nash again as the First Queen prepares to shoot him again.

A second dart slips out and hits Nash in the arm. He weaves across the room, toward the door, as she aims again. I'm counting in my head, hoping against all hope that he'll get out before I get to *three*. A third dart flies through the air and pierces his leg.

Jaku jumps across the room in a few long leaps and knocks the dart flinger from my hand.

Tinkling laugh fills the room. It comes from my mouth, but it doesn't sound like me.

The presence of the First Queen withdraws as sudden as it came.

"Nash, are you all right?" is the first thing out of my mouth. "Jaku, send for Venda. Quick."

"I'm fine." But Nash's words are slurred.

Jaku's at the door, calling for a servant to run and get Venda. Puneah stalks out of my room and reaches Nash as he falls to the floor. She nudges his face with her nose, but he doesn't respond.

"Nash, you have to wake up. You have to be all right." I'm desperate.

Venda said only three darts wouldn't kill, but I'm still worried because the poison has the potential to be lethal. Three is a lot—almost a deadly amount. What if something bad happens to him? What if there are long-term side effects? Why—oh why—did I agree to take the dart flinger from Venda?

Jaku is at Nash's side, feeling for a pulse underneath Puneah's watchful gaze. "He's still alive."

"Venda said only three shots wouldn't kill. She said it takes all five, but I don't know. I don't think he's been exposed to something like this before." And then, I remember. "Quick, grab my poison pouch from around my neck. There's a powder in there that counteracts most poisons."

Jaku rushes to me and reaches for the cord that holds the pouch around my neck. It takes him a moment of fumbling with the cord, and then he gets it and pulls it over my head. It becomes tangled in my hair, and he stops to loosen it.

"Just yank it," I yell.

He does, and I grit my teeth against the pain, but the pouch comes free. Jaku opens it and rifles through the contents. He pulls out another, smaller, black pouch. "Is this it?"

"No. That'll kill him. It's the light green one."

He flounders before pulling out a green pouch.

"Not that one. Light green." I try not to let frustration creep into my voice, but it's there.

Finally, he pulls out the right pouch.

"Yes, that one. Give him several pinches' worth. Put it under his tongue, if possible," I say.

He scrambles back to Nash. Between him and Puneah, I can't see what's going on. I want to know if Nash is safe. Want to know Androlla didn't end his life. She can't take away the man I love, even if I can never have him. We've been through too much for me to lose him.

Venda bursts through the door, guards pouring in after her.

"Nash is injured. You have to help him." The words tumble from my lips.

She takes in sight before her and says, "What have you done, you foolish girl?"

Jaku jumps out of her way, and Puneah comes to my side and nudges my hand. My traitorous hand.

We're quiet while Venda looks him over and pulls the darts out of him. "Only three?"

"Yes," Jaku answers for me. "Ryn had me give him some type of antidote."

"It was hulic," I say.

"That will help." But her words come out angry. She takes something out of a pocket and waves it over him while chanting something under her breath.

The air is heavy with my betrayal. The lack of noise makes me want to scream for Nash. Tell him to wake up. To come back to me. That I didn't mean it.

But Nash lies still.

"Is he…" I can't finish the thought.

Venda glares at me. "Silence."

I swallow my guilt as she goes back to chanting and waving the object over his body. The image is too much like what I last saw of Wilric, struggling for breath. He didn't make it. Will the same happen to Nash, or will Venda be able to save him?

She drops her hand. "A bowl. Quickly."

Jaku hurries to my room and is in the door with my washstand bowl in his hands when Nash jerks and vomits. Venda rolls him onto his side as he continues to be sick.

As much as I don't want to see him like this, my worry eases from seeing him react—do something other than coldly lie there.

Until Venda says, "He's not clear yet."

"What do you mean?" Fear ebbs its way into my chest.

"If he has a bad reaction to it, the poison can be as deadly as if he'd been hit five times."

"Bad reaction? He's throwing up," Jaku says.

"You should have told me there could be a bad reaction," I practically yell.

Venda looks at me. "I didn't want to scare you. I wanted you to protect yourself." She turns her gaze to Jaku. "He would vomit regardless. What we are watching for now is seizures."

Please tell me this isn't happening.

Venda calls servants in to clean up the mess as she keeps an attentive eye on Nash. He's still on his side, pale as pale can be. He has to come through this. He just has to.

I want to send a note to his mother, but I don't want to scare her without knowing if he's going to be fine or not. "How long do we have to wait?"

"We'll know within the next five minutes." Venda keeps her focus trained on him.

That's not enough time to get his mother here. I'll have to settle for finding out what happens before I bring her wrath down upon me.

Time ticks by slowly. Is he getting paler? I wish I could go to him. There's a deep ache inside me, to comfort him. To fix him. I don't know how to do either. Besides, I can't move, and even if I did, I'm not supposed to touch him, unless it's to save my life, not his.

Valcora and its stupid rules. Things have to change. If not for me, then for those that come after me.

Puneah whines.

"Here it comes." Venda's words send a shock of fear through me.

His body tenses and then starts convulsing. I watch in horror as he shakes uncontrollably and Venda sits by him, doing nothing. "Help him," I say.

"Anything I do now will only harm him more."

This is it, then. Tremors wrack his body violently, and I can only watch. We all do. It feels like an eternity. It doesn't seem fair that this is happening now, when he was doing better. When he was getting over the shock and pain of being tortured.

It's too much. I want to close my eyes, but I force myself to keep them open and keep watch over him. All I can do is hope this isn't the end. It's not how he's supposed to go—killed by his own queen, the woman who loves him.

It's not fair or right. The movements wrack my heart with pain. I'd give anything to take his place. For Androlla to have shot me and not him. Though it wouldn't be easy, with my limited mobility, it would be better than this pain and torment.

Finally, his shaking eases, but he's so pale. So still. I want to ask if he's alive, but I can't bring myself to say the words when he looks so deathly.

Jaku does it for me. "Is he going to make it?"

Venda holds up a hand, palm out, and continues to stare at Nash. He gives a shuddering breath, and she's over him like lightning, moving her object and chanting like her life is on the line. She has to help him. Has to bring him back to me.

Her murmured words only last a few seconds when his eyes flutter open. She stops and sits back, watching him. "He will live."

Relief pours through me—I didn't kill the man I love. But it was close. Way too close.

His eyes are glassy, looking around but seemingly not taking anything in. He blinks several times, and the glassiness fades while he tries to sit up.

"Not yet," Venda says to him. "You need rest."

He stays down but looks around the room until his gaze stops on me.

Does he remember that I tried to kill him? It was my fingers, my actions that put this thing into motion.

Dagger the First Queen and her controlling ways. I should have realized what she was when I met her, shouldn't have been taken in by her soothing voice and ways. There has to be a way to fight this, but I don't know what it is.

"What happened?" Nash asks.

Venda shoos everyone out of the room, except me and Jaku. Once the door is closed tight, she looks at me. "Tell him what happened."

"I—I…" Can't manage to get the words out. I clear my throat and try again. "I shot you with the darts. The poison got in your system, and Venda saved you."

He grimaces, opens his mouth, looks at Venda, and snaps it shut.

"You people want to tell me what is going on?" Venda asks. "Why Ryn shot Nash, who she clearly cares about?"

A blush heats my cheeks, but I ignore it. Now is not the time to worry over who knows about my feelings. I glance at Jaku, who says, "It's up to you."

Would it be better for her to know or not? She's helped us so far, and she believes in magic. I'd like to think that she's on our side. "It may have been my body that shot him, but it wasn't me." I take a steadying breath. "The Mortum Tura does more than choose a queen. It makes the very first queen of Valcora part of whoever it chooses. At first, she said she was here to guide me, but I've since learned she's there to try to take me over, so she can rule once again. It's happens every time someone survives the Mortum Tura for the past thousand years."

Venda purses her lips. "I was afraid a darkness was over your country, though I had no idea it was this bad."

"Do you know a way to break the bond?" I ask.

She shakes her head. "None. It is dark, *dark* magic that made this. My people stay away from such things. Is this why you are practicing magic?"

"It's why I'm trying to learn. Yes."

"I see." She turns her attention back to Nash, who's trying to sit up again. Instead of scolding him, this time she helps him up. "Jaku, please fetch him a glass of water."

Nash leans against the wall, head back and eyes closed. If only I could go to him.

Jaku leaves the room and returns a moment later with a cup of water. Venda helps Nash drink. The room is too quiet for what I've revealed to Venda. Do they blame me for drinking the Mortum Tura and bringing this down upon them all? Because I do.

CHAPTER 23

THERE'S no way to protect myself, and at the same time, protect those I love. The thought plagues me as I sit, unable to do much in this dreary, dark room. In my mind's eye, I can still see Nash on the ground, jerking and twisting in ways he couldn't control.

"Ryn?" Inkga's voice pulls me out of my trance.

When did she get here? I want to berate myself for not paying attention, but I can't find the enough energy to do so.

When I don't respond, she says, "They've got Nash in the healing wing. He's doing fine. They said he needs a couple days, and he'll be back to himself."

That stirs me. "Good."

"Also, someone is here to see you."

Who would want to see me? Jaku insisted on standing guard by himself, and Inkga is the only other person to come in my rooms. Venda left with Nash and hasn't been back all evening.

Inkga opens the door, and Jem comes in. Inkga gives me a small smile before leaving.

I pull my thoughts together. Doesn't matter how I'm feeling; I have a job to do. "How are you?"

"Is it true that the woman from Faner used magic on Nash?" she asks.

"Hello to you too."

"Answer the question."

This riles me. "Why are you being so rude?"

"Sorry, Ryn. I just want to know. It feels important."

I contemplate denying it, but a whole slew of guards saw Venda. "She did."

"And do you know magic?"

Not where I expected her to go. I thought she'd curse Venda having magic. "Why does it matter?"

"Because something hasn't been adding up for a while now, and it's surrounding you."

"What if I practice magic? I'm free to do as I please." It's not true. As the queen, I'm trapped by more expectations, laws, and scrutiny than any other individual.

"People are calling Venda a witch. Some are wondering if you brought her here on purpose."

I give a fake, sharp laugh. "I have no say in what Venda does. She's more her own person than anyone I've ever met before."

"I'm serious, Ryn. People are upset. Some are saying Venda was the one who hurt Nash and anyone could be next."

"Now that's just stupid."

"Maybe, but fear changes people. Makes them think of the worst."

"And magic would be the worst?"

She hesitates. "I'm not sure. As your Head Advisor, I need to know where you stand."

I let out a long breath, wishing it was long enough to bore Jem and make her leave. When she doesn't go, I say, "I have been enchanting items, yes, but it's not what you think. You have to promise me you won't say a thing. What I'm about to tell you is the country's greatest secret."

"I promise."

Do I trust her? I make a swift decision. "The Mortum Tura is magic."

"I could have guessed that."

I go on, like I didn't hear her. "It has a dark magic that imbues the very first queen of Valcora into the partakers that live."

She takes a step back. "No. Ryn, you can't talk like this. It's going to get you executed for insanity."

"It's true. I know it's hard to believe, but you have to trust me."

She bites her lower lip. Her words come out as a whisper. "This is crazy talk."

What can I say to reassure her? "Haven't you wondered why I don't always act like myself? Why I do unexpected things?"

She tilts her head to the side.

I bite my cheek. I hope giving her a moment to process all of this will help and not have her running for someone to haul me off to my death.

"This is bad, isn't it?" she asks.

I hold back a sigh of relief. She believes me. "Very. The First Queen is not kind, and she's trying to take me over, like she's done to countless women before me. She wants to reign over this people forever. I'm determined not to let that happen."

"This is why you pardoned Daros, isn't it? He has something to do with this?"

"Unfortunately, yes. He claims he has the knowledge to defeat her."

"But does he?"

I proceed to tell her the information he's given us and how we've put it to use. By the time I'm done, she's scowling.

By the time I'm done, she's scowling. "It sounds like he doesn't know what he's doing."

"But he must have some sort of plan. Not even Venda knew what to do about Androlla."

"Who?"

"The First Queen."

146

She takes a seat next to me. "I will try to help you the best I can."

"Thank you. We've been reading a lot of books from the library, but there are so many, and with only a few of us and limited time, we're not making as much progress as I'd like."

"I can assist you with that, and I'll keep your secret, but are you… safe to be around?"

I press my lips together, remembering what it felt like to watch Nash get hit with dart after dart, and not be able to do anything about it. "It's definitely not safe."

She's silent a moment before nodding. "I can handle that."

"Even if it means your death?"

"From what you've described, it's going to be more than just my death, should we fail, so yes."

"Thank you. Your assistance will be much appreciated."

"I'll do what I can. I'll try to tamp down the rumors of magic."

A sudden thought hits me. "No. This country is going to have to deal with magic sooner or later. Might as well get them started."

"All right, but I recommend keeping quiet on Androlla. I don't think people will like magic to begin with, and having a voice in your head doesn't sound good."

"That's what I was thinking," I say.

Inkga comes in. "If you're finished, I'll help you get ready for bed."

I realize it's late, and I have some words for Androlla.

Jem gives her goodbyes, and Inkga to helps me change for the night.

Jaku comes in the room when we're done.

"You're going to wear yourself out," I say.

"I'll be fine. Julina should be on shift tomorrow."

"She's feeling better?"

"For a while now. She's aching to get back on the job."

I bet she is. "Thank you for letting me know. Don't push your-self too hard."

"Just taking cues from you."

I shake my head and turn my attention to Inkga. "Thank you."

"Of course, Ryn."

She makes to go, but I ask, "Have you heard rumors about magic?"

She freezes. Without turning around, she says, "I have."

"What do you think of them?"

She faces me. "I trust that people will comes to terms with it sooner or later."

"You're not worried about being caught doing magic? We have spent a lot of time with Venda."

"I am a little worried, but I have hope that it will turn out all right in the end."

Good enough for me. Especially since I don't share her optimism. I'm not about to knock it away from her, though. "Goodnight, then, Inkga."

"Goodnight, Ryn."

She's gone, and I close my eyes. Sleep doesn't take long in coming.

The colors of sunset sweep into view in a blur across the sky. I whip around and spot Androlla, sitting serenely nearby. I march up to her and smack her across the face. The sting smarts my cheek but doesn't wake me. I was prepared for it this time.

She widens her eyes for a brief moment before she starts to laugh.

I back up, watching her until she calms.

She says, "My methods are wearing you down."

"You will not bring the people I love into this."

She stands, growing bigger and taller than ever, until she's looking down at me. "I will do whatever I want to win this war."

She shrinks back as she returns to her sitting position, and I pretend what happened doesn't bother me.

"Aren't you going jogging today?" she asks.

"I'll do what I want, when I want."

"Because this is the only place you have that type of control."

The urge to smack her again is so strong, I have to take several steps back to keep from hitting her. "I will win."

Her only reply is a giggle.

"Why did you do it? Why hurt Nash?" I ask.

"The truth?" Her voice turns menacing. "Because if I can't kill you, I will kill everyone and everything you love."

I turn my back to her and run.

CHAPTER 24

INKGA ROLLS my chair into a meeting room with a window. Though I can see guards standing outside, I'm grateful for the view. Without it, it's like being in Daros's room of torture.

Eldim and Julina are in the room. It's the first I've seen of her since she was injured, but this isn't the time to talk because others are here.

Nash was supposed to join us since he's feeling better after days of resting, but he didn't show up. Is he avoiding me? I wish I could see him, but I focus on the couple that is here. A weight lifts from my chest, and I give them a genuine smile.

They curtsy and bow.

Kapeni, the woman who taught me to read, has the biggest grin on her face. It dims as she looks at my chair, but returns when she meets my gaze. "We're pleased to join you here, Queen Ryn."

"We're friends. Please call me Ryn."

"I might not be able to do that, but I'll try."

"Coplo, how are you? How was the journey?" I ask.

"Truth be told, it was long. My old bones aren't used to such trips." He is older than I thought; there's gray in his hair and wrinkles at the corner of his eyes. Kapeni is the same, but her appearance seems as it did in my youth. When I met them on my journey, I was so excited to see her again. I didn't pay attention to their appearance.

They both wear fine clothes. She has her gray hair pulled back into a bun, at the nape of her neck. Her smile makes me want to smile back. He's gruffer, not grinning as much as she does, but when he does, it lights up his face—even those gray eyes of his.

"I'm sorry it wasn't easier on you," I say. "I'm grateful you'll be staying a while. Hopefully that'll give you time to recover from your journey."

"Only to be worn out again. But that's not what we came here to talk about. I've had my man of business draw up all the papers needed to sell you the mine."

"I've looked them over, as has the rest of the council." I snuck them in between practicing magic and dealing with Daros. "We are all in favor of the contract, and I'm ready to sign it today."

"Good."

A servant comes forward and offers Coplo a quill. He scratches his name on both contracts before returning it to the servant. The servant then takes the papers and places them under my hand. He dips the quill in ink and closes my fingers around it. As I sign, I realize it's easier than before. It gives me hope for the future, that I may gain some of my strength back. My name is even legible. I sign the second copy, and it's as clear as the first.

Kapeni claps. "I'm thrilled that the mine will be put to such good use. We worried so much over it, since we don't have children to pass it down to."

"I'm grateful we could purchase it from you," I say. "I'm hoping it will help a lot of people."

The servant hands Coplo his copy of the contract and takes the other away to be stored with official government papers.

"Now, tell me more about yourself," I say. "I want to know it all. I've missed out on so much."

They glance at each other, and something passes between them—the type of communication only possible between people in love.

"The truth is," Kapeni says, "we wanted to come to Indell, now that the mine is sold. It may take some work to sell the house, but we can do it. Then we can come back to the place I grew up in. Although, I'm not certain. I heard you pardoned Daros?"

I don't want to have to explain this again, though she deserves to know. "I did."

She nods, a faraway look in her eyes. "I won't pretend to understand your reasoning, but I would like to know that you and others are safe from him."

"Including you and your husband."

"Yes."

But I have nothing to give them. I shoo the servants out of the room. Everyone leaves, except for Eldim and Julina. This will be news to her, but Eldim understands what's going on. I hope she takes it well. Then again, she's probably heard the rumors. "We are doing what we can with him. I can't guarantee anything, but we've got him closely guarded."

"And you think that's enough?" Coplo asks. "You have to understand my concern for my wife. If I bring her back here, I don't want anything to happen to her."

"I do understand. While I'd like to assure you that you'll both be one hundred percent safe, I can't. No one can. The most I can offer is that we're doing our best. That, and Daros may not even remember her, since many years have passed."

Kapeni nods. "I suppose that will do for now. Do you expect the situation to last?"

"Honestly, I don't know."

"Very well." She hesitates.

"What is it?" What is she's not willing to say?

"I don't know if I should ask."

"This is me, remember? I used to tell you everything, even though it's been some years. It's time you did the same."

She pauses before saying, "When we last saw you, everything was fine. What happened that put you in this chair with wheels?"

I was worried she was going to ask something like that. "I was poisoned." I hope they don't ask by who.

"That's awful. Who would do such a thing?"

Knife it all. "It was Daros."

She gasps. "And you still pardoned him?"

"The circumstances are not ideal, but I'm doing the best I can with what I have."

She's quiet for so long. She must be disgusted with me.

I say, "He's not the same man he was. Not that I'm excusing his behavior, but he's… worn. He's lost most of what he had before, including many of his material possessions and much of his physical stature. His mind isn't as sharp as it once was. This doesn't excuse anything, but it does make me feel a little better about keeping him around for what I need."

"You don't have to explain yourself to me. I was thinking how hard this must be on you."

I clench my jaw, willing my emotions away before they get the better of me.

"I have to know," she says. "Is he working as an assassin for you?"

I burst out laughing. "Daggers, no." If only it was that easy. I'd hire a different assassin and be done with him. "Our arrangement is more complicated than that."

"You don't have to tell me about it, dear." She leans over and goes to pat my hand. Her husband grabs her arm and gently pulls her back, and she gets a knowing look on her face. "I want you to be safe."

"I'm doing what I can. It's not as easy as it was when I had full control over my body." The admission stings.

"Maybe it's not about how much control you have over your

body, but what you do with your mind that will make the difference."

That's a happy thought, except for the fact that Androlla is taking over my mind. Not that I can tell Kapeni that. I don't want her to think I'm insane.

I glance at the clock. "I'm afraid I have a meeting to attend. You're welcome to stay at the palace as long as you'd like, even while selling your house and finding a new one. Whatever is best for you. I'm happy to have you here."

"Thank you," Coplo says. "Your generosity is something we're grateful for."

"Yes, dear. We hope we can visit again soon." Kapeni gives me a big smile, and I'm taken back to when she used to teach me how to read, the few times I was let outside. Happy moments. She was the only mother figure I had in my life until Shillian came around, and look how that turned out.

I shove away the thought. "I'll visit as soon as I can. It means a lot to me that you're here."

"We're happy to be here, dear." As a servant wheels me away, I wish I could stay with them.

CHAPTER 25

THE COUNCIL ROOM seems emptier than usual. There aren't as many assistants here, helping the councilors. Julina and Afet are on guard duty. It's nice to see they have another guard helping so they don't get worn out, but I hope Julina is fully recovered. I need to find the time to talk to her. Things have been so crazy lately. I haven't done much of anything.

Puneah is curled up at my feet, under the table. It's always nice to have her near. Funny to think I used to not like petting her because now it's a joy to do. Even more so that I can move my hand enough. Inkga is behind me, out of sight but not out of mind.

Except Nash.

Since Androlla shot him, he's been avoiding me. I wish I could talk to him—find out what he's thinking. It's difficult enough, getting through each day. Not knowing how he is makes it harder.

"Are we ready to start?" Timit asks.

"Kada and Mina are missing," I reply.

"We've been waiting for them for ten minutes. Let's get started without them. It may teach them to be on time," Jem says.

She does have a point, though it feels odd to start without the whole council there. I send a servant to track the ladies down and find out what's taking them so long. Then I say, "We have officially bought an emerald mine in the outskirts of Wolta. It's been a highly productive mine, and with what we can tell, will continue to be so in the future. Now what's our first step to get it working for us?"

"Posting jobs should be our first goal," Jaku says. "Though I believe Timit should delegate tasks so the council is free to focus on bigger matters."

"I second that notion," Sidle, Head of Military, says.

"I agree." Which has been happening more and more with my council. It's strange but welcome. "We'll have Timit find someone worthy of overseeing this project and bring them before the council to be approved. Anyone disagree?"

Timit scowls but doesn't protest. Everyone else stays silent.

"Good. Now our next item of busi—"

There's a crash in the hallway.

Jaku stands. Cocks his head to the side. He yells, "Get the queen out of here."

My chair rolls back. I glance to see Inkga moving it. Before she can get me out the back door, the sound of blades clanging against each other comes through that hallway.

"What do I do?" Inkga sounds panicked.

"Roll me over—" I don't have a chance to finish the sentence. Attackers pour in the room from both directions. Inkga moves her arm forward long enough to slip something into my hand before getting back behind me to move my chair away from them. I glance at what she gave me.

My dart flinger, loaded.

A mix of joy and fear shoves its way through me. Is this good or bad? I hope Androlla doesn't use it to hurt someone else I care about.

There's no more time to think about it. The room has erupted in chaos. Men and women are fighting everywhere, with the council scattered throughout the room.

An attacker lunges for Inkga. Puneah flashes out from under the table and latches onto his arm. I glance toward the doors, but they're blocked. We can't stay out here in the open.

"Get us to a corner," I yell back to Inkga amidst the shouting, metal clanging, and confusion in the large room.

She runs away from her would-be attacker, heading straight for an empty corner. All around us, people are fighting. Timit crawls under the table, other council members following him. One of the attackers sees this and aims his sword toward them.

I shoot a dart at him.

It lands, and he whips around and sees me.

"Faster, Inkga."

She gets us to the corner, but the man is still coming. I shoot him again. I don't want to kill him, but I have to protect her and myself.

He's only a couple steps from us when he slows and staggers to the ground. The poison is working. Puneah finally drops her victim and lopes over to us.

More attackers pour in the room, men and women. Is this another Kurah attack? Something Daros set up? Or something more sinister, that I can't fathom?

Now isn't the time to speculate. I'll have the chance to do that later. A woman aims for us and charges, her sword at the ready. I aim the dart flinger. Before I can let go, Julina's sword blocks the attacker's with a *clank*. They go back and forth.

Nash is at my side. Where did he come from? He blocks another attacker that's coming at us from a right angle. His swift movements and strong muscles are a sight to behold—until the attacker's sword bangs against his breastplate.

It doesn't faze Nash, who swings his sword upward, effectively stopping the attacker.

"Inkga, take my dart flinger," I yell over the noise.

"But then you won't be able to defend yourself."

"It did its job. Now let the others defend me." It's dangerous to have both them and the dart flinger in the same room when I'm holding it.

She takes it from me and shields me with her body.

"Inkga, I can't see what's going on."

"Better than harm coming to you."

I grumble in frustration as I try to see what action I can around her. Nash and Julina are in front of us, staving off attackers. Puneah at my side seems antsy, ready to get in the fight but unwilling to leave me behind.

I know the feeling.

Jaku joins the line holding the assailants away from Inkga and me. How long can they hold out? How many people are there? Do we have enough guards fighting? I hope so, because they seem to be going for killing blows.

I wish I could be in on the action right now. My body aches with the memory of moving and fighting, joining in the fray. It feels like my place is among them, but I suppose it's here now, even if I can't protect the ones I love. It's their turn to protect me. Though it's hard to let them, I'm grateful.

At my right side, there's movement where Julina blocks off attackers. She moves aside and lets in Monkia, my Head of Staff before jumping back into action, blocking a sword going straight for Monkia's back.

If the attackers are this desperate to kill not just me, but also my councilors, who are they?

Inside, Androlla is laughing.

Stupid First Queen. She needs to get out of my head.

Monkia grabs Inkga by the hand, drags her next to me, and squishes her in before blocking off her escape. What is she doing?

"Mom, stop it," Inkga says. "I'm trying to protect the queen."

That's right—they're related.

"I'm trying to save you from getting hurt. The others will protect the queen. Let me protect you." Monkia's tone is sharp.

"Just stay behind the line of defense, both of you, and we'll all be fine," I shout.

And I'm right; the fighting is dying down. I can't see well, other than to know that Afet joined the line, but the noise of sword against sword is dying down. My people are standing. This is a good sign. I hope none of the councilors that dove under the table got hurt.

"Give up," Jaku says. "You're surrounded."

A woman I can't see yells, "We can't give up. The Kurah will continue on until we have what we need."

Another Kurah attack then. Lovely.

There's a scuffle, and then all is silent.

"Carefully check the ones who are down," Jaku orders. "Make certain they aren't going to cause more trouble."

And hopefully some are alive, so we can interrogate them, though I fear we'll get the same answer as before. A medium-built man in a dark cloak. Not helpful.

"Your Majesty, are you all right?" Jaku's voice is so formal, I'm not used to it.

"Fine. Thank you all for your swift action and protection. Are any of our guards or councilors hurt?"

They all sound off that they're fine.

"You can come out," Jaku says. "Julina, Afet, go help the councilors."

As they go, Jaku and Nash spread out an even distance apart in front of me, opening up more of the room for me to see.

Bodies lie on the floor. I don't look too closely, not wanting to relive the horrors of my past. As Julina and Afet help those hiding come out, they appear to be whole, though pale and shaken.

Sidle is across the room, helping other guards tie up the prisoners who are still alive.

"Are any of the attackers conscious?" I ask.

"Some, Your Highness," Sidle says. "We can take you to them, but they're not very cooperative."

"Very well. Inform me the moment Jaku is ready for me." We have to get to the bottom of this. Here I am, trying to make things better for the Kurah, and they send attackers after me. I refuse to help them any more until this behavior stops.

Nash never looks at me. As soon as everything is given the all clear for my safety, he leaves, not glancing my way.

I try to ignore the pain in my heart—the giant, crushing pain that makes me want to weep. But I am stronger than that. I won't let a man bring me down, whether it's with a sword or my heart.

Still, I wish he would have at least taken a peek at me.

CHAPTER 26

Afet, Julina, and Jaku are with me and Puneah as I get ready to talk to the first conscious prisoner. Before we go in the room, I say, "There wasn't any news from the previous prisoner trying to escape?"

"No. I'm afraid there isn't," Jaku responds.

"Tsk. It would have been a good plan, had she ever tried to escape. Let's get the interviews going. I have more important things I need to be doing." Like practicing, to take down the First Queen.

No one mentions that I don't have to be here. It's true, but it's easier to get the information I need by being present.

We enter the room. The prisoner is slumped back against the only chair, hands and feet bound.

"What do you know?" I ask.

"Brown cloak." He groans.

"I thought he was awake," I say.

"Sort of," Jaku concedes.

At least he's answering my questions. "Do you mean the person who asked you to do this was wearing a brown cloak?"

"Yes."

"What else do you know about them?"

"Man. Nothing else. Please spare me."

I huff. He's not giving us any useful information, but he is cooperating.

"Why did you do as this man said?" Julina asks.

The prisoner rolls his head on his neck and then sits upright, like the question wakened him more than anything else has so far. "He threatened my family."

Ah. Now we're getting somewhere. "Be more specific?"

"If I didn't help, he'd track them down and kill them."

"Do you know if he used the same threat with the others?" Jaku asks.

"I can't talk more until I know you'll keep my family safe."

"I'll send someone for them right away." Jaku gets details from him before going out of the room. Moments later, he returns, asking if the man in the cloak used the same threat with the others again.

"Those I spoke with said the same thing. Ask them yourselves."

We will.

We spend the next several hours of the morning interrogating attackers to no avail. We learn nothing new, other than that they're a mix of having things or people they care about threatened or have a deep belief that the Kurah are being wronged. The last thought grates on me, making the back of my neck and shoulders ache.

It's been difficult on them, but I've been trying so hard to make things better. I want to lower their taxes, and will be in a position to do so soon, but if they are going to bully me, they've got another thing coming.

Inkga's wheeling me back to my room when Shillian appears in the corridor. I don't know whether or not to acknowledge her when she curtsies, mumbles a thank you, and hurries on her way.

I'm still contemplating the interaction while I say to Inkga,

"Take me to Jem, instead of the sitting room. I need to speak with her."

"All right." She turns left when we come to the next hall, following the guard ahead. Eldim's behind us. It's a sure thing that I will be attacked again, sooner or later, so I may as well keep guards on me at all times.

It doesn't take us long to come to the quarters of the ladies-in-waiting. When I moved my rooms, they moved theirs to be closer to me, but they didn't get inside rooms, like I did. We stop at the first one, and Inkga knocks. A servant answers the door, and her eyes widen.

"Jem, Her Majesty is here to see you."

Jem rushes out and ushers me in, the servant getting out of her way. Inkga wheels me in. The room is not at all what I expected. It's flat and unadorned. Not very Jem-like at all.

"Ryn, it's good to see you." Her eyes are puffy. "How are you?"

"Well as can be expected after interviewing offenders. How are you?" It's clear she's upset, but I don't know if she wants to talk about it.

She gives a forced smile, tight around the edges. "I'm all right. What can I do for you?"

I debate pushing her, seeing if I can get her to come around and tell me what's wrong—if there is more than losing Wilric, which is bad enough on its own—but we have four other people here that are all witness to it. While I trust my three people, I don't know about her servant. Besides, if it's about Wilric—like I think it is—I don't want to make her go through that pain in front of so many others. "I assume you know the situation with the Kurah."

"The attack was terrifying. I was able to hold off a man with some tricks you taught me until help arrived. It saved my life."

Maybe that's what spurred the tears—thinking about me and Wilric teaching her how to fight. "I didn't see you in action. I wish I had."

She waves away the thought. "You were safe, where you needed to be."

"You should have joined us."

"Honestly, it was a thrill to fight for my life. I can see why you like it." Her smile loosens, becoming more real.

Mine feels forced, but I push on. "There are a lot of reasons why I liked it. I'm glad your skills are improving, but that's not what I came to talk to you about."

"The other ladies-in-waiting are getting better too. Even Inyi isn't so squeamish," she says. "What did you wish to discuss?"

"I wanted your opinion, as my Head Advisor, about what I should do with the Kurah. You've given me sound advice in the past, even if I didn't always listen to it. I'd like to know what you're thinking on this matter."

She quickly hides her surprise. "Of course. I've spent a lot of time thinking about it, not just with the recent attack, but also since this started coming into play. I think you need to meet with them again and outline exactly what you've done for them and how you want to lower their taxes. What's more, you need to tell them what will happen if they don't change their ways. How much worse things are going to be."

"It's a good plan, but do you think I should lower the taxes?"

"Not unless these attacks stop. We can't let them rule the country through fear and intimidation."

"That's what I was thinking. And we need to discover who is behind everything. Serious punishments are warranted because this behavior is unacceptable. We need Kada to set up a meeting."

"What happened to Kada and Mina at the council meeting, anyway? It's not like them to be late, though I'm certain they're grateful they were."

Maybe or maybe not, given the circumstances. "They were found tied up in their rooms. They were unhurt, but both claim the attackers came in through their windows, to get through to the council rooms."

Jem taps a finger to her lip. "Interesting. I'm surprised the attackers didn't hurt them."

"I am as well, though grateful." And slightly suspicious. What is it about those councilors that kept them from harm? "They've requested to have their rooms moved and are in the process of making that happen right now. Jaku's looking into how the attackers got to their rooms in the first place."

"Their rooms are right next to each other, I believe."

I didn't know that. I'm surprised she does, but then, she keeps on top of things. "They were. We're moving all the council members into different rooms, away from each other."

"Wise move." She turns to her servant. "Would you please get Kada for us?"

"Yes, Mistress." The servant scurries off.

"How is everything else?" Jem asks.

I wonder if she means the search for ending the First Queen. "It's a slow process. I'm grateful for all the extra help I've received lately. It's been significant, but I don't know if it's enough." Will it ever be?

"I understand. I will continue doing what I can."

I change the subject, not wanting to focus on Androlla when there's nothing I can do to fight her at the moment. "How's your family?"

We spend the next half hour talking before her servant finally returns, out of breath. "Forgive me for taking so long. Kada was downstairs, looking for a new room. Everyone else is looking up here, and I expected her to be with the rest. She will be here shortly."

"Don't worry over it," Jem says. "Go get a drink and rest."

Jem would have made a much better queen than I… if she kept Ranen and Fraya from controlling her.

I'm antsy by the time Kada walks in and gives a curtsy. "How can I help you, Your Majesty?"

"I would like a meeting with some of the Kurah tomorrow afternoon. I don't want to delay this any longer."

"Certainly. I'll get something set up, but I must tell you not everyone will be able to come on such short notice."

"That's fine. Just get the word out to those you can."

"If you'll forgive me, Your Highness, I must be going. There's much to do."

"You're excused."

I leave as well. Kada's right; there's much to do, and I have little time left to do it.

CHAPTER 27

THE GROUP of Kurah are so noisy, I can't talk over them, though I've been trying to for several minutes. They're loud and unruly, and a pain I wish I didn't have to deal with on top of my growing headache.

It's almost as if Androlla is applying pressure to my actual brain, sending shooting spikes of pain through my head.

Perhaps that's why I haven't been able to get the Kurah's attention. I don't have the fortitude to do so.

I insisted that the council be here to back me up. They stand on both sides of me. I glance at Jem, and she gives me an encouraging smile. As much as I appreciate it, I wish she was Nash. I could really use him right now.

In front of us, guards line the way, blocking the Kurah from getting to us. It's needed, because even with them, the occasional person slips through, and Afet, Eldim, or Julina has to deal with them. It hardly seems fair that they have to deal with them, but there's no one else to do it. All the guards are somewhere in this room. And yet, it is still so loud.

"Silence." Jaku is standing, his voice booming over the room.

That seems to settle them. They quiet and finally turn their attention to the front—not to me, but to Jaku.

He says, "You will listen to what your queen has to say."

Before they can start talking again, I ignore the pain in my head, hurrying to say, "My people, I know you're upset at the high taxes, but physical violence isn't the way handle it. The government has purchased a mine for Medi and Poruah to work at, if they so wish, thus providing them jobs. In return, the profit it will make will enable us to lower your taxes."

A cheer sounds through the room.

I wait until it dies down and talk over the few still making noise. "I refuse to lower your taxes despite my ability to do so while my councilors and I are being attacked, though."

That silences them.

I meet as many of their gazes as I can. I want them to know how serious I am and that I'm not going to back down. "I want to lower your taxes, so I suggest you stop fighting and start cooperating."

I pause, letting the words sink in before changing tactics. "If any of you know who the man behind these attacks is, bring the information to any of my guards. You will be rewarded, and we will see that this person is dealt with."

A loud noise comes from the back of the room. People are parting, making an aisle for a group that's growing bigger as they pass, pushing a man in front of them. The man gets to the guards and sneers at me. The rest of the crowd are so loud, it's difficult to make out what they say.

But that's not important. The sneering man is wearing a cloak with the hood down. A brown cloak.

"Seize that man," I say. He moves to flee, and I yell, "Bring him forward."

He tries to back up, but hands push him forward. Guards go at him as he pulls a sword out from under his cloak. I clench my teeth, wishing I had the ability to go down there and take him out myself. Jaku's probably grateful I can't.

A circle forms around him, tight enough it would be difficult to get out of, but big enough there's plenty of room to fight. Several guards flash forward, surrounding him and protecting the crowd. It's not adequate, though.

The cloaked man dives, slicing a wound in one of the soldiers' thigh. The soldier backs away, limping, only to be replaced by another guard. The other guards move at the cloaked man all at once. There's a scuffle of limbs and torsos, piled atop one another.

I bite my lip, hoping none of my men get hurt and the cloaked man survives to be questioned. "Bring him in alive."

The men help one another up until they get to the last guard and the cloaked man. The guard has the man's hands twisted behind his back, his weapon left on the floor, several feet away. A couple other guards help the prisoner stand and take custody of him, while others help their fellow man. They cross toward me, and Eldim steps forward and hands them a rope that they use to tie the man up.

The crowd quiets, waiting in suspense.

"Who are you, and why did you try to escape?"

When he doesn't answer, a woman in the front of the crowd calls out, "Your Highness, this is the man who tried to get me to join the Kurah attack."

"How do you know?"

A man steps forward. "Most of us know. He's been threatening us for months, hiding behind his cloak, but I know his build and voice."

"Why didn't you say so sooner then?" I ask

The man who stepped forward glances down. "Personally, I was afraid. I didn't know so many others would back me up, and I worried that something would happen to my family." He looks up. "I believe this is the right thing to do though, even if it endangers us."

169

"We'll do what we can to get this sorted through so no one is endangered." I glare at the cloaked man. "Is this true? Who are you?"

The man is unfamiliar. Why would someone who doesn't know me try to have me killed? It makes no sense. "Tell me."

He offers no response, his gaze darting around, watching my council.

Threatening him with my dart flinger might get him talking. Not that I would use it, but he doesn't have to know how soft I've become.

Jaku steps forward and whispers something in his ear.

The cloaked man jerks his head into a bowing position. "I did it for the money."

Whatever Jaku said must have worked.

"What money?" Something isn't adding up. What is he talking about?

"Kada Pinoch offered me money to lead a group of Kurah to rebel against you."

"You dirty son of a maggot." Kada stands and throws a dagger at him.

It misses by several inches. No wonder she had to hire someone else to do her dirty work; she can't even hit a large target.

"Guards, arrest Kada Pinoch for crimes against the crown," I say.

She runs for the door, but Julina is quicker, stopping her before she's halfway there. Julina drags her in front of me, and Jaku comes forward to help hold her.

"Why did you do it?" I ask, still in shock that she was the culprit behind this plot.

"Because you have what I want. I'm stuck, being Head of Relations with the Queen. Do you know what that means? I book your appointments. That's it. I'm nothing but a glorified secretary. Of course, I betrayed you. I want nothing to do with you and would give everything to be you. Not the queen, but the one with all the power." Her face grows snarlier with each word until she's raving.

"Why didn't you come to me? I could have given you a different job. Given you some recourse besides attacking innocent people."

The room is silent, watching on as we converse. Maybe we should take this somewhere else? Then again, this might be good for them to see.

"What? And be turned away, like by every other queen I've been under? No. I wasn't going to risk it again. I saw an opportunity to exploit the Kurah, and I took it. I took it, and I used them to get to you. But no, you had to be so blasted powerful, taking down everyone I sent at you. Even with you maimed, you still have protectors, and I hate it, and I hate you."

"I'm sorry you feel that way." I keep my voice soft. "The council will decide your fate tomorrow." To the guards I say, "Take her to the dungeons."

The pressure in my head is pounding to the point I feel sick. Or maybe that's the feeling of being betrayed by someone on my council. What was she going to do? Kill me, and have someone she controlled drink the Mortum Tura? It likely wouldn't have worked. She wanted the throne too bad. Right now, I would be more than happy to give it to her.

CHAPTER 28

SLEEP IS my only relief from the headache, but it's its own type of torture with Androlla taunting me the entire time.

The council sentenced Kada to execution. I want no part of it, but as the queen, I don't get much choice. The council refused to have her just locked up, like I talked them into doing with Daros. Now that he's free despite his crimes, they don't want that happening to another criminal.

Sure, she was wrong and cost people their lives, but I'd rather lock her up for life. Maybe try to help her see where she went wrong. We've seen how well locking people up works, though. We need something stronger than that. It hurts to have to do, though, even if the council is the one doing it.

We interrogated Mina thoroughly, and Jaku had guards searching through her things and past. Despite this, we never found anything against her. She seems to be worthy of staying on the council, despite being detained by the attackers.

A servant enters the room. "Kapeni Nola is here, Your Majesty."

"Send her in."

She enters the room with grace and poise, moving like she's going to curtsy.

"You don't have to do that," I say.

She bends low. "Of course, I do. You are the queen."

"And you are my friend."

She beams. "That doesn't change the fact you are the queen. You wished to see me?"

"I have a proposition for you." And it would be much easier to think about it if the pounding in my head eased. "I am in a conundrum. My Head of Relations with the Queen had some problems."

"I heard, but what has that got to do with me?"

And this is the hard part. "I was wondering if you would be willing to take the position."

"Me?" She stumbles backward until her legs hit a chair. She sits in it. "Why me?"

"Because I know you and trust you. This would be a good position for someone like yourself, who has experience in dealing with things such as the sale of your mine. I heard you helped with the sale."

"That is true, but I'm not sure I'm qualified to do such a job."

"Not qualified or not sure you're up for the task? I know this is a hard thing I'm asking of you, and if you're unwilling to do it, there's no hard feelings."

She's quiet for a moment. "I think—I believe I can do the job. I'm just not certain you're picking the right person."

"As far as I'm concerned, you're perfect for it, but I don't want to push it onto you."

"Why do you think I'll be a good fit?"

How do I tell her? I suppose there's no better way than to say it. "There aren't many people I can trust."

"What about the sale of the mine? Will that create a conflict of interest?"

"Not since it's already sold and dealt with," I say. "Listen, if you don't want the job, that's fine. Or if you need time to think about it, that's fine as well, but I would consider it a great favor if you were to assist me in this matter." Thank you, ladies-in-waiting, for helping me know what to say in a situation like this. Whoever thought I'd believe that? It's true, though. My time with them has become vital, even if it doesn't feel like it on a day-to-day basis.

"You make it a hard choice."

"I don't mean to. You really are welcome to turn it down." But please, please don't. There's no one else I trust more with the position. "Like I said, you can have some time to think about it."

"I don't need the time."

Great. She's going to say *no*. "You can speak with your husband about it, at least."

"Unneeded. Coplo will support my choice whatever it is, and yes, I would like to help you. I will take the position of Head of Relations with the Queen."

Relief fills me. I don't know what I would do if she rejected me. "Thank you. I know it can't be an easy decision."

She sits up straight, looking much more like herself than she did a moment ago. "I don't know about that. It was a shock, all right. I didn't expect anything like it. But, if truth be told, I'm excited you asked me. I need something to do with my time, now that the mine is sold, since I was assisting Coplo in running it. He is the one who wanted to retire, and I supported him. But since we sold the mine, life has been boring. This will be perfect for me."

I give her a wide grin. "I'm grateful it works out so well for the both of us. You will attend the next council meeting, and I will announce you there."

"Perfect. Thank you for this, Your Majesty."

"Please, call me Ryn."

"All right, Ryn. I look forward to working with you."

"And I with you."

One less thing to worry about. Someone I trust on the council besides Jaku and Jem. There's still a long way to go if I'm to do a good job as the queen, though. I need to find ways to help my people. Ways to keep them in mind. In any case, Kapeni is a great start.

CHAPTER 29

"Are you well?" Venda asks me.

"Sorry. I was thinking." About more than I should, with such wracking anguish.

"More practicing, less thinking, then. It will do you good."

"We've been practicing for three hours," Inkga says. "Isn't it time for a break?"

"Ah, perhaps you are right." Venda gathers the ingredients we were using. "We will eat and begin again."

As much as I want to protest, because of the pain in my head, I have to press on for that same reason.

Inkga goes to bring lunch. When she returns and helps me eat, the pressure in my head suddenly releases. It's like a cool breeze slipped across my head. It's a welcome relief—until I realize that I'm not the one moving my mouth and hands.

I struggle to take over as Androlla says, "You know you are all doomed to fail."

"What are you talking about, Ryn?" Inkga pauses with the fork halfway back to the plate, a look of pure confusion spread across her face.

I struggle to regain control. It comes crashing in with the pain. I wince. "Nothing. Sorry. I'm not feeling well."

"Perhaps we should break from eating," Inkga says.

Jaku speaks for the first time from his corner. "Maybe you're right." I almost forgot he was there.

I didn't forget about Nash, though. I've been trying to pretend he's not here for the moment. Jaku insisted on him guarding me. He says, "She's looking a little pale."

"No. We need to continue." The words come out harsher than I intend, but they are my own. "I'm not even hungry anymore. Just help me with the spell."

There's a knock on the door. When Inkga answers, it's Jem. "I thought I would check in on you. No one has seen you in several hours," Jem says.

"Come in. Maybe you can help us."

She takes in the ingredients on the table and hurries to close the door. "Magic?"

"What else?"

"She knows?" Inkga asks.

"She does, and she'll keep our secret. Maybe even help us." The pain ebbs and flows, moving through my skull.

"Of course I'll help." She pulls a small book from her skirts. "I've been reading up on magic, and although I haven't found the spell I want to"—she gives me a meaningful look—"it's very interesting stuff. Did you know the only way to make a spell is to enchant an object, and then that object casts the spell according to the user, usually in a manner tied to them?"

"We did," Inkga says. "But it's good you've found that. It means you might be able to find more on magic."

If only she knew what we're looking for…She'd probably take it well, but I don't want to burden her more than she already is.

"What spell are we working on, again?" I ask.

"Are you certain you're all right, Ryn?" Venda asks.

"Fine." Puneah, curled up at my feet, nudges my hand. I pet her, enjoying how soft she feels. The pain eases. "The healing spell, right?"

"Yes." Venda sounds matter-of-fact again. "Here are the ingredients, Jem. Will you help Ryn with the mortar and pestle?"

"Of course."

"I've gotten pretty good at it," I say as she brings over the mortar and pestle.

My hand aches as I grind the items together, but it's a feel-good sort of ache. A nice change from the throbbing in my head. I've gained much mobility compared to how I was previously but still get tired more easily than I used to. As I chant, the rhythm feels familiar. I've gotten close with this spell several times but never quite got it.

There's another knock on the door. Inkga throws a piece of fabric over the items, and Jem hides the mortar and pestle behind her back.

"Begging your pardon, Your Highness, but Daros Durkin is here to see you. Said you would want to see him," a servant says.

I exchange a glance with Jaku. "That'd be fine. Tell him I'll meet him the receiving room," I say.

"Or you could meet me here." Daros shoves his way past the servant, his guards coming in after him. "My... this room is quaint and squishy."

He takes in everything, from the flickering candles everywhere, to the fabric laid across the ingredients and the fact that Venda's here, to Jaku.

"If you wish to discuss anything with me, you'll have to do it elsewhere." I keep my voice firm. Despite that, he ambles in and takes a seat next to Venda.

"Never met someone from Faner before. Tell me, what's your country like?"

Her expression goes blank, not revealing anything to him. "Different."

He takes a piece of fruit from the plate she had set on the table in front of her. "Different how?"

"This has gone far enough, Daros." Jaku takes several steps toward him, only to stop when Daros lifts a hand to stop him. Jaku takes another step when Daros speaks.

"You'll find I can do whatever I want." He pops the fruit into his mouth.

A chill creeps over me.

He continues. "I have all the power here since I know how to get rid of Androlla. So if I want to come and talk with everyone, I can."

"That's all you want to do? Talk?" There has to be more.

"Is that so wrong?"

I take a closer look at his fraying clothes and sunken cheeks. Though I know he's still powerful and not to be trusted, I don't fear him. He's a shadow of who he used to be. Why? He's practically a free man. What has forced him to go through such a transformation from when he was my boss? Not worth worrying over.

Everyone is silent.

Jaku looks at me, and I shrug. We could keep working on spells since he knows about them anyway, but part of me is reluctant to do that.

Jem discreetly puts down the mortar and pestle and stands in front of them while Daros is looking at Puneah.

"What does this creature do anyway?" he asks.

Inkga shifts to uncover a corner of the table, exposing the basil. There's a tension in the air. A feeling that something is going to break any moment. But it doesn't.

"She bites people who attack me or those I care about," I say.

Puneah continues to ignore him, choosing instead to purr under my hand.

Daros bursts out laughing. "Classic. It's the perfect animal for you, girl."

Jaku looks like he wants to lop off Daros's tongue, but he doesn't say anything.

"And you will address the people around me with courtesy and respect." I won't budge from this. If I gave him a little, he'd take me for everything he could.

He glances around the room as if noticing the tension for the first time. He nods and takes another piece of fruit from Venda's plate. She picks up the plate and hands it to him. "Put some meat on those bones."

Though she's thinner than is fashionable in Valcora, and I've wondered if that's how all people from Faner are, she must see what I see. Daros is a hollow man, living only because of the information he can give me.

It's quiet as he finishes off the food and hands it back to Venda. "There's a good person, then. You can put that away."

I've never seen him like this before. It's almost as if he wants to... make friends? That can't be. If he did, he wouldn't choose this group to try it with. What is he playing at?

"So, Queen Ryn," he says, the words sounding sarcastic from him, "how's your magic coming along?"

I glance at his guards, who have spread themselves out at the walls of the room. They remain stoic, like they hear this type of thing every day. For all I know, maybe they do.

"How are your guards working out, Daros?" I ask.

"What?" He looks around the room. "Oh, them? They're fine. Not chatty people, but there, nevertheless."

What happened to his ruthlessness? His cunning? Unless he's hiding it well—and I mean, *really* well—there's something odd going on here.

"What's happened to you?" I ask.

"I don't know what you're talking about." His gaze evades mine.

"Why have you lost so much weight? Why are your clothes tattered? The Daros I knew would never have worn something so unfashionable. What's changed?" I don't expect him to answer.

He sniffs. "Someone had the gall to run away from me. Took away my business when those who hired me realized the Shadow Wraith no longer worked for me. No one cared about my other people, and as I lost jobs, they all abandoned me." He sneers, his haggard skin crinkling. "No one wanted my skills. Said they weren't as good as yours—like they would know. Money goes quicker than I thought, without an income."

I was the one funding him the years I was the Shadow Wraith? If I knew that, I might have had the oomph to run away sooner. Of course, if I'd left sooner, maybe Daros's skills would have stayed sharper.

It's still so strange that he let himself go instead of working harder to become the man he once was. Time and age can change a person, I suppose.

"This is all your fault, you know," he says. "You should have never run away, and if you still chose to, you should have let me tell you how to be a queen. Things would be so much different if you had."

Things would be worse, but I don't want to argue with him. It does no good. "What is it you want, Daros?" I ask.

"To figure out if you're getting this magic down. We all know you don't have much time left." There's a hint of the old Daros I knew.

"What does he mean, Ryn?" Inkga asks.

I stare Daros down, waiting for something else to come out of his mouth. He grins. He's missing a tooth. Not in front, where it's obvious, but a little to the side.

I'm about to ask him about it, when Monkia comes in the room, gaze searching until it lands on Inkga.

"There you are, darling girl. I know you're serving the Queen, but I heard you wanted to talk with m—" She stops as soon as she lays eyes on Daros. Her face goes pale. "What's he doing here?"

Unlike her, his expression seems to gain life. He stands and walks over to her, to whisper something I can't hear. Next to me, Jem shifts from foot to foot. I exchange glances with Jaku. Something really strange is going on. Do Daros and Monkia know each other?

Though I still can't hear what they're saying, the discussion becomes heated, Monkia's face turning red.

"You can't," she shouts.

"I'll do whatever I like." He whips out his dagger and drags Monkia into a corner. She's facing us, and he has his back to the walls while his dagger is at her throat.

My heart stops. Is he going to hurt her? Kill her? If he does, it'll be on me, for not taking care of him in the first place.

The guards step closer, but Daros pushes the blade harder against her, stopping them in place.

"Tell them," he yells.

"Daros, put the dagger away so we can talk about this," I say in my calmest voice, though I want to scream at him.

"No. She's going to tell you what I want you to hear because no one can hurt me anymore. I've got the power here."

Has he gone mad?

"Please. We can talk about this," Jaku says. "You do have the power, and we respect that, but you don't have to bring Monkia into this."

"Of course, I do. She's the one who betrayed you. She's the one who should be going to prison."

"My mother wouldn't betray anyone." Inkga's face is scrunched as if in pain.

"She would," Daros says. "She would do whatever I told her to."

"You manipulated me." Monkia sounds calmer than most would under the circumstances.

He jams the blade harder against her throat, making a line of blood appear. "No. You were a part of this all along, and I'm sick of hiding it. I want everyone to know what you've done."

She thins her lips. Daros presses the dagger in deeper.

"No," Inkga calls out.

Monkia whimpers. Is this to be the end of her? If only I could throw one of my daggers.

As if my dream comes to life, a dagger flies through the air and lands in his eye. He drops the blade and falls to the ground.

Jem stands firm, hand still in suspended in midair from where she flung the dagger that just killed Daros.

CHAPTER 30

I'M unable to process what just happened. Is Daros really dead? After all this time of him tormenting me and playing games with my mind, am I finally free of him? And am I lost to Androlla, never to be free of her clutches? I don't know whether to be elated or mournful. Mostly, I'm confused. "Did you throw a dagger at Daros?" I ask Jem.

She puts lowers her arm, standing tall. "I did."

"Well done." It's all I can think of.

"I'm sorry, I know you needed him, but I didn't want him to take another life." Jem sounds panicked, as if finally realizing what she did.

"We'll figure this out." Though I don't know how. Daros may have been malicious and heartless, but Androlla is downright evil. She's going to take me over and rule the country with her iron fist.

I'm shaking. Whether it's from shock or fear, I don't know.

No one moves. They're either staring at Daros's still form or at Jem. I have to take control of this situation, even though I'm falling apart on the inside. "Inkga, please get someone to clean up this mess. Jaku, secure the area. Monkia, are you all right?" I want to ask her what Daros was talking about, but a few things need to happen first, to make certain everyone is all right.

Inkga and Jaku spur into action. Monkia dabs at the line of blood on her neck before nodding.

"Venda," I say, "would you please look over Monkia? Jem, sit down before you fall."

As the rest of them move, I twist my fingers in Puneah's fur and try to ignore the body in the room. What am I going to do? I'll never defeat the First Queen now. She's mocking me, singing a song of victory inside me, knowing she won't be stuck there long.

*   *   *

I MAKE Monkia stay as they take away the body. The others choose to stay as well.

I still can't believe he's gone. Daros, my most hated master, is dead. *Dead* dead. As in not coming back to haunt me—not ever.

Jem moved across the room from the rest of us a while ago, and now she keeps shifting from standing straight and tall, like she's glad for what she did, and twitching nervously from foot to foot, which is easy to tell even with her dress on.

Inkga is speaking with her mother in a corner. They've gone from hugging to crying to wiping away tears and back again. Nash, Jaku, and Puneah are close by my side while Venda stays on the couch.

"I think it's time we discuss what happened," I say. I want to get over the shock and understand.

Everyone faces me. Jem goes back to holding her head high, as if she thinks I'll be angry, despite my telling her she did good. Am I mad? It's difficult to tell. The fallout with Androlla will happen because of her actions, but I'll deal with that after I've taken care of my friends. "Jem, why did you kill him when important information was about to be revealed?" I didn't mean to snap, but it's too late to take it back.

Her bottom lip quivers until she purses her lips. "I'm sorry. I thought he was going to kill Monkia. I couldn't let another person I know die because of his actions, especially not in front of me."

"How do I know you weren't trying to silence him?" I'm pretty certain she wasn't, but I have to ask.

She straightens. "I would never trust what that scum would reveal about another person, after all he's done. He knows too much."

I know the feeling. It's not something I ever wanted to do. The man was ruthless and cunning, and would do anything to further his agenda. "You did what you needed to. None of us were sure if he was going to kill Monkia. It certainly looked like he was, so you did the right thing."

Her gaze jumps around the room. "But you needed him alive."

"Others are more important than my needs. You did the right thing." Even if the good of the whole country might suffer, I can't imagine watching Daros kill Monkia, though it looked like that's exactly where he was headed. "Besides, it was a very good shot."

She finally looks at me, a timid smile forming. "It was?"

"Very, very good."

She dips her head. "Thank you."

I turn my attention to Monkia. "It's time you tell us what was happening."

She goes pale. "I don't know what you're talking about."

"Daros alluded to your knowing things that he thought we should know. As your queen, I would like to know what those things are."

"He was crazy. The man didn't know what he was raving on about." She won't look at me.

I soften my voice, but take on a warning tone. "Monkia, I know there was something going on. You must tell me, and you must tell me now."

She breaks down sobbing. Inkga puts a hand on her back. "Mom?"

"I refuse to tell you while my daughter is present," Monkia says between sobs.

Inkga jumps back like she's been burned. "I'm not leaving. I will hear what you have to say."

"I can't tell you. I can't."

What do I do? Do I force Inkga to go? She has a right to be here, a right to hear this, but if Monkia won't speak in front of her, what do I do?

"You have to, Mom. I'm going to find out, one way or another. I'd rather hear it from you."

"You'll hate me."

Inkga sighs. "Maybe, for a while, but you're my mother. I'll always love you, even if I'm upset with you."

Monkia sniffs. "All right. I'll say what happened."

Guess that settles that problem. I can't think of what she's going to say, but I can't imagine it's going to be good. Not if it has to do with Daros.

"It started many, many years ago." She takes a shuddering breath. "Inkga, at least go sit on the couch. I can't do this with you standing next to me."

Inkga hesitates but makes it over to the couch next to Venda.

Monkia looks straight at me, as if she's ignoring everyone else in the room. "You have to understand, Your Majesty, I was young and stupid. I didn't know what I was doing. I was already married by this time, but it was a marriage arranged by my parents, to make my life better. They wanted me to live here, at the palace, where there was food to eat, so they found a young man working in the stables, who agreed to marry me."

I didn't know Monkia and Inkga's father had an arranged marriage, but I suppose since they don't live together and seem happy with the arrangement, I shouldn't be surprised.

Monkia goes on. "While I was out one day, I met a charming young man. He swept me off my feet. I returned to the palace, thinking I would never see him again. Except next time I went out, he was there. He courted me over the course of several months."

I don't see this ending well.

"After a time, he convinced me that he loved me, and soon after, I got with child," she says.

Inkga gasps, and Venda puts an arm around her.

Monkia continues as if she didn't hear anything. "I didn't know what to do. I was torn between my duty to my husband and my love for a man who I thought loved me back. I didn't see the man for some time. It was like he disappeared. After I determined for certain I was pregnant, I resolved to find him. I knew it was his child, and I wanted us to run away together. He was rich enough that he could afford to feed and take care of both me and the baby.

"It took some time to find him. He was never at any of the usual places we met, but I eventually tracked him down. He was not who I thought he was." Her voice cracks. "He said he didn't care about me, but he'd take the child. Only, while I was there, I saw another little girl. She was quiet and sad, and after his treatment of me, I knew he must not be kind to this girl. That was when I decided to keep the baby as if it were mine and my husband's.

"The man was Daros, and he said if he couldn't have the child, then he would tell everyone what I had done—that I had broken my vows—and he would take me away from my life at the palace I had grown to love unless I did what he said. I promised, as long as he would have nothing to do with my child."

Inkga is sobbing, but I don't dare drag my gaze away from Monkia, afraid it will break her concentration and she'll never finish the story that should have been told years ago.

"As the years went by, Daros didn't ask much of me—just a few small favors that ended up helping me get higher up in the palace until I reached the position of Head of Staff. After that, he had me doing all sorts of dirty work for him. Changing my vote on the council. Helping his people in and out of the palace. Things like that. He's used me my entire life, and I hate him."

"You're the one who snuck him into the palace disguised as a healer," I say.

She looks down. "I did."

I want to ask why she didn't come forward then, since her word would be better than Daros's at that point, but I know better. He had that type of control over people. He knew their weaknesses and how to exploit them. And he could send forth someone else in his place with damning information about her. Someone who we considered trustworthy.

It doesn't excuse her actions, though.

I clench my jaw so I don't end up saying something I'll regret. Because of her poor choices, she risked many lives and was the reason others were lost. She's the one who brought him here, causing Wilric's death. She might not have stabbed him, but she brought Daros. Instead of telling someone, anyone, about her indiscretion, she chose an eviler path.

Is she the person who told him how I could get to Queen Deedra's room so I could kill her? It wouldn't surprise me. The only thing that does surprise me is that it's taken so many years for her deception to come to light.

"Does Dad know?" Inkga asks. Tears stream down her face, but her sobbing has subsided.

"He doesn't know the details, but he knows I betrayed him. It's why we never fought harder to live together or cared that we couldn't be together. But he was a good father for you. Never question that."

Inkga jumps to her feet. "My father was a brutal man who you should have never even looked at." She runs out of the room.

Monkia moves to go after her, but Jaku stops her. "I don't think so. I believe the council will be having words with you."

"They will," I say. "You are stripped of your position as Head of

Staff and are to remain on the palace grounds with guards, until your fate is decided by the council."

"I understand."

I don't. How could all this have happened? It sounds like Inkga almost wound up living the life I did. I'm so grateful she didn't. Her sweet spirit would have been broken. At least Monkia did the right thing by not letting Daros raise her child.

CHAPTER 31

DAROS'S SKIN is painted the black of death, but there are no honoring markings of stones or gems on his face. It's silent. So very silent.

Only my guards and I are here to see him off. I don't know why I came, except perhaps I feel some sort of connection to him. Granted, a bad connection, but a connection nonetheless.

There's no one to say words about him. No one to sing him to the other side. No one to mourn him. I'm not stupid enough to do that, though I do mourn opportunity lost because of his passing. Despite that it's been two days, I haven't come to terms with the fact that I don't have his knowledge of how to defeat Androlla.

I'm doomed.

I sag, not caring to be queenly in this moment. I need time to mourn the loss of my life, my love, and my country.

"The Ryn I know wouldn't be pouting at her old master's funeral." Nash's voice shocks me into sitting straight. "That's more like it."

"What are you doing here?" I haven't seen much of him.

"Do you mean at the funeral of the man I despise more than any other, for hurting you, or next to you?"

"Both."

"I'm at this joke of a funeral because you're attending it." He bends down, so he's on my level, and whispers, "And I'm with you because that's where I want to be."

"But you've been avoiding me."

He has the decency to look away. "True."

"Why?"

"Because I thought it would hurt you too much if you were the one to kill me, so I stayed away. But if"—he says so low I can barely here him—"Androlla"—he resumes a conversational tone —"kills me, you'll have to understand it wasn't your fault because I'm not leaving again. I demand to be placed back on your personal guard."

I give him a faint smile, though my heart is bursting with joy. "They do need the help."

"It's settled, then."

"Are you sure you're ready to come back?" I can't help but think he may need more time to heal.

"If you don't want me to, I'll stay at home a while longer, but I feel ready. I've got a plan. I'm going to keep talking to Jaku, train less, and see my family more. I think all these things will help." He leans in close. "Besides, I've missed you."

"I've missed you too." My words are so soft, I'm not sure he hears me, until the corners of his lips turn up.

He says, "I think it's time we were away from this place, don't you?"

I glance at Daros's still form. He'll be entombed with those who have no money or family. In the paupers' graveyard. He would have hated that.

"Yes, it's time." And I can honestly say that without any guilt over leaving Daros behind.

One of the guards goes to move my chair, but Nash takes it from her. "I've got this."

I hold back a smile. It's a bumpy ride back to the palace, but it feels good. Feels like my last taste of freedom, out in the open air. While I'm not ready to think about Androlla and what's to become of my future, I am ready to enjoy what's left of my time.

The birds are out, singing, though it's late in the year and the temperatures are falling. It's not cold but cool, the sun warming the slight breeze. As we enter the palace walls, the sound of metal clanging reaches us. The guards are practicing their skills, heedless that they are about to once again be under a mad woman.

I take a deep breath, enjoying the scent of leaves and dirt that come together to make it smell of late year. I don't want to say *goodbye* to this life yet, but the end feels soon and inevitable.

Does Nash feel it? Jaku? Jem? Is there anyone else who has an inkling of what's to pass? I wish there was a way to protect them. To make it so Androlla wouldn't rule over them, but the only way to get rid of the queen altogether would throw the country into one natural disaster after another, according to what history says.

Better to live life under the rule of a mad woman than face certain death.

It's hard to make that choice for my people, but I feel most of them would rather have it that way. Besides, if Androlla pushes on the Poruah and Medi's taxes, I have a feeling they'll push back. They're tired of being toyed with. The assassination attempts on her life would increase, until this body is killed. But that's what she wants—to get rid of a body with limited mobility.

While it's not the ideal body, I've gotten used to it. I still ache to be able to climb onto the roof at night and stretch out my body in a way that has me feeling free, but there are no longer such luxuries. At least for a while. I seem to be improving, but not fast enough for my liking. Anything other than instant improvement would be too slow. I should stop thinking of myself. I'm not the only one suffering.

Poor Inkga, going through everything that she is with her mother… Monkia is in the dungeons, awaiting her fate from the council, and I can't imagine it will be a good one. How does Inkga feel about that? About everything? She's been so quiet, and I don't want to pry, but at the same time, I wish there was something I could do for her.

I tell Nash to take me to Jem. Jaku is already here in my room and joins us. With him and Nash, Venda, Jem and me, we are now the only ones who officially know about the First Queen. It's a sobering thought, even if I'm the one who's tried to keep it that way.

Nash takes me through the twisting hallways of the palace until we arrive at Jem's rooms.

She lets us in while the rest of my guards wait outside. They look to me, waiting for me to say something.

I don't want to say it, but I must. "We know what's coming. Without Daros's help, we don't have a way to defeat Androlla."

"That's not quite true," Jem says.

A flame of hope flickers inside me. I want to douse it before it becomes too big to control. My hope has been squashed too many times to believe it won't be again. "What do you mean?"

"I talked to the men you had guarding Daros. They said he had some paperwork locked in his desk."

"What does that have to do with anything?" Nash asks.

"Don't you see?" She grows excited. "He must have learned how to defeat Androlla from somewhere. The guards said these papers looked old, though Daros would never let them get close enough to read them. I think the answer to our problems might be there."

I tamper down hope, but it does no good. My hope flames into existence, melting any doubts in its path. "We need to go to his house. It's been too long. Someone could have ransacked the place."

Jem nods. "I agree. I should have come to you sooner, but I've been lost in my own problems."

"Is it safe?" Of course Jaku has to be the voice of reason.

"Have there been any attacks since we dealt with Kada and Daros?" I ask.

"Actually, no. Not a one. I'd say the people are starting to settle into your rule happily and don't want to disturb the good news they've had of late."

Yet another reason they'll be furious if the First Queen takes over and changes things up again. "Then I say we should go for it. Nash?"

"I'm up for it. We'll take Afet, Eldim, and Julina with us. They'll help keep you safe, should anything happen, but I think we'd be fine even without them."

"Just in case," Jaku says, "don't tell anyone where we are going."

Nash nods his agreement and goes out to round them up.

"Are you up for this, Jem? It could be dangerous." I don't want her to face something she's not ready for.

"I was trained by the best, even if I still need work. I know I can take down anyone I need to."

It's settled, then. We're going to Daros's, and we will find a solution to dealing with Androlla. I refuse to let it be any other way.

CHAPTER 32

IT'S DECIDED that I shouldn't worry about going incognito. It's not possible to hide my chair, and everyone knows I use it. We have to hope we don't gather too much of a crowd.

My guards surround me as we go through the portcullis, Nash pushing my chair.

The going is slow and bumpy, but I refuse to be left behind. Even if it's hard, I want to see this through. I didn't do enough where Daros was concerned, I need to do more. Much, much more. Going with them feels like the only way to accomplish that, and Nash is willing to deal with my chair.

It's difficult to see much, through the bodies of my protector surrounding me, but there are a few curious onlookers. Nobody stop us, though. They watch from a distance, staying where they are.

The pressure in my head increases the closer we get to Daros's. That house. How often will I have to come back to where so many horrors await for me? I wish I could leave it behind, never to return, but it doesn't seem like I'm going to be that lucky.

When we arrive at the house, no one is in sight. That doesn't mean no one is watching us, just that they're being discreet.

The house is dark. Lifeless. Then again, it may have had a lot of comings and goings, but otherwise it was never full of life.

"I'll search the house to make certain it's secure," Jaku says.

"No. If there's a group of people in there, you'll need more than a few people," I reply.

He gives me a stern look. "I'm not leaving you out here."

"Then we all go in together." I'm not budging on this. I need to keep my people safe.

"I don't like it," he says.

"What are we even doing here?" Julina asks.

Nash and Jaku look at me while Eldim and Afet avoid my gaze. They must be curious too; they're just too well trained to ask. "We need to see if there's paperwork to retrieve."

"What type of paperwork is worth risking your life?" Julina persists.

"The type that will save the country." Which is all I feel like giving her for now. "Let's go."

She purses her lips.

Jaku sighs but strides forward without any further dissent. The front door is unlocked, and he opens it easily. Not good for keeping robbers out. Maybe Daros hoped his reputation alone was enough to keep them away. Eldim and Jem join Jaku, and Nash pushes my chair after them, with Julina and Afet taking the rear.

The house is dark, curtains drawn. There's a musty smell in the air, as if no one has been here for a while, despite the fact that Daros came back here to live with his guards. Dust is spread across the room and furniture. Not as much where we're going, which looks like it's been tread on before, but the farther I look into the house, the dustier it gets.

"Where to?" Jaku asks.

"The back office," I say.

Everyone's weapons are out as we move through the house,

except mine. I have nothing, not even the dart flinger, to protect myself with. It's safer for the others but leaves me fidgety.

The deeper we go, the more pain radiates through my head. The pressure on the back of my eyes is so great I feel as if they'll pop out, and the pain travels down my neck. I keep my gaze focused before me, trying to ignore it—to work past it—but I must not do a good enough job.

"Are you all right, Ryn?" Nash asks.

They all turn to look at me.

"Fine," I squeak out. They look like they don't believe me. At some point, I hunch over, my hands in fists. I have to give them an excuse. "Headache." *Problems with the First Queen.* Do I tell them? Have them worry over me? I'm in good hands right now. Jaku and Nash will take care of everything, should the worst happen.

Julina nods and turns back to the front, but Jem and Jaku are frowning. It's a good thing I can't see Nash. I'm not certain what he's thinking, and I don't want to know not while we can't do anything about it.

As we enter the office, the ache turns into a torment of blinding pain. I close my eyes against it, fighting Androlla for the right to control my thoughts and not be in such misery. It's to no avail. Short of discovering how to defeat her, nothing will work. She's too powerful, soaked with magical power unlike anything I've ever countered before.

The sound of wood scrapping against wood makes me open my eyes. Jem is searching through the drawers in Daros's desk. She goes through all of them as we wait.

"Nothing." She slams the last drawer closed. "I was certain we'd find something. The guards said they were right here."

"Daros wouldn't make it that easy," I say. "Nash, wheel me over where I can see the what's going on, please."

People shuffle around, while Nash moves me into position.

I say, "Go through each drawer again, Jem. Slowly."

She opens each one, this time taking the time to run her

fingers along the edges and corners, looking for possible hidden compartments. The first drawer turns up nothing, as does the next and the one after that. When she pulls out the last one, I watch with bated breath.

"Nothing." She slams the drawer shut.

"Is there anywhere else it could be?" Jaku's gaze darts to where the hidden room of torture is.

I shake my head. "He never kept anything like that in there. Important documents were always in this room, though we should check the rest of the house, just in case, since his bookcase is empty too. It doesn't look good, though. Maybe someone got here before us."

"There's something funny about this desk," Nash says.

"What do you mean?"

"Not sure yet." He steps closer, pulls out all the drawers, and places them on top of the desk. "I've worked with wood a lot in my spare time, which is how I made Ryn's chair. Something about this isn't coming together right."

"What do you think it is?" I keep my voice quiet, both in case he needs to think instead of answering, and to keep my headache from getting worse.

"I don't know." He crouches down, so he's at eye level with the desk, and goes through it, tapping the framework as he goes. The *thud*, *thud*, *thud* adds to the ache in my head, until I hear an empty knock.

"What was that?" I ask.

"I think I found a hollow spot." He taps around a bit more. "It's big enough to fit a few pages inside."

I bite my lip to keep from asking anything further.

He slides his hand across the wood back where I can't see.

He slides his hand across the wood, back where I can't see. "Anyone have a dagger they don't care about?" he asks. "I may be able to pry this open. I'm not sure how to get inside otherwise. He must have a switch or something, but I can't find it."

"You can use this one." Julina takes a dagger out of her boot. "I've been meaning to replace it."

"Thank you." He takes the proffered dagger and works a piece from the bottom up. It's hard to see from the angle I'm at as the metal scratches against the wood.

"Don't do it," Androlla says from my mouth.

Nash glances at me, eyebrows furrowed. "What's wrong, Ryn?"

The headache is gone, but this is much worse. I want to scream that it's not me, that I have no control over myself, but there's no way to do so.

"I said don't. Stop it right now. I refuse to let you go any further."

Everyone in the room stares at me. The confused expression on Nash's face clears, and he turns away from me. He continues his work as if I didn't say a thing.

I want to tell him he made the right choice. That he's doing great. Instead, my body betrays me more. Androlla lifts my hand, trying to for a fist. Though my hand won't close all the way, she shoves it forward with all her might.

Thankfully, it doesn't move much, but it's enough to get even more strange looks from everyone here but Nash.

Jem's expression flattens, and she comes to my side. "It's all right, Ryn. We'll take care of this. You don't have to worry."

She's right. They'll take care of everything. My body is too weak to do any real damage if Androlla tries. There's nothing the First Queen can do in this moment, and I'm free of the headache.

"I command you to stop," she says.

Nash ignores me. Jem continues to say soothing words, but Afet, Eldim, and Julina put their hands on the hilt of their swords.

"You need to stop, Nash," Eldim says. "The queen demands it."

Jaku steps forward. "You have to understand something, and I'm swearing you all to secrecy."

The three exchange looks. Julina says, "What is it?"

"Promise you'll not utter a word of what I'm about to tell you."

Do I want him to reveal this? Not that it matters—there's nothing I can do about it in my given state. Androlla mustn't care either, as she stays silent.

They promise, and Jaku says, "The queen is not always herself. The papers we're trying to find are supposed to have information on how to help her."

Good. He told them what they needed to hear without bringing magic or the voice in my head into it. But how will they take it?

Eldim takes a step back, running a hand through his hair. "I don't know… You realize this would make the queen incompetent, right?"

No. An incompetent queen is a dead queen.

Inside, Androlla laughs her wicked laugh. This was her plan, then—let them think I'm crazy, so they'll put a death sentence on me and she can get a new body. Works well for her. I'll be daggered. I wish I could throw a knife.

"Not incompetent," Jaku says, tone soft. "If you utter that word again to a single soul—any of you—I'll have your tongue cut out."

Would he do that?

Whether or not he would, the three have taken their hands off their swords, the tension going out of their muscles.

"Is she going to be all right?" Julina asks, peering at me with a worried expression.

"Only if we can find the papers," Jaku says.

"How is that going to help her?"

"It's a long story. And the less you know of it, the better."

"That doesn't sound promising."

Afet says, "I protect the queen, and I gave my word to keep this a secret, but it had better be fixed soon."

"It makes sense, though," Julina says. "She's done things that don't mesh with how she works and thinks. Throwing Jaku and Nash in prison is one example of how she's lost it. The Ryn I know would never do such a thing."

"The Ryn you know is gone." Androlla spits the words out.

Panic overwhelms me. Is she right? Am I gone for good? Has the time come that she's taken control of me and there's no way for me to get it back?

Nash whips around, staring in my eyes. "Fight, Ryn. Fight this off."

I want to scream that I'm trying. That I can't find purchase on myself. There's nothing to grab onto. Nothing to attack Androlla with. I have no idea how to get myself back.

He turns back around and works on the drawer again, the *scritch scratch* the only sound filling the room until Androlla's laugh comes out, tinkling and evil.

I want to slam against her, let her feel my rage, but it only makes her laugh harder.

Suddenly, I snap back to myself, the laughter cutting off mid-laugh. I clamp my mouth closed and try to think of what to say that will make Afet, Eldim, and Julina think I'm less crazy.

There's nothing but the truth.

Do I dare?

I open my mouth to tell them.

There's a *snap*, and Nash says, "Got it."

The others' attention is diverted to him, and I'm free for the moment.

Papers flutter toward the ground, but Nash catches them before they fall all the way. He scans them over before holding them up before me.

"Maybe we should do this back at the palace, where it's more secure," Jaku says.

I want to growl in frustration, but he's right. "Let's go."

It takes longer than I want to get back to the palace and get in a secure room—another inside suite that's become mine. This one has a sitting room, a bedroom, and a bathing chamber. I've barely used the premises. The sitting room is dark, and Nash and Afet hurry to light the candles and liven it up. Even with lots of candles, it's dark. The deep-brown floor and dark furniture don't help. I want to have it changed, but it doesn't matter since I'll never use any of it.

I'm parked next to a table with a lit candelabra and a vase of flowers—Inkga's attempt at making the place cheerier. Or maybe she's trying to distract herself from the awful happenings. I haven't been able to speak with her about it.

Afet, Eldim, and Julina are excused from the room. Nash doesn't waste any time holding up the first paper for me to read. The big, looping handwriting is fading but readable.

I scan it, at first looking for something useful, but it's talking about different spells. Nothing I ascertain would help with Androlla.

"Let's look at the next one," I tell Nash. "And you both can read what papers you want. I trust you."

Nash moves next to me so he can read over my shoulder, and Jaku picks up the paper I finished.

The next several pages, while interesting and filled with little bits of history, don't have anything to do with how I could defeat her. I groan. At least it's not in Daros's handwriting, so he didn't write the pages. "What was Daros doing, hiding these pages, if they don't have any useful information? Just that a search said they were written by some woman named, Tula."

"Maybe there's still something here. There are several more papers to get through," Nash says.

I hope he's right, but the next one isn't useful either, though it does have the luck charm and healing spell that Daros had me doing. "Why would he have had me doing those spells if they weren't relevant to Androlla?"

"He said they were to practice, right?" But Nash sounds as skeptical as I feel.

"Let's see the next page," I say.

He pulls out the next one, and I begin scanning it. I have a feeling he and Jaku read much faster than I do, but they're patient.

It's frustrating, being a slow reader, but more frustrating to not find anything.

"Wait. Did you see this?" Nash points to a part a couple paragraphs below where I'm at.

I glance where he's pointing.

SOME OF MY research leads me to believe things aren't what they seem in this country. Something is strange about the queens throughout my lifetime. Perhaps I'm getting senile in my old age. My children and great grandchildren say so. Because of that, I don't dare tell others of my suspicion.

WHAT IS HER SUSPICION?

The next paragraph talks about her family, and how sweet they are with her though they believe she's not all there. Nash points at the next paragraph. "Here it is," he says in an excited voice.

I'VE DETERMINED that the queens are really one person. Though they may start out as different women, they all end up looking the same and bringing about the same laws. I don't know what to do with this information. I'd like to confront the current queen about it, but I'm old and can't withstand much. Besides, part of me does wonder if I'm crazy. Why would these girls all look and act the same after some time?

The more I think about it, though, the more sense it does make. As the queens age and change, they become private, hiding themselves away from the public eye, where they would be scrutinized. Because of my position in the palace, I've happened to see more queens than most, and with my age, see them through much.

All I can think is that the Mortum Tura does something to these women. Something that changes them after a period of time. The death drink is the thing they share, except for the fact that they all live in the palace. I've lived in the palace almost my entire life, and I haven't changed, except perhaps being more stubborn. I can admit that.

Even the softest of queens turn hard, their rules ones of tyranny.

Further spying has shown me that there's evil at play. A woman named Androlla taking over all the queens for generations. There has to be a way to stop this woman. For too long has she reigned over this people with terror and cruelty. I can't handle my great grandchildren growing up in this climate. It's unpardonable. But what do I do?

Not much, without getting close to her. I'm not sure even that would help. It's not like I can kill her. There needs to be a way to kill not only the body she's inhabiting, but also the soul of the creature that's usurped the power for years.

THE PAGE ENDS.

"Can she have found out about the First Queen?" Nash asks.

"I don't know. It makes sense, if she lived in the palace and was close enough to the queen to see her go through those changes over the years."

"Who was she?"

I want to know that too. It would be nice if there was a way to talk to her. Get her firsthand experience instead of reading about it. But the ink is faded with age, and she's long gone.

Nash hands the page to Jaku and grabs another.

After much research, I have an idea of how to get rid of the queen, but I worry she's going to find out my plans. She's been very suspicious of me as of late, not letting me attend her as much, and when I am there, she keeps a close eye on me. What will happen if she finds out what I have planned?

Doesn't matter. I'm going forward with it, anyway. The magic I must use isn't one I've studied before. It's new to me, but it could work. I have to make a golem and send her soul into it. Then I can destroy that golem, and she will be vanquished with it.

"Would that work?" I ask.

"Would what work?" Jaku leans over to see what's on the paper.

Nash hands it to him, though I didn't finish. When Jaku is done, I ask him, "Do you think that would work?"

"I don't know," Jaku says. "It sounds plausible."

"It's the best thing we've got. We'll have to give it a try." Nash scans the last paper. "There's nothing about it on this one. We're going to have to figure out two different things—how to create a golem and how to send Androlla's soul into it."

"And then we have to determine how to destroy it." Because I won't have her around any longer, even as a golem.

How am I going to create a golem and put the First Queen's soul into it?

CHAPTER 33

JAKU SENT a servant to get Venda. While we wait, we reread the pages, searching for more clues, but finding none.

"What I don't understand," I say, "is why Daros had me doing luck and healing spells. How does that help make a golem and put Androlla into it?"

"I don't know," Nash replies. "Maybe he's using the other spells in here to make you strong enough at magic to do the transferring spell."

"I guess we'll never know." And I don't feel bad about it anymore. Mostly, I feel terrible for Inkga. I have hardly seen her since she found out Daros was her father, and when I do, she doesn't want to talk about anything. Not even mundane things. It must have been shocking for her.

There's a knock, and Jaku lets in Venda.

"You sent for me," she says.

"Yes, we're wondering how to do a spell." For some reason, I hesitate to tell her. "We found some papers at Daros's. They are enlightening."

"What do they say?"

I rush to get it all out. "That we need to make a golem and send the First Queen's soul into it."

Venda scowls. "This is dark, black magic. I am uncertain how to accomplish it, though I have a few ideas."

"I was afraid of that," Nash mumbles. "What are your ideas?"

"Black magic always requires blood sacrifice. Human blood."

"I'll volunteer for that disgusting job," Nash says.

"I can do it." The words tumble from my lips.

"We don't need to waste your precious blood," he says.

"I'm afraid, in this case, we do," she says. "Her tie with the First Queen will require her to be the one to sacrifice her blood to the golem."

Nash fists up his hand. "I don't like it."

"It's called *dark, black magic* for a reason."

"Are there any consequences to doing black magic?" If I'm going to use my blood for something, I want to make sure it's not going to have repercussions for my country and those I care about.

"I do not know all about it."

"I'm sensing a *but* in there," Jaku says.

Her lips thin. "Very well. I have heard rumors. People talk in Faner, in hushed tones. It is forbidden to practice, but that doesn't mean no one does. They're careful about how they do it, so they don't get caught. They say those who practice the dark magic will have someone close to them perish. The more horrific the magic, the more people die."

My throat tightens to the point I can't talk. I clear it. "If I do this, people I care about will die?"

"It is the rumor. But I would take it seriously, yes."

I glance at Nash. He's the closest person to me. Would that make him the most likely candidate for death? "I can't do this," I say.

"It's fine, Ryn. I'm willing to die for this cause, as I know others are. It's more important than a few people. You have to make this happen if it's the only way to stop Androlla. If she survives, we're all as good as dead, anyway."

My constant headache increases to the point where I close my eyes in pain, unsure if it's from the headache itself or from his words. No matter what happens, I fear he is right.

People I love are going to die.

"How do we do it?" I ask.

"We will need something to make the golem out of. A structure that can stick together, though if you want to kill her after she's in it, you'll also want it out of something that can break easily. It's mostly a guess, but I think you will need to mix your blood with the object you're going to enchant as her golem. I would recommend clay, since that is what golems are typically made of."

"Clay would be a good choice," Jaku says. "A sword can slice through it easily enough, but it would have enough consistency to stay together."

"Agreed," Nash says.

I don't know what to say. "Can we do this soon and get it over with?"

"We'll need to find a space where we can make the golem. It will have to be big enough to fit a person inside."

"So we can't make her tiny and then step on her?" I ask.

"No."

It was worth a try. "Why not? Does the soul take up space?"

She nods. "At least as much space as they took up in life, though they can grow bigger."

"Then how does my body contain both my soul and Androlla's?" I ask.

She crinkles her eyebrows. "I'm not certain. It can't be good, whatever the reason. We have to assume that she'll need at least enough space for her soul moving forward, though. Our plans will all be for naught if it isn't big enough and the First Queen takes over before we can fix our mistake."

Good point. Doesn't matter, though. No matter her size, we'll be able to defeat her. The swords will do damage to her, though. I'm certain of it. We have a way to kill the First Queen, and judging by my headache, she knows it, and she's furious. Now we need to make it happen.

"You think you've won, but you haven't," Androlla says through my mouth.

Curse her, for taking over me again. It's getting old and frustrating. I've got to do something about it, but what?

Nash gets in my face and snarls. "Get out of her."

She smirks. "Don't like that very much, do you, lover boy?"

He jumps back, glaring.

"That's right," she says. "Ryn and Nash have been touching, and even kissing. Guess that's lover boy's death." She giggles.

"I know, and we're not going to do anything about it," Jaku says.

What?

"What?" Androlla screams.

How did he know?

Jaku comes closer and gets down on my level. "Ryn, I know you're in there, and you're probably upset. You don't need to be. I figured that you and Nash were close, and Julina saw you kissing through the window one night. Came to me, not knowing what to do. We talked about it and decided we wouldn't turn you in as long as you didn't get pregnant. We care about both you and Nash too much to do that to you."

I can't believe he did that for us. He's a better man than I knew.

"I wouldn't get her pregnant," Nash says. "But that doesn't matter. I should never have kissed her."

Jaku puts a hand on Nash's shoulder. "You clearly love her. Things happen. But I promise I'll do all in my power to keep you both safe."

"Well, isn't that cute?" Androlla says. "Risking your career and life for something as stupid as love? It won't last. It never does.

Look at Monkia and Daros. Or Wilric and Jem. Love never wins. I win."

As much as I worry she's right, I'm done dealing with her bad attitude coming out of my lips. I mentally shake her from my mind, whipping her around until we're both rattled. I control myself again, whether it's because I tried to knock her loose or because she was done with me. I'm glad to be back.

"First," I say, "you and Julina didn't have to risk yourselves like that." Jaku goes to speak, but I raise a hand to stop him. "But I'm glad you did. Thank you. I will never be able to repay you."

"It is an honor to protect not only my queen, but also true love," he says.

"And I will keep your secret as well," Venda says. "It is not right to dictate love, and I want you both to know Androlla is wrong. No matter what she says, love can last. I've seen it among my own people."

Inside, the First Queen scoffs, but I ignore her and the ache in my head. "Thank you. I'm honored that you value love so highly." I smile at Nash.

He smiles back but looks a little pale. Must have been a shock to him; it was for me.

"Second," I say, because as much as I want to linger over this, we need to deal with some things, "I want a law enacted that says nothing can change within the next thirty days. That way, if Androlla gets out in public again, she won't be able to do any damage." I keep my worries about Nash to myself.

"Good idea," he says. "I'll get on that with the council as soon as we're done here."

Jaku says, "What do you plan on doing after those thirty days, if Androlla is still with you, though?"

"If she's still with me, I'm afraid it will be too late." Because I'm already under so much pressure, I can't imagine lasting much longer.

CHAPTER 34

I'M up for the day after a night of running from the First Queen. I've long gotten over the fact that she's always there, hounding me, and enjoy the feel of my legs stretching. As much as I wish I was still there, there are too many things to be done today.

Inkga is helping me with my hair. The blonde is coming out in it much too strongly. Even in my gaze, I see Androlla peeking out. I want to stab her in the face. Of course, that's impossible.

Instead, I focus on something I can do. Something I've tried to do, but never had any results. It's time to change that. "Inkga, how are you?"

"Fine." She doesn't look me in the eye.

"I really want to know. You've listened to me through so much. I'm happy to do the same for you."

She pauses mid-brushstroke and sets the brush on the table before wheeling me around so she can sit across from me. She's silent, though. I keep waiting for her to say something, anything, but she sits there, looking at her hands.

Looks like I'll have to play her role today. How do I start? I didn't know this was so hard. "What are you thinking?"

She sniffs. "I can't believe Daros was my father."

"I couldn't either." When she stays quiet, I say, "How do you feel about that?"

"Awful." The tears start. "I don't want to be his daughter. He's a cruel man who was vicious to so many, including you. What if I turn out like him? I couldn't handle it if I betrayed people like he did. Or worse, what if I turn out like my mother, who kept such a horrid secret for all these years—a secret that cost others their lives?"

I wish I could lean forward and put a hand on her arm. We've been able to keep her true parentage a secret, but that doesn't change it or the fact that her mother has been sentenced to execution, which must be weighing on her as well. "You are not like him or her. You are good and kind and true. You would never do something cruel, like Daros, or stupid, like Monkia. You're a wonderful person. You take care of me with no thought to yourself when the other servants have pretty much abandoned me."

She gives a warbly sigh. "Do you really think so?"

"I do. I'm grateful and happy to call you my friend."

She pulls out a handkerchief and dabs at her eyes. "Thank you, Ryn. I'm glad to call you a friend too."

"It's a good day when you're willing to talk to me."

She laughs, though it still sounds a bit watery. "I thought for certain I was about to receive the lashing of my life."

Blasted Androlla. "Never with me. I promise you that." Though if Androlla gets a hold of me, Inkga will suffer her wrath. I've got to find a way to protect the people I care about if she takes over. Maybe I should just tell her. She's certain to understand. Before I can do so, she continues.

"Can I tell you something?"

"Anything."

"I'd love to hug you right now."

I grin. "I'd love to hug you too." And if Afet and Eldim weren't hiding in the corners of my room, I'd do it. Another reason I can't tell her now. Too many people present. This secret is getting out of control.

"Do you want me to leave your hair down or put it up?"

Normally, I have her put it up, but there's so much to do, I don't want to waste time. "Leave it. I need to speak with Nash. Send for Jaku as well, please."

"I can do that." She wheels me into the dark sitting room and lights the candles as Afet and Eldim take their places.

I watch the two men, wondering about them. They've been steadfast through everything. I wish there was something I could do for them. A way to show them how much I value them.

"I'm going to get Nash and Jaku," Inkga says. "I'll see you at lunch."

"I look forward to it." After she leaves, I say to the two men, "Thank you for always guarding me so faithfully."

"It is what we do," Eldim says.

"If you don't mind me asking, why are you both so devoted?"

The exchange a glance. Afet says, "You are the queen."

"Is that all, though? If I was a bad queen—which I try not to be, but if I was—would you still guard me with such loyalty?"

They hesitate.

"You can be honest with me. I'm not going to get angry," I say.

Afet shifts his weight, the loss for words uncharacteristic for him. "I don't know that I would, Your Majesty. I would be more likely to try to get in a different position."

"And you, Eldim?"

He stands straighter. "I am the same as Afet."

I must do something for them as well, in the likely case that Androlla takes over. "Thank you for your honesty. I want you both to know I'm grateful all you've done for me, for putting your lives on the line for me over and over again."

"It's a pleasure," Eldim says.

Nash and Jaku enter the room and relieve the other two guards. As soon as we're alone, I say, "We have a problem. When the First Queen takes over for good, those who have been loyal to me will be under her scrutiny and rule. I get the feeling she has wicked plans for them, including the both of you."

"You mean *if*," Nash says.

"I'm sorry?" What is he talking about?

"You said *when* the First Queen takes over. It's not a *when*. It's an *if*. We're determined to do everything we can to not let that happen."

I don't want to tell him *when* seems much more appropriate, especially with the pounding and persistent feelings of victory in my head. "All right. *If* she takes over, it's going to be dangerous for the people I care about. I don't want to sit helplessly inside my own head, watching her torture the people I love. I'd like for you both to plan how to get everyone out and away from Androlla, without telling me what you decide."

They exchange a look.

"What?" I ask.

"We'll take care of it," Nash says. "You don't have to worry about any of us. Just worry about defeating her and taking care of the country."

It feels as if a huge weight has been lifted off of my shoulders. I sit taller, ready to face the challenges of the day. Now, if I could concentrate on defeating her and protecting my people... The headaches make it difficult. "Thank you. Now, I believe I have a state dinner tonight to get ready for. Is there any way we can skip it? I'm worried about Androlla taking over during it."

Nash gives a slight grimace but covers it well.

Jaku says, "I'm afraid you've skipped so many, people are starting to wonder if you're ruling or not. It could be detrimental if you didn't go. Nash and I will try to stick close to you, so we can get you out if something happens."

I was afraid of that. "Very well. Go ahead and send Julina in, and Inkga in a few minutes, so I can get ready."

"Of course," Jaku says.

Nash walks over to me and takes my hand.

"What are you doing?" I shoot Jaku a worried glance, but he's looking at the wall.

"Jaku and I talked about it. It's all right. You need the contact, and I'm going to give it to you."

His hand feels so good in mine. It's tender and gentle. A nice, firm grip that leaves me feeling breathless. The calluses on his hand are familiar and welcome. I want to pull him closer, but no matter how Jaku feels, I worry about kissing Nash in front of him. I'll have to settle for this touch; that's what I need.

He takes both hands and grasps one of mine. He leans forward and whispers, "I love you, Ryn. We'll make this work. I promise."

"I love you too." Even if I know he can't make that promise come true.

He gives my hand a final squeeze and leaves. The loss is immediate. I want to call him back and latch onto him—not let him go until this is all over. It may be unfeasible. Doesn't matter.

"I'll get Julina for you." Nash leaves the room, and a moment later, Julina joins Jaku.

"You wanted to see me?" she asks me. "Or is it my turn to guard you?"

"I suppose you should guard me, but I'm more interested in talking to you. We haven't done that in a long time."

She grins and sits down near me.

"How are you doing?" I ask.

"As well as can be expected. I'm happier now that you seem to be safe. There haven't been any attacks on you in a while. That's a record, not just for you, but for any queen I've protected. You're bringing stability to this country."

"Thank you for the kind words. I'm grateful my work is paying off with the people. I hope they're happier." And now maybe I can focus on defeating Androlla. I've spent too many long hours practicing spells, but I need to figure out how to make that golem. I won't have a chance today, but hopefully tomorrow, I can end this all. And if it doesn't work, then I can practice until I lose myself to her.

"Are you all right?" Julina asks.

"Fine. Why?"

"You looked sad, all of a sudden."

I sigh. "I'm afraid I have some heavy things on my plate. But I want you to know something. No matter what happens in the future, you are my friend more than my guard. I've appreciated all you've done for me. I never had sisters, but if I did, I'd want you to be one of them." Her and Inkga. My two surrogate sisters.

Her eyes glisten. "Thank you, Ryn. I consider you a sister as well. Although we get on better than some siblings I know."

I laugh. "That may be. Tell me what you've been doing the last while, since you healed. I haven't seen enough of you."

We spend the next half an hour talking. It's nice to sit down with her. I wish we could have done this sooner. I'll never forget the time we were hiding, and she sneezed. It was memorable, and I don't want to forget it or any moment like it. I'm afraid that when Androlla takes over those memories will be all I have to comfort myself with.

CHAPTER 35

As Inkga gets ready to roll me into the dining room, I want to tell her to take me anywhere but here. I know the council and court need to see me, and I need to be strong for them, but in a day or so, I'll know if I can defeat the First Queen and be able to come out among them.

Only I don't believe it's going to happen. Not with me. Perhaps Nash and the others will figure it out and defeat her eventually, but the spell seems too difficult for me to carry it out. Though if I can, it will take a single swipe from Nash and Jaku's swords for her to be gone forever. I need to focus on that, and not the negative.

But in case I don't survive, I should spend one last night with the court. "I'm ready."

Servants open the doors, and Inkga wheels me in. The sight before me is like many I've seen before, though this time, someone seems to have paid attention to how much food we serve. There are no obscene mounds of it, like there were in the past, for people to gorge themselves on. Modest amounts are spread across the tables—still probably too much, but not so that I worry we're taking food away from those who need it the most.

Everyone stands as Inkga rolls me forward toward the only setting without a chair. Nash stands on my left, Jaku on my right with Jem next to Nash. I wonder how they pulled off not sitting in the seats protocol dictates. It doesn't matter, though; I'm grateful they did it.

Once I'm rolled to my place, the others take their seat, and people start chatting. There are many sideways looks at me. I smile and pretend there's no pounding in my head or fear in my heart. That everything is as it should be.

Silence once again spreads through the room. What is going on? I glance around to see Inkga bringing me the Mortum Tura.

Oh no.

I can't drink it. If I do, Androlla will have even more power over me. Her strength will increase while mine decreases. There's no saying I'll keep myself from drinking it if it gets near me. She will likely take over and drink it for me, and who knows what announcement she'll make then?

I breathe slowly, trying not to let my panic show. Nash must see it, because he whispers, "It's all right."

It's not all right. It's all wrong.

The pounding in my head lessens as Androlla laughs inside. She revels in my fear. I have to work past it. Inkga's almost here. What do I do? It's not like I can accidentally knock it over; it'll refill itself.

Inkga reaches me, and her huge grin dims when she sees my faces. Still, she holds the tray out to me.

"Do you need help?" she asks when I don't grab it, concern lacing her words.

I've gotten more mobile and I'm able to move my upper body some, but have yet to drink without spilling. Perhaps she thinks I'm worried about embarrassing myself.

"Drink, Your Highness," a male voice calls out. "We want to see the glory of your glow shining over us."

"Yes, drink," a female yells.

"I can't," I whisper.

The ground begins to shake. The tremor is faint at first, but soon it's rolling. Nash grabs one of the handles of my chair. People scream. Things go crashing to the floor. The platters are shaking and clanking together.

How long has it been since I last drank the Mortum Tura? Is that why this is happening?

Everything sways beneath me. I've brought my country to their knees because I won't drink. Androlla's tinkling laugh becomes louder in my mind. Either way, she's won. The city will continue to deal with this earthquake, and she'll still take me over. I'll drink, and she'll be that much closer to getting what she wants.

"Drink it," someone hollers.

Soon, everyone is yelling it, adding to the chaos of the ground shaking and things falling. The chandelier in the middle of the room sways dangerously, like it's ready to fall. The people at the tables beneath it scramble to get away from it.

There's no time to waste. I'll have to deal with the consequences later. "Help me, Inkga."

She doesn't hesitate. She reaches for the cup, but before she gets to it, the floor shakes harder than ever. She staggers, and the cup falls to the floor, its juice splattering across the wood.

"Get it," a woman calls.

"For the queen. Get the Mortum Tura."

"The Mortum Tura."

"Get it before we all die."

The voices overlap, so I can no longer make out words. People are hurrying to get the cup, but it rolls away in the heaving of the earth. While Nash helps me move toward the cup, Jaku jumps into action, joining the others trying to grab the fleeing object.

Finally, Jaku gets a hold of it. Liquid sloshes everywhere, but he's not close enough in this wavering world. "I'm going to throw it," he says.

Good thing it refills itself.

"I'll catch it," Nash hollers.

Jaku swings his arm back and then forward, and the cup goes sailing through the air toward us. Nash reaches out with one hand and catches it midair. He says, "I'm so sorry." And then he brings it to my lips.

I swallow, hating the sickly-sweet taste of it.

The shaking stops, the room going deathly quiet. Until Androlla's tinkling laugh fills the air.

No, I scream in my head. I slam against her, trying to regain control. Nash must know that's not my laugh, because he pushes me toward the closed door.

"What's going on?" people ask.

"Where's he taking the queen?"

"What just happened?"

"Are we all going to die?"

The questions keep coming, but Nash ignores them as the tinkling laugh stops. She's going to say something, and I'll regret it. It will be a taste of what's to come—one that leaves me with a foul feeling. Someone's hand slaps across my mouth before Androlla can speak.

Jaku opens the door, and Nash races me out. It's his hand on my mouth. Him protecting me from the First Queen.

Behind us, I hear Jaku yell, "We're securing the queen after this earthquake. There's no cause for alarm. Jem, please see to the room."

Behind us, voices speak all at once. Androlla tries to bite Nash's hand, but he keeps a firm grip on her. I've never been as grateful to have him around as I am in this moment.

Jaku races ahead of us, clearing the way of both people and debris. Voices sound about both Nash's and Jaku's actions. I shove myself against Androlla's presence, vying for a way back to myself. A way to stop this chaos.

But nothing.

Suddenly, Androlla relaxes. Nash doesn't move his hand, but as he hurries down the hall, he asks, "Are you back, Ryn?"

She nods, while inside I'm screaming. What is she doing? What is her plan? And then I sense it. She's going to act crazy when we next see someone. Have me declared incompetent, which will bring my death and a new life for her.

I can't let that happen.

I fight against her, trying to get her to focus her attention on me. She doesn't react to me or Nash, just continues to sit quietly.

Nash slowly takes his hand from my mouth. I hope they don't kill him for touching me because everybody saw. No. I won't let that happen, and Jaku will help keep him safe. I need to focus on getting my body back.

"You all right, Ryn?" Nash asks.

"Shaken," Androlla says.

Is that something I would say? Will Nash believe her?

"It's all right," he says. "We'll be somewhere safe soon."

What does he mean by *safe*? Nowhere is safe.

Inside, she's laughing. I do my best to knock with force against her. She trembles and the laughter stops, but she doesn't give me control.

Will she ever, or am I permanently stuck here? I thought I would have more time. At least, a little.

Jaku bounds ahead, and I realize we're not headed toward to my room. Where are we going? Outside? It'd appear safer, after the earthquake, but that's not the danger we're facing now. Outside, Androlla will have a bigger audience.

Footsteps echo behind us. Androlla hears them too because she speaks nonsense about magic. That's how she's going to bring about my downfall—with talk of the mystic.

Nash says something under his breath but doesn't clamp him hand over my mouth. Does still he not realize it's not me? Doesn't he get that Androlla is playing him, using my body to betray us all?

"There are others coming," Venda says from behind. "We must move quickly and get her out of earshot."

I relax for a brief moment. No wonder Nash wasn't worried. He probably knew it was Venda the moment she started after us. Androlla isn't so happy; she lets out a piercing scream.

Nash clamps a hand over my mouth again as Jaku looks back at us, a crease forming between his eyebrows.

"Almost there," he says.

We're not in a part of the palace I'm familiar with, but we were heading toward the outside wall. When did that change? Probably when I was too busy fighting the First Queen. I give her another good lashing, but she goes on screaming underneath Nash's hand. It leaves me mentally exhausted and doesn't seem to do much to her.

Jaku opens a door and disappears into the room. A moment later, he pops back out. "It's clear and looks sturdy, even after the earthquake."

What's going on? Where are we?

I can feel Androlla's curiosity, though she keeps up the screaming. Nash wheels me into the room. A passage is open in the far wall. He goes into the dark passage, slowing as he goes, but not taking his hand off my mouth.

After a brief moment, the darkness deepens as someone closes the door to the passage. We travel a ways. Androlla stops screaming, but Nash won't be fooled a second time. He keeps right on blocking her from speaking.

I continue struggling, though I don't know what good it does. It seems like whenever I gain govern of my body again it's because she loses control, not because of anything I do.

A faint light appears and grows as we continue on. We come to the end of the path with a door that has light shining through its edges. Nash reaches over me and shoves the door open. He pushes my chair into a room lit with candles, like it was waiting for us. And then I see why—Julina steps out from the shadows.

"What's going on? Are you covering Ryn's mouth?" she asks.

"I'm afraid Ryn isn't herself," Jaku says from behind us.

"So you're restraining her?" Julina takes a step closer to me, rage filling her expression.

Nash pulls my chair back. "I promise you this isn't what it looks like."

She folds her arms. "Then what is it? Because from my vantage point, it seems like you're kidnapping the queen and having me help you do so."

I hope they can get her to understand. I should have told her sooner. She's close enough to me she might have accepted that I'm not crazy. Now, though, things look bad.

"Ryn is inhabited by an ancient queen, bent on taking over every queen's body and ruling the country," Nash says.

"R—right." She takes a step toward the door across the room from us. The room is bigger than I first thought, but Jaku beats her to the door, blocking her way out.

"It's true," he says. "I know it sounds crazy. I know magic seems far out there, but that's what's happening. The Mortum Tura causes this and has for a thousand years. Think about it. The queens always end up ruling with a cunning and harshness that doesn't always mirror how they first act."

"I don't know what you're talking about. The queens are women who have drunk the Mortum Tura and lived. They don't get some entity in them through magic, just the glowing power that makes it known they're the queen."

"That's what this evil queen wants you to think. But it's her, not Ryn. I swear to you on my life and on Ryn's life that what I say is true," Jaku says.

"And I add my word to his." Nash's hand is still over my mouth.

"As do I." Venda steps out of the passage we went through and shuts the door.

Nash takes his hand off my mouth, but the First Queen doesn't do anything. She just sits there.

"Is this true, Ryn?" Julina asks.

"Of course not." Androlla's words make me cringe.

Julina takes a step closer, and Nash wheels me into the corner, by a table with a lit candelabra on it. He steps in front of me and says, "I know this is hard to believe, but think about Ryn's behavior recently. Think about the lighter color of her hair and the green of her eyes. She's done and said things very un-Ryn-like. She wouldn't do anything like send me and Jaku to the dungeons. And if she did, why would she turn around and let us back out? Why would she appoint someone she doesn't know to be her Head Advisor? A man who tried to kill her? It makes no sense, unless you know someone else is behind these actions."

"All right." Julina takes a step back and grab the door handle. "I need to run and get something. I'll be right back."

Nash, Venda, and Jaku jump at her. They're fighting against her, struggling to restrain her with their hands. I want to tell them to stop fighting each other—that we're going to have to get along to defeat this. I want to tell Julina the story myself. If she hears it from me, she may change her mind. But I can't. I'm stuck in my own body more than I was ever stuck in this chair.

Androlla stretches my arm, fighting against the weakness, while the others try to subdue Julina. What is she doing?

She snatches the candelabra off the table and tips it onto my lap. My arm slouches to the side after the hard job. I scream at her to pick the candelabra up. To get it off my lap. To tell someone what happened.

She doesn't.

The material of my skirt goes up in flames.

She's trying to kill me.

And it's going to work.

If only one of the others would look my way...They don't, though. They're so absorbed with stopping Julina. Androlla uses my other hand to shove the candelabra to the side, where the flames tickle my chair until it too lights up.

I'm going to burn alive.

I don't feel pain yet, but then, I don't have control of my body. The fire licks up my chair, and soon the whole corner is on fire. Nash notices. He races toward me, but hands reach out to stop him.

I can tell they're talking, but I can't hear what they're saying over the crackle of the fire. Venda rushes to a stand that holds a water jug, several cups, and a platter of food, grabs the jug, and throws the water on me. It barely douses the flames, which grow bigger, now taking up half the room.

Jaku pulls off his cape and throws it on me, though he has to step inside the flames to do so. Nash follows suit, and they both try to put out the fire while being engulfed themselves.

Venda pulls them back, swatting at Jaku's sleeve that's been lit up.

"Can't we use magic?" Nash yells.

"I don't have any anti-fire enchantments," she says.

"We can't just leave her."

The room above their heads and to their sides has now caught. The wall of flames is thick between us.

They won't be able to reach me.

Androlla has won.

"We have to go," Jaku yells.

"I won't leave Ryn," Nash hollers back.

From my mouth, Androlla's tinkling laugh fills the room with the crackling fire.

Nash continues to fight against them, but Jaku pushes a pressure point on his neck, and Nash falls to the ground. Jaku scoops him up and yells my way, "I'm sorry, Ryn. I promise we'll find a way to defeat her."

They are out the door, and I'm left alone. Burning.

CHAPTER 36

I BLINK against the raging light and realize Androlla has given me back my body. To feel the burn for myself, no doubt. Except I don't feel much of anything. Just a slight tickling. And my finger… it's cold. Really cold, now that I think about it.

I glance down to see the wooden ring I took out of the treasury all those months ago lit up but not with fire. A blue-hued light is emanating from it. It wraps around the ring and moves along my body in a fainter pattern. It must be the magic saving my life.

Inside, the First Queen howls at her foiled plan. I smile. I have to wait out this fire and hope someone comes back to get me.

Something cracks beneath me. My chair. It doesn't seem to be receiving the same protection my body is getting; it's going up fast. I try to scoot off it, avoid being injured when it falls, but the thing breaks beneath me, dropping me to the ground, and I hit the back of my head on the wall.

The ache is nothing more than I'm used to—the pain of the First Queen being ever present. But now it seems muted, as if she's not trying hard enough to get through my mental barriers because of her failure. I'm all right with that, even if I'm sitting on a half-broken chair that's going up in flames. As long as I survive this, I can do anything.

Except maybe get rid of the Androlla for good.

As soon as this is over, I'm not wasting any more time. I'm going to defeat her once and for all. My friends have been taken care of. It will be fine, even if I fail.

I wait what seems like an eternity before the flames have scorched everything in their path next to me. The fire still crackles in other parts of the room, but here, it's nothing but coals. The stone wall behind me held in place, but the floor is a mixture of dirt and ash.

I'm filthy, my clothes covered in soot. Why aren't my clothes burnt? How did they survive and not my chair? Doesn't matter. Better dirty than dead. I've got to get out of here. I let myself slump so my arms are stretched out in front of me. I use them to pull myself forward. My legs are tangled in the wreckage that was my chair and aren't budging. I don't have the strength to do this.

I try again and again, screaming for help. Hours pass. My eyelids grow heavy. I let them close, and I'm off to a dream, where I can run and dance and mock Androlla.

* * *

SOMETHING WET NUDGES MY HAND. I open my eyes to find Puneah pushing up against me. "Hi, girl." My voice is a little raspy, but otherwise I feel fine.

Puneah licks my hand.

"How did you get here? Is anyone else coming?" I ask.

She sits back on her haunches and stares at me. Last I saw of her was in my room, before the meeting.

"Go get Nash or Jaku. All right, Puneah?"

She stares a moment longer, then gets up and strolls away like she has all the time in the world.

"Can you go a little faster, please?" I say.

Surprisingly, she speeds up to a lope.

Time passes. It's difficult to tell how much. It feels like a lot, but must be less than I think. People should come back and make certain the fire didn't spread. There's a noise in the distance that grows closer.

"Darned cat. Are you taking me to see Ryn? I'm not certain it's safe to move her remains yet." There's no life to Nash's voice.

What is better—to have him see me alive or hear me? Hearing me may be less startling. "Nash?" The word comes out croaked.

"Ryn?" The word is filled with disbelief.

"Nash, I'm here."

The footsteps grow louder and faster. He enters the room with Puneah behind him.

"Good girl, Puneah. Good girl." I look up at Nash, grateful to see he's unharmed, though he is covered in dirt and soot too. He even has a smudge of it on his jaw.

He stares at me. "I'm dreaming."

"Fortunately, no. I'm quite alive and really uncomfortable."

He rushes to my side and pulls me into his arms.

I sigh. "That's better."

"I can't believe you're alive. How did this happen? Last I saw, you were engulfed in flames."

I lift my hand and wiggle the finger with the ring on it, before dropping it back to my lap. "Magic ring, I think. It kept me from burning."

"That can't be."

"But it is."

He buries his face in my hair. His body shakes. Is he… sobbing? I let him and enjoy the feel of him. He's much more comfortable than the ground, and though my head still hurts, it's nothing to what I could be like. His chest plate is hard against my side, as are his arm muscles, yet they're better than any pillow I've ever felt.

Puneah bumps her head against my shoulder. "That's a good girl, Puneah. Good, good girl," I say.

Nash lifts his head from my hair. His eyes are wet, but he's smiling. I grin back. He leans down and brushes a kiss across my lips, light and feathery. Perfect for making me want more.

"We should get you to the others. They were going to come looking when the heat died down, but Puneah here decided I needed to show up sooner."

"It's still hot? Did you burn yourself? Can you breathe all right?" I'd hate for something to happen to him.

"I'm fine."

He stands and lifts me with him, an impressive display of muscles. I lean my head against his shoulder, and Puneah follows us out.

We travel through a blackened hall, the sky visible through the roof as Nash makes his way across the debris. "Where are we?" I ask.

"In a safe house outside the palace walls."

"What are we doing here?"

"Keeping you safe from Androlla's outbursts."

"That's a good idea. How long have you been preparing for something like this?" They must have planned this out.

"Almost since we first found out she was taking you over."

That's wonderful. I can't believe I'm in love with someone so thoughtful. Well... I can, but it's still amazing. "Who else knows I was in the fire?"

"Just the few of us that were there. Jaku, Venda, Julina, and I."

"How is Julina taking this?"

He winces. "We had to tie her up so she wouldn't go raving about how we were all crazy. We didn't want to get banned when we were going to try and take out the First Queen."

I grin. "You're the best."

"I still can't believe you're alive. The others won't believe it either."

We've left the building and are headed toward a small house. When we get there, Nash kicks the door with his foot to knock.

"It's I," Nash says, "and I've got a surprise."

The door opens, and Jaku pokes his face out. He stares at me, his mouth dropping. "But that's impossible."

Nash pushes past him and brings me into a large room, where Julina is tied to a chair, a gag on her mouth. In the corner, Venda doesn't look nearly as surprised to see me as the others but still has wide eyes.

"Magic?" she asks.

Nash sets me on the couch.

I say, "I'm getting everything filthy."

"Doesn't matter. It's just stuff," he says and turns to Venda. "She thinks it was her wooden ring, the one Puneah detected as magic."

"Ah. I see."

I focus on Julina. "Are you all right?"

She shrugs, her arms not moving much since she's tied up.

"We should let her go," I say.

"I still can't believe you're here," Jaku says.

We have a lot to do and little time left to do it. "We should let Julina go," I say again.

"That's like you, to worry about someone else when you were almost burned alive," Nash says.

"As much as I'd like to take the time to deal with it, Androlla's power over me is stronger than ever. We need to get to work. Venda, I'm glad you're here. We must gather supplies to make the golem."

"We gathered them at the house that burned down. I'll see what I can recover and get the rest."

She leaves, and I turn my attention to Nash and Jaku. "We need to let Julina go," I say for the third time.

"She will tell on us. Tell people you've gone crazy. That we all have."

I purse my lips. We can't have that. "Can you at least take the tie off of her mouth so I can talk to her?"

Nash and Jaku exchange a look. From what I gather, the two have become so close they're like an old married couple, able to read each other at a glance.

Nash goes to Julina. "I'm going to let you talk, but you have to promise not to scream. All right?"

She nods.

"Good. If we have any problems, I'm going to put it back in place." He unties it.

She looks right at me. "How are you alive? Last I saw, you were burning in an inferno."

"Like Nash said—my ring. It's magic and protected me."

"That's impossible."

"So is my being here," I say.

She stares at me, gaze searching.

"It's true. You have to believe me. Everything—from me living through the fire to the First Queen's trying to take me over—is all true. Why else would I have set myself on fire? I wouldn't do that."

"No, you wouldn't. But why would someone inhabiting your body want you dead?"

"Because I'm stuck in this body. She wants freedom, not —well—this."

"That makes sense, but I'm still not sure I believe it. It's too farfetched. Too out there. It doesn't come together."

"Just because we didn't grow up knowing about magic and its possibilities doesn't make it impossible."

Her forehead creases. "Say I do believe you. Not saying I do, but pretend it is so. What's the next step?"

"We're going to try to get the First Queen's soul out of my body and into a golem made of clay. Then Nash and Jaku will destroy it. This will happen, whether or not you believe us."

"How do I know you're not crazy?"

I think about that a moment. How do we know that, other

than by Androlla's saying and doing things I never would? I explain Androlla's words to her. "But even if I am crazy, would it hurt to try?"

She sighs. "No, it wouldn't."

"I'm glad you agree. I'm willing to let you go if you promise to give this a chance and not go running to the council and telling them you think I'm incompetent."

She bites her bottom lip. "I promise. Whether you're crazy or not, I don't want anything to happen to you. You're my friend, even if you've lost touch with reality."

I give her a small smile. "I'm glad. Let's see what we can do. Nash, will you help Venda gather supplies? I don't want to wait longer than we have to."

I'd ask them all to help her, but they won't want to leave me unprotected and Julina free to tell the council.

"I can do that." Nash heads out.

Puneah settles down in a ball next to me. Once this is all over, I'm making sure she gets the dinner of her life.

CHAPTER 37

IT TAKES a while to get all the supplies, but we get them in the end, and we put together a golem made of clay. It looks rather lumpy and sloppy, but it will do the job.

Even Julina helps, despite her disbelief.

Venda comes over to me. "Are you ready?"

"Is it ready for me?" I'm suddenly worried this isn't the right thing to do. That it's not going to work. That we're doing something wrong.

Probably because we're doing dark magic.

Who am I going to lose as part of the consequences of this spell? I hope the rumors were false and there are no consequence beyond the usual ones.

"It's ready when you are."

"Let's do this, then."

Nash walks over and picks me up. "No matter what happens, I have you."

"If this doesn't work—"

"It will. We have to believe."

My chest tightens, but I nod. No matter how I feel, we're going to make this happen.

Jaku, Venda, and Julina have their weapons out. Julina was given hers back under my direction. So far, it's been the right choice. She hasn't tried to run off in a misguided effort to protect me.

The pressure in my head grows so great, it's hard to concentrate, but I force myself to. "What do I need to do?"

Venda instructs me as she holds her sword ready. "We need to mix your blood with the lemongrass, oak leaf, and honey over the top of the clay. If my research is right, it should bring the golem to life and send Androlla's spirit into it." She sounds very matter of fact.

"How do you know it won't send my soul in it?" I ask.

"Honestly, I don't. This is guesswork. But I believe it will work —that's half the battle right there. Believe it yourself, and all will turn out okay," she says.

I let out a deep breath and let her take my hand. She slashes it, and I'm taken back to Daros and how he used to treat me. I throw the feeling aside and force myself to concentrate. Venda guides my hand to the top of the clay. I tip it to the side and let the blood flow out.

I push my injured hand into the mixture and direct my attention on the sensation inside me. The pull of power.

"I don't know what to chant," Venda whispers. "As long as you find something in the magic to focus on, you can do this."

I tut under my breath and let that be the chanting. I continue as the magic pulls at me. I don't know what it is, but something feels different. It's heavier than any spell I've done before. I don't have a lot of experience with magic, but I have enough to know there's a strange, slimy, feel to this.

The pull is strong, achingly so. My instinct is to stop it. To keep it from tainting inside me. Instead, I force myself to deal with it. To take it and let it out. The darkness coats my insides, making me cringe.

I continue chanting and let the oily feeling spread across me. It tugs and pulls, leaving me the impression like I'm about to be gutted.

This is for my friends, my country, and for me. I have to let it happen. I focus like I've never focused before, sending waves of energy through my body, across my arm, into my hand, and down into the golem. The mixture is slick in my hand as I rub it into the top of the clay. My palm stings, but it's nothing compared to the ick inside me.

It rips me to shreds—the power bursting from me. I call out as the pain doubles, jolting through my body and out my palm.

All is quiet.

I take my hand from the golem. Did it work? There's no pain in my head, no pressure of another, but there's no life in the golem either.

"Get ready," I say.

The golem's crude mouth opens, and the swords are raised. "Don't attack. It's me, Ryn." The voice is strangely feminine, coming out of such a creature.

They hesitate. Nash looks from me to the golem and back.

"Don't believe her," I say. "She's trying to trick you."

"No," Androlla says through the golem. "It's me, Ryn. Please don't hurt me. Something went wrong."

"Venda?" Nash asks.

"I don't know. I suppose it's possible the wrong spirit went into the golem. I didn't know what I was doing."

Nash growls and starts to move me away from his body. I force my arms around his neck and cling to him. "Please, Nash. It's me."

"What do we do?" Jaku asks.

"I don't know," Venda says.

Nash looks between me and the golem, as if trying to decide something. "Maybe Puneah knows?"

"Give me a dagger, and I'll prove I'm me," I say.

Androlla laughs.

Nash pulls me away from the clay creature. "Kill it."

"Are you certain?" Julina says.

"Ryn would never laugh at us like that, and she would most definitely ask for a dagger. That thing is the First Queen." Nash takes several more steps back.

I clutch onto the arm of his shirt, wishing I could be the one to deal the killing blow. Not that it matters as long as we get rid of Androlla and her influence.

The blades go slashing down onto the golem. But instead of fighting or crying out, Androlla just stands there, laughing.

Nash takes another step back, but I have a feeling it's not enough.

The clay of the golem's body reforms where the slashes from the swords cut through it. She giggles as the edges of the cuts come back together. "You fools. All you've done is given me a body that can move until a new queen drinks the Mortum Tura."

Her big, uneven hand takes a swat at Jaku. He cuts her arm before she gets to him, but it doesn't fall off. Instead, it reattaches itself and resumes its motion until it hits Jaku in the side of the head.

He slams into the wall.

"Jaku," I yell.

Venda and Julina rush to step in front of him before Androlla's golem can do more to hurt him. They keep cutting at her as she swipes at them, but again, she heals faster than they can cut.

Puneah dives at her, snarling, but Androlla whips the animal away. Puneah shakes herself as the others continue to try to hurt the First Queen.

"Give me a dagger," I tell Nash.

He sets me on a chair from where I watch Venda and Julina get shoved to the side. Androlla steps toward Jaku. Nash pulls out a dagger and hands it to me before picking me back up and whispering, "We've got to get you out of here."

"And leave her on the loose?"

"Only until we figure out what can defeat her."

I don't like it, but it's probably for the best. Still— "Can't we lock her up somewhere?"

Nash darts for the door, and Julina gets to her feet. She screams something unintelligible as Androlla goes to stomp on Jaku. At the last moment, Jaku rolls out of the way, and Julina runs her sword through the clay all the way up to the hilt.

Right. No locking her up, then.

Androlla whips around, the sword yanked out of Julina's hand. Androlla shoves Julina aside and strides straight for Nash and me. He turns and runs as fast as he can while carrying me. He stops at the door, and I glance over his shoulder.

"Faster," I say. "She's gaining."

The door bursts open, and Nash takes a step, Puneah at our heels.

"Turn around," I yell.

He pivots to face the golem, and I throw the dagger at her where the indents for its eyes are. The whole blade slides right in.

She howls before ripping it out with a ragged hand and throwing it to the side. "What? Did you think you were strong enough? That you would slay me?" The tinkling laugh sounds odd, coming from such a creature. "Nothing you can do will stop me now. Not anything."

"Run, Nash." She's coming straight for us.

CHAPTER 38

Nash runs, weaving through the streets as he carries me, Puneah staying faithfully close by. "What now?"

I glance behind us. "She's coming, but she's slower than you."

"Where to?" Nash asks.

"Good question. We don't want to lead her to the market. Too many people to get hurt." Though maybe it's a good idea to have them see her. Then they'll be more likely to believe me that magic has been at work at this country for ages. "We have to find a way to destroy her."

"A well. If we can get her to fall in a well, it should do the trick. Clay can be diluted in a ton of water, can't it?"

"That might work."

"There's one a couple of blocks away. Can you make it?" I ask because he's slowing down.

"Making sure she can follow us."

"You can leave me behind."

"Never."

It's just as well. She'd be more likely to come after me than Nash. I'm the bait. Not the first time I've played that role, but first I've done it when I can't attack the thing chasing me. It wouldn't do any good. Even a dagger to the eye didn't slow Androlla down. If the well doesn't work, I don't know how we'll defeat her.

And if we can't defeat her now she's going to kill everyone I love. "She's gaining."

Nash speeds up, but his breathing is labored. He rounds a corner. "We're almost there," he says between breaths.

I look away from Androlla's lumpy, clay body to look ahead. The well is in sight, wide and surrounded by people on their midday break.

"Get away, by order of the queen," I yell.

People glance our way and scream.

"Run," Nash hollers.

They scatter at his word, running in all directions but toward us. Nash takes a leaping bound over the well. For a moment, I think we're not going to make it. His foot catches on the wall of the well, and he stumbles forward, dropping me on the ground.

I tumble forward, scratching my elbows on the dirt and rocks.

"Ryn." The word is breathless.

"Don't worry about me. Figure out how to get her where we want her. She's coming."

He goes to pick me up.

I wave him away. "Leave me. Figure it out."

He jumps to his feet and turns to face Androlla, who's almost upon us. Puneah licks my cheek with her rough tongue before planting herself between me and the golem. Nash pulls out his sword and tosses me a dagger. It's not like I can do much with it, but I feel more secure having it in my hand.

Nash rounds the well. I scoot, using my arms so I'm opposite him, but far enough back that he can jump over it. Pebbles grind into my arms, drawing blood. Puneah keeps between the First Queen and us.

I continue crawling away, but look back when I hear the pounding of feet. Nash is facing me, running from Androlla's golem. He leaps over the well, and then crouches down beside me, Puneah not turning to look at either of us.

Androlla gets a running start and jumps.

"Here she comes," I say.

Quick as a flash, he whips around and slashes his sword through the air to slam it into her mass before pushing against her with his body. She tumbles down the well and lands in the deep water. Half of her upper body is sticking out.

With a laugh, she chants and rolls something in her hand. As she does, her body grows bulkier.

"I think that was a bad idea," I say.

Nash grabs me and pulls me into his arms as he runs. "Where to now?"

"I don't know." If we're both out of ideas, that means trouble.

There's screaming in the distance. As I glance back, I say, "Dagger it all." She's coming at us with thumping footsteps. Her mass has doubled as she towers over us.

"What?" Nash asks, chest heaving.

"She's grown."

He hisses.

Julina, Venda, and Jaku appear ahead. They must have used a shortcut. All of them have weapons drawn, though at this point, I don't think it'll do any good.

But what will?

We've lost, just as we started fighting. I'm not going to give up; I don't know how to contend something like her. At least my head doesn't hurt anymore.

"Get behind us," Jaku calls.

Nash dashes past them, and they block the path, facing Androlla. Puneah stays at Nash's feet. The First Queen's form has smoothed out and taken a more feminine shape, as if her vanity was more important than bulking up, but she's still huge. The creature even has long hair, like a solid wall of dirt and clay, though it's darkened from getting damp in the well.

That's it.

"Get a torch. If we burn her, the clay will harden so she can't move." It won't be a permanent solution, but it should work and won't make her bigger. It may even let us break her apart.

But will that kill her for good?

Nash runs into a house without knocking. The family inside shrieks.

"I need a lit torch, in the name of the queen." He moves to the fireplace.

The family backs up, except for the man who comes over, grabs a torch, and sticks it in the fire. When he hands it to me, he says, "Your Majesty."

I take hold of it. "Thank you. Get your family away from here, and take as many people with you as you can. There's about to be a battle."

The man's jaw tightens, but he nods and gathers his family. Nash is out the door before them, racing back toward the fight.

My hand is tight around the handle of the torch, but aching. "I don't know how long I can hold this."

"I understand." He slows.

"No. Just put me down on the ground, by a house. I'll be fine."

"I've got to take you somewhere safe."

"There's no time. Put me down." I don't want to pull authority over him, but I will if I have to.

Thankfully, he veers off to the side and sets me on the stoop of a house, taking the torch.

"Stay safe," he says to me, and to Puneah, "Keep close to her."

As he runs off, I call after him, "You too."

In the time it took us to get the torch, the three of my friends fighting the First Queen have been knocked to the ground. Not one is getting up.

They'd better not be hurt.

Androlla stomps forward, looking like a giant warrior, except she lacks the weapon and grace. What she lacks, she gains in brute strength. Making her out of clay was a bad idea. Putting her in an area she could make herself bigger, a worse one. I hope fire will work.

I squeeze my hands into fists so tight they hurt as Nash gets closer to her monstrous form. Puneah paces in front of me like she's not certain if she should join the fight or stay with me.

Androlla puts one hand on her hip and stretches the other out to the side, palm up. "What do you think you're going to do with the torch, little man?"

Nash ignores her words but slows as he approaches her. One of the figures on the ground pulls itself up behind Androlla. Julina. She's alive. The others might be as well. Maybe they just got knocked out.

Julina sneaks behind the golem as Nash grows closer. When he's almost upon the golem, Julina slices across Androlla's legs and kicks her, so she falls forward, toward him. She did it fast enough that the bottom halves of the golem's legs are now disconnected from its body, far enough away that they didn't reattach.

Why is Androlla even after me? What good would it do to kill me? Would she go back into the next person who drank the Mortum Tura, or would she stay a golem? I don't know, and now isn't the time to worry about it.

Nash slams the torch into the middle of the First Queen's chest. She tries to bat him aside, but he doesn't budge, holding the fire on her. The legs try to move toward the body, but Julina kicks them back.

It doesn't look like Nash is doing any good with the torch. The flames lick the clay, but it's not enough to harden the thing. We need a bigger fire.

Venda gets up and runs into the nearest house. Jaku also stands and goes to Androlla's arms, trying to cut through them as Nash holds steady. The arms reattach faster than Jaku can slice, but he provides a distraction. The clay around the fire is turning a lighter color, but not fast enough.

I want to crawl out there and tell them that this isn't going to work, but I'll never make it in time. What can I do to assist them? I hate this helpless feeling. I scan the area for something, *anything*, that can take her down. I wish I could send Puneah to them with a message, but there's no way, and I doubt she'd leave my side anyway.

Smoke is coming from the house Venda went into. As the others continue to fight Androlla, Venda races out of the house and yells something I can't make out.

Androlla takes another swipe at Nash, this time knocking him off his feet. The torch tumbles to the ground. She goes to stomp on him with her nubs, but Jaku dances around her, wielding his sword. She swats at him and misses as he skirts around her. Julina is coming from the back with her dagger, except when she diverts her attention from the legs, they jump toward their master.

The First Queen turns her back toward me and bends to put the bottom half of her legs back on. Venda runs up to the others and points toward the house that's now engulfed in flames. A moment later, they're all on the opposite side of Androlla, slicing her and shoving her sideways into the inferno.

Androlla stumbles back and falls into the flaming house, crashing through the wall. Her legs go hopping after her and disappear into the house.

All is quiet, except the crackle of flames.

I hope against all hope that this will work. That it will dry her out so much and harden her, like her heart, so she won't be able to move.

Jaku takes a step closer to the raging fire. Thankfully, the house isn't close to the others around it, so with any luck, the flames won't spread. Venda chose well.

Androlla jumps from the flames and knocks Jaku to the ground with a powerful strike.

He has to get up.

But he lies still.

He'll get up in a minute. I know he will. Though that was a hard hit, he'll be fine.

Except, with her new, lighter colored body that looks like rock, she slams her foot down on him, crushing him.

I gasp, helpless.

The others run for Androlla, their swords drawn. They try to slice up her body, like they did before, but this time instead of going cleanly through, they clang against her. There's no piercing her. How's she even moving? Magic? Something else?

Whatever it is, we've made her an even worse monster.

CHAPTER 39

Julina steps forward, toward Jaku. Androlla shoves her with one swift movement, and Julina goes flying to the ground. Venda faces the golem alone while Nash runs toward me. The creature takes a swipe at Venda, but she jumps out of the way with a grace I haven't seen before.

Nash blocks my vision and scoops me up into his arms. "We have to go."

"What about the others?"

"They're doing this to keep you safe. We have to find somewhere to hide." He darts into an alley next to the house and weaves his way through buildings, Puneah beside us.

"I don't want to leave them behind. They need us." I grip him with one arm and my dagger with the other hand.

"They want you safe. That's why they're distracting her. Know anywhere to hide? Most places I know are by my mother's home, and I don't want to take Androlla around there. Wait. We'll borrow this cart."

He puts me in a cart on the side of the road and starts pushing. I'm jostled and keep knocking against the cart, but we're going faster and Nash isn't getting as worn out.

I consider our options. We can't hide from the problem; she's never going away. We need to stop her, but how? I wrack my brain for an answer. Fire didn't work. Water didn't work. Fighting her doesn't work. Besides, she's bigger and stronger.

There has to be a way to defeat her for good. Even with the black magic she used to create the Mortum Tura, there has to be a loophole.

Wait.

The Mortum Tura. It's the key to everything. "Take me to the palace," I say.

"We can't. She'll look for you there."

"We have to. I need the Mortum Tura."

He switches directions, peering at the streets before running onto them. People watch us go by. I can't let them be hurt.

I yell, "Get out of the city. Danger's coming."

No one moves.

"Go," Nash hollers. "If you care for your lives, go."

Something crashes behind us. Androlla?

The people run, gathering their children with them as they go. Nash hurries past them, heading for the palace. I keep an eye out behind us, waiting for the golem to show itself, but she never appears.

What feels like several minutes later, the palace is within sight, and the portcullis is open.

Eldim strides toward us. "Where have you been?"

"No time to explain," I say. "We must get to the chalice room."

"Everyone's been worried. You left without a word. What happened?"

"What did I say? We have to go. Now." My voice is stern.

Puneah growls.

He gets the message because he turns and pulls out his sword. "Make way for the Queen."

Androlla's hulking form comes into view from our left, running full speed toward us.

I cry out, "Nash."

"I see her." He puts on a burst of speed, but it's no use. We're several feet from the open portcullis when Androlla knocks into him, sending me flying from the cart.

The guards surround her in full force, but she rips through them like they're paper. Nash is under her arms, but she doesn't seem to realize it as she attacks my other guards.

I wish none of them would get hurt. What she wants is me. My heart thuds in my chest, leaving me breathless. My body aches from the fall, but that's nothing compared to the hurt in my heart at seeing my guards thrown around like dolls.

Nash attempts to crawl away, but she hits him on the back and sends him to his stomach. Even through the distance, I feel his pain. My body wants to join the fight. I try to get up but fall back to the ground.

Puneah lunges forward, snarling at Androlla. The First Queen swats at her, but Puneah is quicker, darting out of the way and lunging forward to bite her leg. When that doesn't work, she backs up with a sort of growling noise I've never heard from her before.

Nash tries to stand up, but the golem shoves him back down, not taking her attention from the fila. Puneah's two tails stand on end, her fur spiking up. She dances around the creature, while trying to edge closer. I cringe as Androlla tries several times to swat her and fails.

The First Queen strikes hard, making contact with Puneah. My heart twists in agony as the fila yowls and collapses to the ground. Androlla goes to smack her again, the buildup making my muscles tense.

I am about to scream, to get Androlla's attention on me, when from behind her, Eldim starts hollering, "You big, ugly beast. Why don't you fight someone who can take you on? Come and get me."

She turns, hitting several guards with her big hand in the process.

"That's right," he taunts. "Face my wrath."

As she steps toward him, Nash gets to his feet and comes toward me. Puneah doesn't move from the ground. Eldim holds out his sword toward the golem, ready to fight. She towers over him, bringing all my fears with her as she lumbers closer.

Nash scoops me back up and heads for the open gate. As we're through, Androlla smashes Eldim to the ground with one of her hands, bending him and his sword. Last I see, she's stepping on him.

I whimper, feeling the loss of not only him, but also other guards that are out there, fighting her.

The noise has drawn the attention of those practicing in the courtyard. They run toward us.

"Be careful," I call out. "She's dangerous."

They run past me, several of them nodding in my direction. I glance over Nash's shoulder to find them blocking Androlla's path as she tries to bend down and make it through the open gateway. As she slaps at them, they dodge out of her way.

We make it inside the palace, with her hulking frame not where I can see.

"Close the doors," I yell. It may slow her down. I hope Puneah and the others are better than they looked. I can't have people I care about getting hurt, even if I knew it was coming.

A group of guards rush to close the doors, and the rest draw their weapons. We whip around a corner, but I still hear the guards wondering what's going on. I'm not about to stop and explain it to them.

Nash continues onward when someone enters the hallway we're running down. I holler at her to leave. "It's not safe."

"Ryn?" My mother's voice fills me with a cold panic.

We may not be the best of friends, but I can't allow anything to happen to her. I've lost enough people in my life without losing the woman that gave birth to me. "You have to get out of here. Danger is coming," I say.

Nash slows as we approach her. He's got to be exhausted, even with all the training he's done. I'm not heavy, but I'm still a weight he has to carry. The cart must have helped some, but this has to be putting a strain on him.

"I want to help with whatever it is," my mother says.

Nash dodges past her, not stopping.

As she follows us, I say, "Leave the palace. You have to go out a side entrance. I don't want any harm to befall you."

"I'm your mother. It's fitting that I help you, even when there's danger."

I should have never let her back into the palace. Then she wouldn't be in trouble's way now. We continue, and I'm happy at least that she keeps up with us.

This is the same path I took when I first drank the Mortum Tura, bringing the First Queen back into this world. Hopefully, this time I'm taking it toward her destruction. A darkness inside me whispers I'm wrong, but I shove it away. I can't think like that when it's my only option.

There's a *crash* behind us as Nash slips into the chalice room, Mother right behind us. As Nash runs across the wide expanse toward our destination on the dais the sound of crashing becomes louder. The mirrors around the walls of the room reflect our flight.

We're halfway there when Androlla's form smashes through the door.

"Get back here, little Queen," she says, voice full of anger.

Is she angry because we've taken her on a chase or because we're on the right track? Either way, we have to hurry; she takes loping steps forward.

"What is that?" My mother sounds frantic, as well she should.

There's no time to answer.

"Faster, Nash." The pounding inside me grows stronger with each step Androlla takes. I glance at the chalice. We might make it. Maybe.

She ramps up her speed. Nash tries as well. Between breaths, he says, "Love. You."

Now's not the time for the *goodbye* I hear in his voice. I panic, wishing there was more I could do than be an extra weight on him. We're almost there. We can make it. We don't have to say *goodbye*.

I'm shoved forward and fly through the air. Nash goes with me and lands flat on his face while I tumble to my side. Instinct says to go to him, but I've got my country to think about. Besides, if I waste any time now, all will be lost.

The sound of multiple footsteps approaches, but I don't look back. I crawl the last foot to the chalice, using my arms, and pull myself up to it with a strength built from pure desperation. I reach for the Mortum Tura, my arms aching. My fingers brush against it, and it wobbles. I strain, putting everything I have into getting that cup.

I about grab it, and something slams into me from behind, sending me, the pillar, and the cup crashing to the floor. Red liquid splashes across the floor and up onto the closest mirror.

I haul myself forward as Androlla's laugh fills the room, echoing across the expanse. The footsteps are ever closer, but they won't be here in time to do anything. The cup is almost within reach when my muscles give out. I collapse, reaching out my arm toward the overturned cup laying on its side.

"You've lost, little girl," Androlla says. "Give up now."

Ignoring her, I stretch forward. I'm not going to make it, no matter how hard I try. There's not enough strength in my body yet. If I had another week or two, I might be strong enough, but now… I've failed.

Shillian appears in front of me. She scoops up the chalice and hands it to me. There's no time to thank her. I grip the stem of the chalice and roll onto my back to face Androlla.

I can't read her expression through the golem's thick clay, but her voice is calm as she says, "You won't win."

She reaches for me. Nash hurtles himself from the side, knocking into her. She wobbles but doesn't fall, instead grabbing Nash with both hands. "Give me the Mortum Tura, and I'll let Nash go free," she tells me.

I grit my teeth. I want to save him. Want to live out my days with him. But I also have to do what's best for my country, even if it means his death. Cringing, I make my decision. "You are nothing but the bringer of death, and I am death's assassin."

I think on the spell I read about weeks ago, for destroying an object. It was simple, but I have a feeling it's going to take a lot of power to get rid of the Mortum Tura. It didn't take any ingredients, except the object itself.

The pewter is cold in my hand as I pull out the power inside me. I let it flow to the cup while chanting Nash's name. It's all I can do, to focus on it and not him, though he's still within her reach.

The power flows through me and into the cup. The ground beneath me rumbles. Thunder rolls outside, and what sounds like large pieces of hail smash against the windows.

Still, I hold onto the power, focusing on it and on Nash. The rumbling grows deeper as the power pours out of me. Androlla throws Nash aside, almost making me lose my focus, and turns her attention on me and the Mortum Tura.

She comes running at me.

I close my eyes so I don't see the imminent danger.

The magic takes a chunk of me with it, but I let it flow, free and clear. Even if I don't survive this, my people will finally have a chance at freedom.

The rolling beneath me grows worse, violently shaking the room. I open my eyes in time to see Androlla reaching for me as the cup crumbles to dust.

Everything goes dark.

CHAPTER 40

I SHOVE against the heavy blocks of clay on top of me, but I have no strength left to move them. Androlla's last remains lay on top of me, crushing me. Not the way I wanted to die.

"I'm in here," I call out for what feels like an eternity, hoping someone can hear me. I hear the sound of rock moving against rock, and the pressure lifts. My body feels the sharp pain of having been crushed by a pile of hard clay, but doesn't seem worse for the wear, other than for a few bumps and bruises.

An unfamiliar male guard pulls me from the pile. "What just happened?"

I ignore him and look around for Nash. *Or Nash's body.* My throat tightens. I spot a prone form lying on the ground. "Take me to Nash Zorris. Is there anyone else hurt?"

The man carries me toward Nash, my eyes not leaving him to see if he's breathing, but he's on his stomach. The guard says, "A few, but they're being tended to. I regret to say that we've had several casualties. We were worried about you. What was that thing?"

We're surrounded by guards, and more pour in the room. I ignore them and stare at Nash's lifeless form. My eyes and nose burn, but I force back the tears. I was told I would lose at least one person close to me. Jaku may or may not be alive. Who knows what happened to Venda and Julina? Eldim is certainly gone, and more may have followed him. I hate to think of Puneah being no longer with me as well.

I chose this. I picked my country over love and friendship. More lives will be spared than taken, but it doesn't make it hurt any less. After all we've been through, I was hoping Nash would survive, even if I didn't. I stare at his still form. It looks like I am going to have to carry on without him.

When we reach Nash, I say, "Put me down and check him."

The guard sets me down.

My gaze doesn't leave Nash, though out of the corner of my eye, I see Shillian join us. We're all here because of her. If she hadn't followed us in, I would have never reached the Mortum Tura. I owe her much.

The guard carefully rolls Nash's body over and presses two fingers against Nash's neck, where his pulse should be.

I want to cry. There are cuts across his face and arms. His chest isn't moving, but he's wearing his uniform with the steel vest, so it wouldn't be noticeable anyway. He's not just pale but almost gray. There's no way he could have survived, after everything and with how he looks now.

I squeeze my eyes shut against the blinding pain and the torrent of aching rage toward the First Queen and toward myself for not being able to save him. If only I hadn't let Daros poison me, things might be much different now. Then again, they could be worse.

The pain increases as the guard says nothing. The love of my life is gone. I turn to look at his face. Even gray and scratched, it's perfect to me. He was everything I could ever want.

The guard still has a hand to Nash's throat. It doesn't take that long to find a pulse.

Nash is gone.

I let a tear roll down my cheek, not caring who sees. Not the guards. Not my mother. It doesn't matter anymore whether or not they know I loved him since he's paid the ultimate price. There's nothing I can ever do to bring him back. My life will be so much colder and darker without him.

Puneah limps toward me, nuzzling my hand. I don't know how she found me or how bad she's hurt. I'm just grateful for her being alive and for her comfort, as I look on at the man I love.

His eyes open—those hazel eyes with hints of blue that I've grown to love.

My heart soars higher than the clouds. "Nash?"

He tries to speak, but all that comes out is a croak.

I glance at the guard. "What's wrong with him?"

"I don't know." He points to one of the guards surrounding us. "Run and fetch a healer."

I turn my gaze back to Nash, not wanting to ever let him out of my sight again.

"Is she gone?" Nash chokes out, voice rough.

"She's gone."

He closes his eyes and sighs.

"Don't you dare leave me, Nash. Don't you dare."

His eyes flutter open as some of the color returns to his cheeks. "Just tired, but I'll live."

"Are you certain?"

"Positive. We should get you off the floor."

I hadn't paid much attention, but I'm lying in rubble—smalls shards of mirrors that broke during the earthquake, scattered around the wooden floor. My tiny cuts can wait because Nash is alive, and somehow I survived as well. There's nothing I want more than to stare at him for the rest of forever.

"I'm fine here. I don't want to leave your side," I say.

He gives a faint smile but doesn't try to sit up.

"What hurts?" I ask.

"Everything."

"That's not helpful."

"I don't think anything is broken. Just bruised."

I know the feeling.

"Healer coming through," a female voice says. A moment later, she appears between the guards. "Let me have a look at you." She crouches down next to me.

"I'm fine. Look at Nash first."

"You're bleeding," is her response.

I glance down and see a jagged cut in my bicep. It's nothing. I ignore the pain and her probing. She wraps my arm as I stare at Nash, who doesn't take his eyes from me either. I know there's much to do. People who need looking after. A mother who needs to be thanked. A country that needs rebuilding. Damage that needs to be assessed. For now, though, I'm grateful we survived.

* * *

MOTHER SITS ACROSS FROM ME, her fingers knotted together. "You wished to see me?"

"I did." I feel as nervous as she looks, but I'm better at hiding my emotions. Keeping them tight inside. I don't want her to know how much this affects me, but at the same time, I want her to know how thankful I am. What's the right balance?

"I'm sorry for how I've treated you in the past," I say. "When Carver tried to kill me and was later punished for it, I thought the best thing to do was to shut you out. Things changed, though. After you saved me and everyone else in Valcora by helping me get the Mortum Tura, I realized what it would mean to have my mother around." Especially now that I know I can trust her to help me. Not that I won't be cautious around her still, but I can let her in.

She blushes. "I deserved your ire. I should have in seen the truth about Carver a long time ago. There was no place for him in our lives. It took too long to see that. I understand now, but I didn't then. I'm sorry."

Her words touch something deep inside that I've never quite felt before. "Apology accepted, though I don't want you to think it's your fault. He fooled me too."

"Yes, but I lived with him for years. I should have realized how dark his heart was when it came to gambling."

"No more of that. We've both learned a lot. Let us remember but move on to something better." Like perhaps having a real mother-daughter relationship.

"You're right." She lets out a loud exhale. "It will take a while for me to get accustomed to forgive myself, but I'll try."

"That's all I ask," I say. "I've learned something too. It's all right to have help sometimes. If you hadn't helped me get the Mortum Tura, everything would be different now."

"It was nothing. I saw you needed something, and I gave it to you. That was an important lesson, though. We all need it."

It wasn't nothing, but I'm not about to argue. Not now, when I know how much she means to me. We talk for a while longer. It's nice, getting to know her without the constant worry she's not who she says.

There's still much to deal with, though. As I think of the coming days, my heart is laden with sorrow, pain, and worry. I will take care of what I can, but some things can never be replaced.

CHAPTER 41

I STARE at Jaku's lifeless form, the black death-paint covering him and lots of metal studs decorating his face. It's not how I want to think of him, so still in death. I want to remember him full of life, at my side, being stern with me because I'm not taking my safety seriously.

His wife and children are next to me, in the place of honor. I spent several hours talking to them and listening to stories about their father and husband. He was truly loved and cherished. They aren't angry at me for him losing his life, though I wonder if they should be. If I had figured out how to defeat Androlla from the beginning, none of this would have happened. Lives would have been saved and torment avoided.

Doesn't matter. I can't change the past.

As we get ready to follow the funeral procession into the tombs, Nash steps behind my new chair. He had help making this one, but it works about the same as the last, rolling me where I need to go when someone pushes it.

Nash's presence is soothing, a reminder that not all is lost, even if we can never have each other. I'm grateful for the opportunity to be with him. Changes are coming, but without the council's approval—which will be hard to gain when they've been steeped in tradition for so long—the changes may not be what I want.

Julina, Venda, Inkga, and Afet are here. Eldim's funeral was yesterday. It was a good service, honoring him properly. He was a good personal guard. After everything we went through together, he saved my life, Nash's life, Puneah's life, and who knows how many countless others'. He deserved better than what he got. All those who passed away did.

We line up and follow Jaku's body into the tomb for guards. I made sure he has a good place in here that his family can come and leave him presents whenever they want, without having to travel far.

The ceremony continues on while I think of what's happened the last few days. Funerals have been mostly for guards who fought Androlla. The natural disasters that hit seem to have spread across the country from the reports I've gotten, but spared most lives.

The country is being rebuilt with help from the treasury. I'm grateful there's enough money for something so important. The people seem happy, despite the losses. Will they stay that way when they realize the Mortum Tura is gone?

No one has asked me about it yet. Do they even know it's missing?

As we reach the tomb, I turn my thoughts back to where they should be—on Jaku. His funeral is hugely attended. I didn't realize he knew so many people and had such a great relationship with them. I shouldn't be surprised, but I am. I selfishly thought his faith and trust were in me only, but I'm learning he believed in a lot of people.

The ceremony winds to an end, and Jaku's wife says, "You meant a lot to him. He talked about you often. I believe you were like the daughter he never had."

The memory of him saying so brings unexpected tears to my

eyes. "He was like the father I never had. A very overprotective father."

She gives a somber laugh. "That sounds like him, especially where you were concerned. Thank you again for honoring him."

"I only wish I could bring him back."

"We all do." She gives me a small smile before leaving with her sons.

"You ready?" Nash asks.

Ready to be done with funerals for the rest of my life. "Yes. There's much that needs to be taken care of."

He wheels me away from the crowd, only Julina with us. When we're far enough, he asks, "Do you have any idea what to do about succession?"

"As a matter of fact, I do. I'd like a council meeting as quickly as possible."

"That can be arranged," he says.

I sigh. I'd much rather give into a period of mourning, but the country needs to keep running. "How soon, do you think?"

"Not long. Few minutes, perhaps."

"All right. I need to speak with Inkga before the meeting starts."

"I'll make sure you get to."

"Have I mentioned you're the best?" Because he is. Maybe even better than the best. "Jem and Kapeni can help with the tasks, I'm sure."

"I'll get them on it, but you need to eat something."

"You know me too well."

We go in to a side room where a luncheon is being served. Inkga is already here, ready to help me. Nash trades guard duty with Afet and goes to find a servant, Jem, or Kapeni to get things settled. I try to feed myself but find it's easier to let Inkga help, especially after the type of day it's been.

"I wanted to talk to you about something," I say.

"What's that?" she asks, cleaning up the last bits of lunch I didn't want.

"The council is going to be changing. With how I plan on restructuring the government, it's not going to mean as big a role, but if you're interested, I'd like you to take up the position of Head of Staff." Her mother's position. Now that she's no longer in it, I need to find someone else. There's no one I can trust more than Inkga with the position, even if it means other servants will have to take care of me.

She holds still. "I don't know what to say."

"You can think about it if you'd like, but I believe you'd be perfect for the position. You can change your mind later, as well. And if you don't like the new form of government, you'd have your say or you could leave."

She's quiet as she finishes putting dishes to the side for other servants to clean before sitting next to me. "I think I'd like that." She smiles—a real smile that lightens my load a little. "I'd like a chance to undo the harm my mother caused with her dishonesty, and I don't know a better way than to take her old role."

"Thank you. I appreciate it."

"Good. Now that's settled, I'm going to prepare for a council meeting."

"Sounds like you're fitting into the job already, though you don't have to do the dishes."

"I want to." She laughs and gives her goodbyes. I turn my attention onto Julina. "I have the same proposition for you, but for Head of the Guard instead."

She widens her eyes and points at herself. "You want me to be your Head of the Guard?"

"I can't think of anyone better for the job. I'll have Afet and Nash to keep me safe. That'll be more than enough, the way things are changing. You can decide how much you'd like to help with that and your other duties over the guard."

She's quiet, and it's hard not try and influence her to do what I want. After several minutes, she says, "I'd like to take the position."

I give her a wide grin. "Thank you. It's going to be a lot of work, but I respect your opinion and think you'll do the job justice."

"I hope I can do half as good a job as Jaku did."

That sobers me up. "You can. You've all the makings of a great Head of the Guard. Just don't sneeze at the wrong time."

She laughs, and I'm grateful we can still be lighthearted despite the heaviness of what's happened in our lives lately.

Inkga returns several minutes later after Julina and I discuss about what her duties will be.

"I've come to get you for the council meeting," she says.

"Let's get to it."

She wheels me out of the room, through the halls, and to the council room.

"Are you ready?" she says.

Am I? This is a big deal. I'm introducing a new form of government to everyone, and I'm not sure how it's going to work. Will they hate me for it? Will they protest? Or will they agree? Whatever happens, it will take some time for everyone to get used to the new way of life.

"Let's do this," I reply.

Before she can wheel me in, Nash comes running up a side hall. "I'm going to stand guard during the meeting, if that's all right."

"I'd like you to be there." Though he doesn't know my plan for the new government, it's good to have him here, supporting me. "Thank you."

He nods.

The doors are opened, and I'm wheeled in. Everyone stands and bows or curtsies. Rumors of magic and the Mortum Tura's destruction abound. The people are stiff. Hopefully, after this is over, their concerns will ease. If not... well, it's not up to the council any longer. It's up to the people.

After everyone is seated, I say, "Let's get right down to business. First, I've asked Julina Hister to be my new Head of the Guard and Inkga Setum to be my new Head of Staff. Please welcome them into this council."

There are congratulations going around as they both take their seats. Jem looks at me with a smile. "Wise choice."

"Thank you." Jem spoke to me about both, but I hadn't made my final decision when last I saw her. It's nice having someone to keep up to date and bounce thoughts off of. She does a great job of it.

Once things calm back down, I say, "As you all know, the Mortum Tura was destroyed." Oddly enough, the names of those who perished drinking it are still engraved on the pillar that held the chalice. I'm having it cleaned and will find a special place where people can come remember and honor those who lost their lives because of the First Queen's ways. "I know this comes as a disappointment for many of you, but it's time to move on from the Mortum Tura. There's a better way for things to go forward.

"I am changing the form of government, starting today. Instead of the queen ruling, there will be a new ruling council called the Unkai, meaning *united*. The Unkai will have one member elected from each city in Valcora, representing them and their voice. The queen will stay in place, and the current council will be there to guide her still, but final decisions on the laws will be left to the Unkai, with the queen advising them, but not ruling over them. In light of this new change, and because the Mortum Tura is no longer, I have created a new drink that will choose the ruler."

Thanks to Venda's help. She was most generous with her time and talents, to help me make what I wanted to create. "The new cup, the Vitay Tura containing the Life Drink, can be drunk when it's time to appoint a new ruler. It can be drunk by men and women alike, picking from the whole populace."

"And how does this drink choose a new ruler?" Timit asks, sounding very curious.

Does he want to try for it? If he does, he's more than welcome to it. "It is similar to the Mortum Tura in that it will choose the new ruler, but it will choose those who hearts are pure and who want nothing more than to do the best for our country. Those who fail the test will not die, but will not glow either." Less sporting way to do it, but also much more humane.

"This is a matter I will not be moved from, though the new Unkai will be able to choose a different method of picking a new ruler if they so choose in the future." Not that it will matter, since the king or queen will have much less influence over the laws of the country. "I trust you will all support me in this matter."

"I will," Sidle says. "I think this is the type of change this country needs."

"As do I," Mina says.

Nidon strokes his chins. "I agree as well. It will be what's best for the country."

"I suppose I'll have to agree as well," Timit says, sounding almost put out.

I work to cover a laugh. Maybe it's better than I thought that I didn't change my Head of Treasury. He's good for this council, even if we don't always agree. "It's settled, then. We will send a proclamation throughout the land. In two months' time, those elected to the Unkai will gather in the capitol and form a new government. During those two months, the Vitay Tura will be available for anyone who wants to try it, until a new queen or king is found."

"You're stepping down?" Inkga asks, a note of discontent in her voice.

"No. I believe the new government should start with a ruler chosen by the Vitay Tura. I will remain on as queen until a new ruler is chosen, at which time I shall give my position over to the new head of state. Anyone who is with me on this council will both have to choose to stay and be accepted by the new king or queen." I don't glance at Nash, though I so want to. What does he think of this news? Of the chance we have at being together when this is all over? I'm guessing it will mean as much to him as it does to me. Though I am sadder than I thought I would be, to no longer rule the country, I need to do what's best for the country, and not what's best for me.

Though it could also be what's good for me. Nash and I will no longer have the excuse that I'm queen to keep him away. Will he still want me, when I become available?

CHAPTER 42

I'VE GOTTEN SO MUCH DONE in the month since the council meeting that changed the government, but it feels like there's more to do. It will be nice when someone else handles this and has the Unkai and the council both to help them. Valcora may not be the biggest of countries, but it's got people with needs that have to be taken care of.

"Mina is here to see you," Inkga says.

"Wonderful. Show her in." I glance at Nash. He gives me a small smile but then is back to his serious job of guarding. Despite hundreds—perhaps even thousands—of people trying the new Vitay Tura, no new ruler's been chosen. I'm certain someone will be picked in time. I need to be patient a little longer.

Mina, my Head of Foreign Relations, enters the room with a curtsy. I motion for her to get up, grateful that I'm getting more of my strength back every day, though I'm still not walking.

"You wished to see me," she says.

"Yes, Your Majesty." She takes a seat near mine. "I have news from the border."

That's not what I expected. "What is that?"

"It would seem that when the earthquakes hit Valcora, it hit the hardest on the mountain range. To put it bluntly, the mountain pass is gone. There is a wide-open path for people to get in and out of the country."

Is this good or bad? Have I opened my country up to more trouble?

"Before you say anything, let me finish," she says. "With this news came a message from the Queen of Faner, delivered by your very own Venda."

"Venda's back?" I'm very much looking forward to speaking with her. At Venda's name, Puneah raises her head. She must be as excited as I am to hear of someone she's comfortable with. She healed well after the encounter with Androlla, making me think she wasn't badly injured in the first place, just knocked out.

"She is, and she brings news that Faner would like to open trade routes with Valcora."

"This is wonderful. When do they want to start? People are going to be so excited. We can try new things and export our precious gems. It will be perfect."

She smiles. "I agree. There's still some paperwork to be taken care of, but I thought you'd want to know about it as soon as possible."

"Indeed, thank you."

She inquires after my health and then takes her leave. As soon as she's gone, I look to Nash. "What do you think?"

"I agree with you. It will be good to open up this country to the outside world."

I grin, wishing we could touch now and not have to wait until the next ruler is chosen. If only someone worthy would hurry and drink the Vitay Tura.

* * *

JEM LOOKS MORE serious than I've ever seen her before.

"Is something wrong?" I ask.

"Not exactly." She fidgets in her seat.

I shift my position, grateful I can do so. The two months since the reform announcement are almost up. Soon, the Unkai will be here and taking over, only a new ruler has yet to manifest themselves. Venda assures me we did everything right when creating the Vitay Tura, but I'm starting to have my doubts. At least one good thing is that I can move more than ever. With the help of the healer assisting me with exercising every day, I'm getting better all the time. It's hard work, but worth it. At this rate, I'll be walking by next month. Thinking about it makes my insides feel like dancing.

When she still doesn't say anything, I speak up. "What is it, Jem? You know you can tell me anything."

"I know." She sighs. "I'm worried how you're going to react, is all."

"I won't be mad at you."

"That's not what I was thinking," she says. "I've come to find out the people are requesting something of you."

"That's not a problem. I'm happy to help the people while I still can. What is it?"

"They want you to drink the Vitay Tura."

Blood drains from my face, my heart feeling as if it stopped. "They want what?"

"They believe the reason the Vitay Tura hasn't picked a new ruler yet is because you are that ruler."

I shake my head. "No. I'm not. I'm an assassin who's stuck in a chair, not a queen."

"The people think otherwise."

I sit back, waiting for the shock to pass. "What do you think?"

She bites her lip and then sits up straighter. "I happen to agree with them. I think you're an excellent queen who should continue to rule, doing what's best for the country, which is what you said the new King or Queen is chosen by, yes?"

"That's true. I'm not sure it's me."

She shrugs like she doesn't care, but the gleam in her eyes says she does. "It's your choice."

But is it?

We talk of several more things having to do with the country and how her life is going, but my mind keeps racing back to the Vitay Tura. Is it really waiting for me to try it? So many already have. Why hasn't it picked one of them?

After Jem takes her leave, I turn to Nash, grateful Julina has decided I'm safe enough to only need one guard with me. "What do you think?"

"I believe you should try." But there's a sadness to his words.

"If I try and succeed, we won't be able to be together."

His shoulders slump, but his gaze is steady. "I know, but Jem is right. I've never met anyone who wanted the best for this country more than you. You make a great queen, and the people know that. It doesn't surprise me that they want you to at least try to continue on in this position."

"And if I fail? What then?"

"Then they will know it's not meant to be, and we will keep trying. This isn't the first time it's taken a while to find a ruler. The people are used to it."

Maybe he's right. Perhaps I do need to try the Vitay Tura. It's not exactly my choice, but it will be able to see my heart better than I can.

CHAPTER 43

THE FLOOR of the chalice room gleams, the mirrors all back in their place. A lot of work has been put into restoring this place. Other parts of the palace are still in disarray, but we needed to help the people before fixing a palace that is bigger than anyone would ever need. The council agreed on the condition we fix up this room.

And now I'm here, like nothing ever happened.

The area is bursting with people silently watching as I sit on the dais next to the pedestal that holds the chalice. Unlike the last one, there's no magic about this column. It's elegantly carved but doesn't keep track of names like the other did.

The chalice is made of pewter but is simple in design. Like the last cup, it automatically refills itself after being emptied. Unlike that one, this didn't require black magic, so it's got a much cleaner feel.

"Are you ready, Ryn?" Nash whispers. He's beside the dais with the other guards surrounding me. Julina is with them. Inkga and Kapeni are not far off with the rest of the council. Venda is close by with Mother, who came early. Both are important to me.

Shillian is slowly earning my trust back, and I think that it's well-deserved trust.

People are noticeably missing. Wilric. Jaku. Eldim. Without their presence, it doesn't feel the same. I miss them and will always honor them by remembering their valor and spirit.

I nod to Nash. I'm going to do this.

One taste. As before, that's all that stands between me and the throne. Not that I want the throne, but I do want what's best for my people, even if that means sacrificing my relationship with Nash. I frown at the thought. I love him, but if the people need me, I'll do what needs to be done.

I reach up and grab the stem of the Vitay Tura. The metal is cool beneath my fingers, reminding me of the last time I held the Mortum Tura. The Death Drink. Now I ready myself to taste the Life Drink.

Fear of what's to come clogs my throat. I think I know, but having it happen is something else entirely. I swallow past it and bring the chalice to my lips.

The liquid is sweet, with a slightly tart aftertaste. It's like wild berries, freshly picked in the summer sun. It tickles across my tongue and is cool going down my throat.

Will it end where it all began? Or will there be a new beginning?

I place the chalice back on its pedestal and wait. A spirit of peace envelopes me, making me feel as if whatever happens, it will be all right. Everything will work out. Nash and I are used to not being together. This would be no different.

I love him, but I also love my country.

I'm not sure where the love came from, but at some point, it developed. It's surging through me now, making its presence known.

But I don't glow with the glow that indicates the next ruler.

Seconds tick by. People murmur amongst themselves. Have I disappointed them? The voices grow louder, filling the vast room.

I have failed.

A mix of knotted emotions fills me, and I'm not sure what to think. I sit back in my chair, readying myself for Nash to roll me away through the crowd of people whose disappointment in me is palpable.

There's a gasp in the group, then silence ripples through them. As one, they bow low to the ground. And then I see it in the mirrors.

I am glowing.

Golden and bright, my entire being radiates magnificence. They think me a goddess.

But I am not.

I'm just their queen, ready to do their will.

CHAPTER 44

THE UNKAI SIT at a huge table that fills the room. Each city has a voice and each voice has a city, all with me, helping with new laws for things to move forward. I can veto their power, should they get too hungry, and they can overturn me, should I get too hungry.

It's a crowd of unfamiliar faces. A mountain of work. But I am up to the task.

Nash is halfway across the room, standing guard over the council of men and women. He doesn't look at me, and I don't look directly at him.

We haven't spoken in the couple weeks since I became officially queen for the new ruling government. There's nothing to say.

We can never be, though our love stays true.

Sneaking around doesn't feel like something we can continue doing. Not with the country looking to me to help guide them. I shouldn't have done so to begin with, but I did. That's going to change because doing so now when I've chosen to be their queen doesn't seem right.

I focus on the task at hand. Thinking of Nash won't help.

Taking care of my people is what I have to concentrate on. I give Puneah a pat on the head, to reassure myself more than her, and say, "I call this meeting to order. The first item of business is to go over the new trade agreement with Faner."

"That's not quite true," a woman two chairs down from me says. "While we will get to that soon, there's something else we, as a council, decided needs to be taken care of first."

"Oh, I'm sorry. I wasn't aware. What do we need to cover?"

The woman nods at the man across from her. I need to learn all their names and which cities they are from.

He says, "We need to change an archaic law."

Something stirs within me, making me sit straighter in my seat.

He continues, "It has come to our attention that the rule stating a queen can neither touch nor marry is out of date. We vote to rescind this rule and put another in place, stating that if a ruler's child should wish to be king or queen, they must take the same route as everyone else, and drink from the Vitay Tura for their worthiness to be tested."

My jaw drops. Did he say what I think he said? It can't be. I can't have everything I want. It's too much.

"All in favor," says the first woman.

Everyone in the room raises their hands and says, "I."

"Any opposed," the woman says.

They're silent.

"Then the old law shall be done away with, and the new one take effect." She faces me. "Unless, of course, you'd like to veto, though I'm certain we could overrule you with all of us taking the vote against you."

My heart drums in my chest, a beat wild and free. My voice comes out strong. "I don't wish to veto."

"Then the new law is in effect, starting now."

I seek Nash's gaze. My breathing becomes rapid as he looks back at me as if searching my soul. He moves from his position halfway down the table and strides toward me. I push my chair away from the table as he nears. I feel like I'm going to faint, but I won't allow it to happen. Not in this moment.

Puneah knocks into my hand, her tails snaking around, as if she can sense my excitement.

Nash kneels on the ground before me. "I love you more than life itself, Ryn. Will you marry me?"

It takes all my control not to squeal with delight. "*Yes*. I will marry you."

He stands and leans forward to press his lips to mine, for all to see. Heat blossoms at my lips and spreads through my body as a cheer goes up around the table.

"You know," I say, "it's still against the law for you to ask for my hand in marriage. I meant to change it so men could ask women, as well as the opposite, but with everything going on, I never got to it."

Laughter fills the room. Puneah tries to push between Nash and me, but I gently keep her to the side, a hand on her head.

"We'll fix that," Nash says, leaning in for another kiss.

Our lips press together, sending that searing heat through me. It's finally time to live.

AFTERWORD

If you enjoyed reading this book, please consider helping the author by leaving a review where you purchased the book and/or on Goodreads. Even a simple one line review helps.

You can sign up to receive notification when Janeal Falor releases a new book at www.janealfalor.com with a Release Notification link on the side bar. Or talk to the author directly at janealfalor@gmail.com

ACKNOWLEDGMENTS

It's bittersweet to end this series. I love Ryn and Nash so much, I'm glad they got their ending, but sad there won't be any more stories from them, at least not in the near future. There are so many wonderful people that helped make this story turn from the lump of coal into what I hope is close to a diamond.

My beta reader that put up with the entire series even when it was a mess, Jessie Wolf, thank you! To my editor, Sotia Lazu, she is beyond fabulous. I'm always amazed by the feedback I receive from her. It's thorough and spot on. She always makes me work to have my books become better, and I love her for it. My proofreader, Yesenia Vargas, is wonderful. She always helps me polish my manuscripts going above and beyond her job as a proofreader.

I'd be remiss if I didn't thank my family. From my brothers and sister to my parents, I don't know what I'd do without you! You read my books and ask how things are going. It means so much to me that you care. I'm the lucky mother of three of the most fabulous children. They are incredible and support me by giving me time to write and telling everyone about my books. My husband is beyond helpful, being my sounding board, listening to me go on and on about my books, and loving me even when times are rough. I couldn't manage this without him. Love you, Erik!

My biggest thanks has to go you to you, my fans. For all those who ask me how my books are doing, who take the time to purchase and read my books, thank you. You're support means so much to me. I wouldn't be able to do what I do without you. Your words of encouragement and excitement over my books keeps me writing. Thank you!

ABOUT THE AUTHOR

Amazon best selling author Janeal Falor lives in Utah with her husband and three children. In her non-writing time she teaches her kids to make silly faces, cooks whatever strikes her fancy, and attempts to cultivate a garden even when half the things she plants die. When it's time for a break she can be found taking a scenic drive with her family or drinking hot chocolate.

www.janealfalor.com
janealfalor@gmail.com